Hot Flush

Hot Flush

Rosy Fenwicke

Wonderful World

Published by Wonderful World Ltd, PO Box 1695, Wellington, New Zealand

Author website: rosyfenwickeauthor.com

This is a work of fiction. Names, characters, places, and incidents either are the product of the author's imagination or are used fictitiously, and any resemblance to actual persons, living or dead, events, or locales is entirely coincidental.

A catalogue record for this book is available from the National Library of New Zealand.

To Georgina, Josephine and Harry, with love.

Chapter One

Euphemia Sage lay in the dark, listening to Kenneth snoring softly beside her and grinned. Moments before she had woken with a prickling feeling on her chest. It felt as if thousands of ants were scrabbling up her neck and across her face, dragging with them a layer of heat so suffocating she had to sit up and hurl the duvet away. Cold air washed her skin leaving behind a film of cooling sweat, and the feeling passed.

Snuggling back under the duvet, Euphemia fizzed with excitement. It was all she could do to lie quietly and not get up and dance around the bedroom punching the air in triumph.

Menopause! Ta-daaa!

She'd been waiting for two years to find out if Maree had been telling the truth. Two years that had dragged achingly slowly since she'd opened the third and final letter on her 51st birthday.

Euphemia looked across at Kenneth silhouetted against the morning light and reached out and brushed her fingertips softly against his back. Should she tell him? If it hadn't been for him, the letters would have been dumped along with that old chest Maree had left her. He'd been the one who told the solicitor to keep sending the letters on the dates as instructed in Maree's will. He'd been the one who had lugged the surprisingly heavy chest up to the attic, even though it was locked and they hadn't been able to find a key. He'd been the one who'd said what harm could it do because one day they might find the key. She remembered the certainty in his voice when he told her Maree wouldn't have left them junk.

Euphemia hadn't been so sure. She knew how determined her aunt had been. Autocratic was too strong a word to describe her, or was it? How else did a woman in the 1960s come to be CEO of a large construction company? Maree had trained to be an engineer when women on building sites were not only rare but anathema. Her dogged determination and undoubted intelligence had seen her rise to the top of this male-dominated field in record time only to give it all up much to her colleagues' astonishment when the three-year-old Euphemia was left on her doorstep.

Growing up in her aunt's house, Euphemia had had to submit more often than she'd liked to expectations and rules, which had seemed at times to come from another life, another century. Euphemia tried to stand up for herself. She tried to show her aunt it was a modern world and things had changed. Their battles could rage for days and eventually, but not always, Maree would win.

Lying in the dark, Euphemia still couldn't quite believe what her aunt had written. On the one hand it was ridiculous, because none of it was serious, sensible or even rational. But on the other hand, what if it was true? The odds against it were enormous but over the years since she'd opened the first letter, now and then when life was tedious she would give the fantasies full rein. She couldn't expect Kenneth to take anything in the letters seriously no matter how much he had liked and respected Maree, and so she hadn't told him.

Outside the bedroom window the tuis were bustling in the branches warming up for the morning chorus. Such enthusiasm and variety so early every morning was at once both charming and very annoying.

"Worse than roosters," muttered Kenneth as he rolled over and pulled Euphemia into the curve of his body, before relaxing back into deep sleep, his arm heavy over her hips.

Normally she would have been out of bed by now. She would have pulled on her running gear, tiptoed downstairs and stepped over the sleeping Petal to slip out the back door, all without waking her husband. Running through the streets, past curtained houses, she would take one of the tracks winding up through the bush into the hills above the city. The narrow ridgeline looking down onto the harbor below, regardless of the weather, was her special place, the place she felt most alive.

But today was different — or it might be. Today, if Maree had been telling the truth, was the day she would find out. Today if Maree had been telling the truth was the day everything would start to change.

She'd been so busy in the years after Maree died, she'd almost forgotten the letters but the first arrived punctually on her 30th birthday. Two young children and their business Sage Consulting occupied her every moment and she was struggling to keep up. Kenneth was supportive but he was as busy and as tired as she was. She envied her friends who had their mothers to help them. His mother tried, but living in Australia, she couldn't do much. Kezia, their eldest, had been planned, but she was followed a little too quickly by Nicky, their younger daughter.

The last thing Euphemia had felt like when she turned thirty was a party, but Kenneth had insisted.

"We both need it," he'd said. "We need to enjoy ourselves. We've been working too hard. Music, dancing, friends, good food and wine, what's not to like?"

Euphemia was just about to ask who was going to organize it all when a howl from one of the girls stopped her.

"I will," he said, and true to his word, he organized caterers, waiters and plenty of wine. He even arranged for the girls to go to a babysitter for the night.

It was late and everyone had gone home when Kenneth gave her the first letter. He couldn't understand what the fuss was about and Euphemia couldn't explain how much she dreaded opening it and reading about her mother, because it had to be about her.

Euphemia shivered. She edged herself back against Kenneth's

warmth, finding security in his size and strength. After all these years she still loved the early-morning smell of him, his unshaven chin scratching against her, his maleness. Downstairs she could hear Petal snuffling in the laundry. Kenneth sensing her need pulled her closer, wrapping both arms tightly around her body.

The night of the party, she remembered, had been awful. When everyone had left, when Kenneth had stood over her expecting her to open the letter and read it there and then, she had rebelled. Fueled by too much alcohol and too little food, Euphemia told him she didn't appreciate his standover tactics. What followed was their first proper fight. Both of them said too much, words and accusations that couldn't be taken back.

She'd run into the bathroom, slamming the door behind her. Unbelievably, Kenneth hadn't accepted her withdrawal and had gone on and on, eventually pushing the envelope under the door. She heard his words again. "It's time you faced this," he'd called. "Maree only ever wanted the best for you. If she thought you needed to know something, then you do. Read it. Find out about the woman you hate so much you can't even talk about her."

Euphemia remembered sitting on the loo, and hearing him walk out of the house, the front door closing behind him and she remembered the rising panic in her chest. She'd listened to his footsteps on the gravel outside as they faded into silence. Kenneth, usually so patient and loving, so tolerant of her moods when she was exhausted, the man who could make her laugh when she was most stressed, had walked out and left her. She'd picked up the envelope and ripped it open.

Dear Euphemia,

Happy Birthday. I remember my own 30th birthday. I spent it with your mother in Rome. We drank champagne and she introduced me to handsome men. After the champagne we went dancing. I woke the next morning in a stranger's bed, with the worst hangover I have ever had, after one of the happiest nights of my life. Fredericka had left by the time I got back to our hotel. She was like that. There in all her glory one minute and gone the next. No note, nothing. Just gone.

The next time there was any contact from her was when I opened the door to you. Three years old and so brave all alone on my doorstep, clutching that blue rabbit. You wouldn't let it go for months. It went everywhere with you, even the bath. Made an awful mess.

Fredericka left me a note — and you. The note introduced you and asked me to take good care of you until she returned. Stupidly, I destroyed it. I thought she would be as good as her word and come back for you any day. That note could have proved she didn't mean to abandon you, but what's done is done.

I know I'm not the motherly type but I did try to give you a good home and hope you have some happy memories. I also tried very hard to talk to you about my sister but every time you closed me out.

As time passed and there was no sign of her, we made do. Any mention of Fredericka brought down a wall inside you, which I could never get past.

This is the only way I can get to you.

Dead... and with Kenneth's help.

He loves you more than you can believe. He won't leave you. I know it but do you? You are lucky to have found love. I didn't. Enjoy the years with your family. They'll be busy years. The two girls are gorgeous. You have so many exciting things ahead of you, more than you could possibly know.

So now for the part of the letter I know you are dreading. Read on...

Fredericka was the eldest daughter of an eldest daughter of an eldest daughter going back many generations. You are her one and only daughter and Kezia is obviously your oldest daughter. Which means you and then Kezia will, if you meet certain conditions, inherit what is called, for want of a better name, Rachel's Switch. Bit dramatic, I always thought, but then maybe I was jealous.

Rachel's Switch turns on something in your genes, which gives you strength in ways you could not imagine. Don't try. Maturity will give you the wisdom to know what to do when it happens.

You've met the first two of the three conditions. You're the eldest daughter of an eldest daughter and you have given birth to a daughter. The third condition will drive you nuts, just as it did Fredericka. The switch is activated by menopause.

I have heard you end up with some sort of enhanced powers but I don't really know. Your grandmother didn't tell me much more than I'm telling you. All I can say is, please don't think you will suddenly turn into Superwoman. You won't. You will be able to do good for others in ways you could never imagine, but quietly. No fuss. None of your grandmothers thought it a good idea to draw attention to themselves after what happened to Rachel.

Time is your friend. Live life and love your family. They love you.

My sister leaving you did diminish you. I saw that. But you have a light, a hunger for the truth, which marks you as special. It's there deep inside, buried under a bit of hurt and shame. You are better than you think you are. I know that and one day, you will too. But you'll only come into your own when the time is right. Then you may find out why Fredericka, who did love you, left and for some reason couldn't come back. I always loved you and I never left.

Aunt Maree

Euphemia had been fast asleep on the bathroom floor when Kenneth came home. Dried tears crusted her cheeks. He'd knelt down and touched her gently on the shoulder. She remembered reaching up, pulling him down to her and kissing him.

Chapter Two

Maree had been right about how busy the next ten years were. Euphemia had had little time to wonder how she knew they'd called their eldest daughter Kezia — Kenneth's idea, not hers. Euphemia had been bullied at school because of her strange name and the last thing she'd wanted was for her daughter to go through the same misery. Kenneth had been remarkably insistent, assuring her the name wasn't so strange and that their daughter would be fine. Too exhausted to argue and for the sake of peace, Euphemia had relented.

Surprisingly, Kezia suited her name. Always happiest in front of a screen solving problems or writing new programs in strange code, Kezia, pale and blonde, didn't enjoy the outdoors. She was tall and willowy with bright blue eyes, and intelligence radiated from her. Nicky, her younger sister by only fifteen months, was the exact opposite — a tomboy, who once she was old enough was never at home. When Euphemia did see her she was covered in dirt or bruises, usually both. Shorter than her sister with dark hair and brown eyes, Nicky was no less intelligent but in a different way. She was a practical hands-on girl who didn't have Kezia's patience but she nevertheless managed to get things done, by fair means and sometimes, Euphemia suspected, by foul.

When she did think about the letter, Euphemia could only assume Kenneth had secretly promised Maree he would name their eldest daughter Kezia. Why he would do that without telling her was another matter. The real mystery was Maree knowing they had two daughters.

The rest of the letter was more concerning.

'Rachel's Switch' for goodness' sake? Superpowers to be used for good but without a fuss? Euphemia tried to remember how much medication Maree had taken at the end. 'Rachel's Switch' was like the plot of some wacky sixties TV sitcom. How could Maree — the engineer, the CEO, the stable sister — write such weird stuff and expect to be taken seriously?

The bits about her mother had been nice, but told her nothing she didn't already know. Maree could try all she liked to explain it but Euphemia couldn't forgive her mother for abandoning her when she was so young. Saying that Fredericka meant to come back for her was all very well, but the reality was she hadn't.

Euphemia remembered every birthday and every Christmas when she'd secretly hoped that this would be the day when her mother would return and take her in her arms and cuddle her. Weeks of hopeful longing were always followed by disappointment, which grew more bitter and angry as time passed. Eventually she built an imaginary cupboard inside her head where she put the pain and emptiness she felt each time her mother let her down, not even acknowledging she had a daughter. Nothing Maree could tell her now would change that. Fredericka Marchamp had preferred her party lifestyle to looking after her daughter, and Euphemia would never forgive her.

Being a part of a happy family and watching her daughters grow and thrive over the next ten years made her happy, but also, at times, exquisitely sad because it highlighted how much her mother had missed.

Chapter Three

"Tell us the story about you and Mummy," said Kezia.

"Yes, Daddy, tell us again," echoed Nicky from the other bed in their room.

"Only if you both promise to go to sleep. Straight to sleep, Nicky, not later after you've climbed out the window, slid down the roof and run off to play soccer with the boy down the road till it's too dark to see the ball."

"But..."

"No buts. His parents phoned this morning. No point in denying it. They were really worried when they found his bed empty."

"Idiot. He should have stuffed it with pillows like I told him."

"So now you're telling the other kids how to deceive their parents? Really? You think this is a good thing?"

"It's only soccer, Dad. Hardly a crime."

"Not yet, anyway. So do you promise? Straight to sleep?"

"OK."

"And promise you won't do it again?"

"OK."

"You have to check she doesn't have her fingers crossed, Dad. She does that," said Kezia.

"You are such a snitch, Kezia. I wouldn't tell on you."

"You did last week. When I got into that porn site and made the mistake of showing you. I was only curious but you told Mum and I haven't been allowed online for a week."

"That was different. That was a crime, wasn't it, Dad?"

"Yes, it was. It was, Kezia. We've had that discussion. Now do you girls want to hear the story about how Mum and I met, or can I go downstairs and do the dishes? Which is it?"

"Story!"

"Thank goodness. I hate doing the dishes."

"You said dishes were fun. Were you lying to us, Dad?"

"Enough."

Euphemia often listened to these bedtime chats. Sitting on the floor at the top of the stairs in the fading light, her back resting against the wall, she enjoyed being part of it, but separate. She picked up changes in the girls she had otherwise missed, and appreciated more and more what a good man Kenneth was.

She'd had her doubts about him early on in their relationship about whether he'd stay with her, worrying herself sick that his commitment to their marriage wasn't as strong as hers. She'd been abandoned once, so by her logic what was to stop it happening again?

Maree's letter helped put her mind at rest — helped by stating in black and white that Kenneth loved her and wouldn't leave her. Strange but those few sentences had settled her in a way that nothing else could.

Despite the silly talk about mysterious changes at menopause, she trusted Maree to tell her the truth about everything else in life. Maree liked Kenneth as soon as she met him. Seeing the two of them laughing and joking together, sometimes at her expense, made her realize how much Maree must have missed the male company she'd had at work. Maree had been delighted when the engagement was announced and insisted they lived with her after the wedding so they could save money for their own home.

But after Maree's death, in the busy years when the girls were small, Euphemia had watched his desperation to leave and play golf with the boys on Saturday mornings. She was scared he'd stopped loving her. It was ridiculous and she knew it intellectually, but fear led to jealousy and irrational thoughts. She imagined other women at the golf club, women who weren't harried by work and two small children, women who had time to look good, flirting with him and stroking his ego in ways she didn't know how to do. The more detailed her imaginings, the more he seemed to pull away. Euphemia had no one she could talk to, no one to ask, no one to tell her it would be all right.

Maree's letter was the reassurance she needed and she started to relax. As the girls became more independent and Sage Consulting more established, the pressures on both of them reduced. Euphemia started running again and entered events where she made new friends, had her own life. Her confidence returned. She realized how much she had given up when she met Kenneth. She understood that her fear of losing him had driven her to be too needy, the exact opposite of the girl he had fallen in love with.

"When I first saw Euphemia Marchamp, as she was then," said Kenneth, "I knew she was the girl for me."

"Really?" said Nicky.

"Yes, Nicky. Don't sound so suspicious."

"I believe you, Dad," said Kezia. "I've been reading about pheromones and the subcortical areas of the brain which release neurochemicals..."

"Will you shut up, Kezia? Dad, ignore her, she's ten and going through puberty."

"I am not!"

"You are. I saw you looking at yourself in the bathroom mirror. Looking at your boobies."

"Oh for goodness' sake. There is no privacy in this house."

Sitting at the top of the stairs, Euphemia had to hold her nose and put her hand over her mouth to stifle her giggles.

"Back to the story," said Kenneth sounding a little uncomfortable. "I saw your mother in first-year Accounting on our very first day at university. She was the only girl in the front row and she looked awful. No make-up, baggy old tracksuit and glasses. And when she stood up, she seemed to go on forever until she slouched over and picked up her bag and hurried off to the next class, which was..."

"First-year Business Studies," chorused the girls.

"Have you heard this story before? Because if I'm boring you... I can always leave..."

"Go on, Dad. Hurry up, get to the good bits."

"Well, for the first year, I watched her. I couldn't talk to her because she never seemed to stop and talk to anyone. She was always the girl who was different from the rest. And I met a lot of other girls. I was captain of the university rugby team and a lot of girls seemed very keen to meet me, you know."

"We know," chorused the girls.

"I found out her name — weird name. I found out she lived in one of the halls and I found out she hadn't gone flatting because she wanted to study. I found out the study paid off and she was top of both Accounting and Business Studies. I knew this, why?"

"Because you were second and you didn't like being second... at anything!"

"Thank you. Anyway, I also found out she was a runner. A really good runner. Middle distance. Who knows what that is?"

"Eight hundred, fifteen hundred and three thousand meters," said Nicky.

"Exactly. And your mother was fast."

"Faster than she is now?"

"Just a little. When I got to know her, she told me she had discovered she was fast when she had to get away from the bullies at school."

"Poor Mum," said Kezia.

"You say that every time, Kezia. But Mum says the bullies soon stopped being mean and respected her."

"Only cos she did their maths homework for them."

"Yeah. One of them still brought the magazines to school though. The ones with pictures of Freder... I can't say that name, Dad. You know, Mum's mum, the one who left, not Maree — the other one, the one who was naughty."

"Fredericka. Yes, Mum was teased and it made her very sad sometimes when she was a little girl. But she had Maree. So... back to the story. It's getting very late. One freezing Saturday morning in second year, I decided enough was enough. I went to the running track and after the fifteen hundred meters, which she won by the way, I stood in front of her and wouldn't let her go and get warm until she said she would meet me at the pub that night."

"And she did and she looked beautiful," said Nicky breathlessly.

"You've ruined it again Nicky," said Kezia. "Tell the story properly, Dad."

"I will. I waited at the pub trying not to look nervous. I was worried she wouldn't come or, worse, I wouldn't see her and she'd run away. All these guys were coming up and congratulating me on the game and getting into the interclub finals. Did I tell you I was captain of the university first fifteen?"

"Yes, Dad."

"I must say, I played well that day. There were some very important coaches there, watching, so it was a nerve-wracking game for lots of reasons. We only won it with a try in injury time, scored by....?"

"You, Dad. Get to the good bits."

"Why don't I have sons? That was a great bit, but OK, your mother. There I was in the pub, a few beers under my belt, waiting and waiting, looking out for a tall slouchy girl in a black tracksuit and I almost missed her. No one else in the pub missed her though. They were all whistling and calling out to a girl I didn't recognize — a gorgeous girl in a red dress. I couldn't believe it was Euphemia. No glasses, hair tied back, and she was wearing make-up. I'd never seen such beautiful eyes. And when she looked at me — that was it."

"You have been together ever since," chorused the girls.

"And not a day goes by when I don't think how much I love her. And also thank Maree for buying her those clothes. Do you know, your mother had them lying in the bottom of her wardrobe, still in the bags Maree had bought them in, for two years? I can't imagine either of you two not ripping your shopping open as soon as you get it home."

"She was a bit weird back then, wasn't she, Dad?"

"Still a bit weird now. That's for the person sitting on the landing, by the way."

Euphemia, cover blown, came in and kissed the girls.

"I am not weird. Just different, which is fine."

She'd once asked Kenneth if he missed rugby, if he ever thought about the injury that ended his chances of playing forever. He'd been quite honest and told her it was the worst day of his life when he was carried off the field on a stretcher, his knee blown to smithereens. But he said that if he hadn't had her to get him through after it happened, it would have been much worse.

And, he'd said, taking her in his arms and hugging her very tightly, what rugby loses, golf gains.

Chapter Four

Turning forty had been no big deal. Euphemia, truth be told, was a little bored with the regularity of her life. She wasn't ungrateful, but she was restless. Life was too predictable, too perfect. The girls were enjoying school. Kezia was doing so well in computing she was already taking classes at the local university. Nicky was obsessed by whatever sport was in season. School was squeezed in between practice.

Sage Consulting had moved to new premises and employed more staff. Euphemia and Kenneth were a good team. They enjoyed advising their clients and building their own business alongside their clients. They made a point of mentoring those just starting out. Some of their best clients had started small and were growing fast under the guidance of the 'two Sages', as they were known at the Chamber of Commerce.

Euphemia envied Kenneth's relaxed mood and his acceptance of everything and everybody. She tried hard not to want more and to be grateful, but it didn't work. The only time she ever felt complete was after a long exhausting hill run when she had pushed herself to the limits of her endurance. But even that feeling of exhilaration was short-lived.

At work, she organized the internal administration, did all the hiring and firing and put the computer systems in place as well as shouldering her share of advising clients. She ran, she gardened, spent time with the girls and with her own friends, but she couldn't escape the nagging feeling that part of her belonged in another world. A world where everything she did mattered, a world where she could use all of her talents and push boundaries. She wanted to make a difference.

The second letter was no help whatsoever and in fact made things worse. Kenneth didn't have to stand over to get her to read it this time. She opened it as soon as it arrived, on the morning of her birthday.

Dear Euphemia,

Ten years have flown by or maybe for you they are starting to drag a little. Entirely normal to feel this way at 40. You have accomplished a lot but maybe it seems looking back it was too easy and there are no challenges for you?

Do you have any gray hairs? Have you looked? You may remember the first time I had my hair dyed was on my 40th birthday. You came to the salon and were so bored, but you tried hard to be polite. You were good at supporting people, even when you wanted to be somewhere else. Keep it up because once you get the basics of life out of the way, it does get more exciting. You have a very interesting life ahead of you.

Just not yet.

Your mother was too impatient for her own good — and yours. She wanted to hurry up the switch, she wanted to get it activated before the proper time and searched for someone to help her. Her efforts made things so much worse. She wasn't ready, physically or mentally.

I kept the circumstances of her death from you as much as I could. The papers reported the sanitized version.

Fredericka was drowned in a pond in a village called Coldsham, in England. My sources later got word to me that she was murdered. The person (or persons) who killed her were never found. I hoped one of the others would solve the mystery, but there aren't many of you left. And with Fredericka gone and you so young, none of them could take the risk of exposure.

I know this will have been a shock. Can't be helped. Best to face things head on, I always think.

Anyway I couldn't inherit any of the talents or powers of the eldest daughter, but I did have you.

You look so much like Fredericka. You have her qualities but luckily not her faults. Of course that's down to me and the way I brought you up.

On reflection, you have more self-control, your actions are more considered. And you have the support of a loving husband and two daughters, who are equally talented in their unique ways. These are the people who will keep you safe until you are ready.

Your life now is a preparation. You are learning and growing in ways that will hold you in good stead, until you can bear the burdens you will have to carry. Trust me and trust your ally — time.

Stay fit. Stay smart. Stay honest and true. You will find out more in another ten years.

Soon, Euphemia...

Your Aunt Maree

Euphemia didn't know whether to howl with grief or vent her frustration when she finished reading the letter. Instead she sat staring at the wall, questions swirling in her head.

My mother was murdered? Some birthday present, Maree. Why tell me? What do you mean when you say she tried to get help to hurry the switch? Who from? Who was in that village? And what others? And now you say I have to wait another ten years. Are you kidding me?

Euphemia shook herself. What am I thinking? Do I seriously believe that Rachel's Switch exists and my life will change in ten years? Really, Euphemia? No, stop it. None of this is true, it can't be. This letter is another part of Maree's deranged fantasy. There is no other explanation. She is right about the years dragging. I'll give her that. Admit it, Euphemia, you're hoping that the switch might be real, aren't you?

She screwed up the letter and tossed it in the bin. For a woman who'd been dead for over ten years, Maree could be very, very, annoying.

Chapter Five

The next morning, Euphemia retrieved the letter from the rubbish bin.

She'd been sixteen and still at school when Fredericka died. Maree had tried to tell her gently but Euphemia had run out of the house in tears, running until her feet ached and there was nowhere left to go. Her aunt was waiting up for her when she got back and could tell by the look on Euphemia's face that it was not the time to say anything.

Back at school and a few days later on the morning after mid-term break, Euphemia sensed a tension in the senior common room as she unpacked her homework. She looked around but no one would meet her eye. That wasn't unusual. She wasn't the most popular of the girls, unless the maths homework was particularly difficult and then she seemed to have lots of friends.

But something about this morning felt different. Those who had their lockers closest to her got their books quickly and left as if in a hurry to get away.

It was a big room strewn with books, rackets and hockey sticks and smelt of socks and sour milk left out over the long weekend. On the far side a group of girls were huddled together. Heads down in a tight circle looking at something, one of them giggled until she was poked in the ribs and shushed to be quiet. The girl looked up and, making eye contact with Euphemia, blushed and, looking guilty, left the group and got her books.

"Euphemia. We were, are, very sorry to hear about your mother."

It was Jane calling across the room, the tone of her voice sounding far from sorry.

Euphemia froze. How could they possibly know? She didn't have long to wait to find out. Jane walked across the room bearing a glossy magazine triumphantly before her, open to a full- page photograph of a woman looking the worse for wear in a crowded nightclub.

"My mother gets this magazine every week and look what she showed me. We were so sorry to read about your loss, Effie. Please accept our condolences," said Jane.

Euphemia didn't look up. For a moment all she focused on was how much she hated being called Effie. Then tears rolled down her cheeks and plopped one after the other onto her bag leaving dark circles in the soft leather.

The girls on the far side of the room shifted uncomfortably, aware they might have gone too far, but Jane didn't notice Euphemia's distress, or if she did, she didn't care.

She started reading aloud. "Fredericka Marchamp, once a well-known society beauty, was killed last weekend in a car crash in rural Warwickshire. Aged 49, she was the only occupant of the car. It is believed alcohol may have been involved."

Jane held up the magazine turning it this way and that displaying the photo to everyone again.

"My mother said Fredericka Marchamp is your mother. Your real mother. The one who left you when you were a baby. None of us knew that. Now it all makes sense. You really live with your aunt and we all know you don't have a father." Jane left the rest of the conclusions unspoken. It was enough. The room was silent with horror at what had just happened, at what they had been part of.

After a few minutes one of the girls she'd helped with her maths came across and stood beside her. Taking her hand, she said quietly, "I'm really sorry, Euphemia."

It only took one of them to be brave enough to break away from Jane's toxic influence. In the next few seconds, every girl in the common room was crowding around Euphemia trying to console her and be as nice to her as they could possibly be. Jane and her mother's magazine stood alone and forgotten. But Euphemia never forgot. And neither did Jane.

Kenneth never understood why she was so reserved when they met Jane and her husband, Justin, at golf club functions, and she couldn't bring herself to tell him why she was always wary around the woman. Especially so because no matter how many times she asked her not to, Jane would persist in calling her 'Effie', much to Kenneth's amusement.

The years had not been as kind to Jane as they had been to Euphemia. Her mother had died with huge debts and Justin, who spoke well and dressed impeccably, always seemed to be between jobs. Euphemia heard that Jane had had to quietly sell most of her antiques to keep their house. Euphemia couldn't help thinking that maybe there was some justice in the universe after all.

The second letter reminded her of that day at school, and it also reminded her that she didn't know any more about her mother's death than the short paragraph read out by Jane in the common room. It had been too traumatic at the time to find out more. She couldn't go back and ask Maree after making her stand about never talking about her mother again, so she'd let the matter drop and got on with her exams.

Euphemia took the letter to work and when she was between clients, shut the door to her office, smoothed it out on the desk and typed the relevant details in to Google: 'coroner's report, Fredericka Theodora Marchamp, Coldsham' and the date of death. And there it was, everything set out in black and white, pages and pages of official information about her mother. It took the rest of the morning to read it all.

Fredericka had indeed been drunk at the wheel and alone in the car. She'd been driving too fast judging by the skid marks and missed a bend in the road. The car had plowed head first into the Coldsham village pond. The back of the car was discovered poking out of the water by the milkman early the next morning. No mention of anyone else and no suspicion of foul play.

The only points the coroner had raised any doubts about were that her seat belt was undone and the pond wasn't very deep. They were easily able to open the doors when they dragged the car out of the pond, so she wasn't trapped and there was no sign of a struggle. He surmised that without further evidence to the contrary, she had so much alcohol in her system that she had been incapable of escaping the vehicle.

There was also a matter of a fresh puncture wound in her right elbow, which the pathologist had pointed out at the postmortem. Fresh, as in some time in the twelve hours before she died. He had postulated it was consistent with having just given blood or a sample being taken. There was no evidence of any drugs in her system. Just alcohol.

The coroner returned a finding of Accidental Death and the case was closed.

One detail caught Euphemia's attention. Fredericka hadn't been living alone when she died. A Dr. Martin Shaker and his daughter were recorded as living in the same house, but they hadn't attended the hearing. In fact they hadn't been able to be contacted at all after the accident. Dr. Shaker and his daughter had disappeared with no forwarding address.

Chapter Six

The hot flushes started in earnest. One moment Euphemia was working quietly at her desk and the next she was pulling open her shirt and hanging out the window, desperate to feel a cool breeze on her skin. They happened when she was running and when she was in the shower. They interrupted her when she was on the phone and when she was shopping. She could no longer enjoy a glass of red wine when she was cooking dinner in the evening without being overwhelmed by a surge of heat driving her away from the stove and outside into the evening air, regardless of the weather. Worst of all, they woke her at night, and she was exhausted. Kenneth knew better than to comment.

Euphemia envied her friends who could take refuge in HRT. They raved about it, telling her with all the authority of Dr. Google that modern medicine meant she didn't have to put up with her flushes. Help was at hand. Their hot flushes had vanished overnight and hers would too. But the third and final letter had been quite specific. No hot flushes, no powers.

In the run-up to turning fifty, Euphemia had thought again and again about the switch, alternating between hope and ridicule. Taking the last letter out of the mailbox on her way to work, she'd dropped it into her tote bag meaning to open it later. She was more concerned that Kenneth and the girls might be planning a surprise party.

Euphemia had caught the three of them whispering together in

the weeks leading up to her 'half-century', as Nicky insisted on refer-
ring to the day itself, only for them to suddenly go quiet when she
appeared. If they hadn't looked so pleased with themselves, it could
have been rather tiresome.

That morning she'd got up early to go for an extra-long run. Kenneth, eyes closed, dribbling attractively out of the corner of his
mouth, his gray hair awry on the pillow, looked to be still asleep.

"Lucky I love you," she whispered as she tiptoed out the door.

"Ditto," came the reply.

The weather was her idea of perfect — stormy and threatening to
rain. Thick gray clouds churned across the sky on all sides of the narrow strip of land circling the harbor. When she reached the ridgeline,
the wind roared in her ears as she broke cover. Below her the trees
bent first this way then that, branches of wilding pines amongst the
native trees creaking alarmingly. She stood leaning into the powerful
gusts buffeting her so hard she could barely keep her footing, revel-
ing in the force of the weather against her body. It's a great day to be
alive, she thought. She checked her watch and realizing she would be
late for work, Euphemia picked up her heels and galloped down the
hill along the bush tracks, leaping over tree roots and rocks all the
way home to a hot shower.

Something was definitely going on when she stepped out of the
lift at Sage Consulting. She could hear hushed voices, doors shutting
and a general shooshing as she greeted Alison at her desk.

Euphemia did a double take. The woman had made an effort. Not
much of an effort, granted, but she'd pulled her hair off her face and
a sprig of daphne was pinned to the lapel of her long gray cardigan.
Alison smiled shyly when Euphemia told her how nice she was looking, and murmured the words 'Happy Birthday' before returning to
sort through the bundle of letters on her desk.

Euphemia couldn't count the number of times she'd tried to
encourage Alison to put more effort into her appearance. Sage Consulting prided itself on excellence, and the dowdy appearance of the
receptionist was not exactly the first impression they wanted their

new clients to have. Euphemia had even given Alison a generous clothing allowance, but no new clothes appeared.

At least the woman was more efficient than she looked. She remembered clients' names and details, she organized appointments and documents without mishap, and she was brilliant with the staff, remembering birthdays and making sure everyone signed the card, the cake was ordered and everyone got a piece. Imagining how difficult it would be for her to find other reception work looking the way she did, neither Euphemia nor Kenneth could find it in their hearts to take the necessary steps to terminate her employment.

"Oh Mrs. Sage,' said Alison looking up from the letters, "there's someone waiting in your office. Mr. Sage said it would be all right."

Laughter in the tearoom opposite was quickly stifled.

"Please, please, don't let it be a surprise party," Euphemia murmured to herself as she walked down the hall to her office. She opened her door slowly, ready to put on an instantaneous smile of delight so as not to disappoint those who had gone to so much trouble to make her birthday special. The room was empty. She turned back to Alison, eyebrows raised, and a ball of cream and black barreled into her legs, bounced off her feet and hurtled down the corridor.

"Quick, stop her," yelled Kenneth racing out of his adjoining office in hot pursuit of the bundle of fat and fur, which was a tiny puppy now incontinent with excitement and leaving a trail of pee all the way to reception.

When the puppy reached Alison, it stopped, looked at her, first one way and then another before it backed away, hackles raised, and snarled. Kenneth arrived just in time to scoop up the little body, saving it from a vicious kick to the kidneys. In gratitude the puppy promptly finished emptying its bladder all over his suit.

"I don't like animals, Mr. Sage, especially puppies," said Alison.

"I can tell, Alison,' said Kenneth before turning to Euphemia and bundling the puppy into her arms.

"Happy birthday! She's a pug and she's from all of us."

At that moment Kezia and Nicky emerged from the tearoom carrying a huge chocolate cake ablaze with fifty candles. Several of the staff started popping the corks from champagne bottles frightening the puppy, which burrowed against Euphemia before looking up at her with bulging black eyes. A collective 'Aaahhh' went up from the staff with the exception of Alison, who had returned to her letters.

"The best birthday present ever. I'll call her Petal. What do you all think?" asked Euphemia, and was greeted with general agreement. "Thank you. Now Kenneth, please tell me there isn't going to be a party."

Chapter Seven

Euphemia had forgotten the sheer exhaustion that came with getting up in the night to crying babies. She was determined Petal would sleep in her own bed in the laundry and Petal was equally determined she wanted to sleep upstairs with Euphemia and Kenneth, where it was warm and there was company. Taking turns to get up became a necessity and the puppy was always so pleased to see whoever poked their weary head around the laundry door. Neither of them could do anything but relent and cuddle her back to sleep.

Eventually Petal realized she was not going to win the war, and the laundry was not so bad after all.

But there was no way the stubborn little dog was going to be left at home alone during the day. When Euphemia went to work, so did Petal; when Euphemia went to the shops, so did Petal; but when Euphemia went for one of her long runs, Petal suddenly needed a lie-down — she drew the line at anything more than a short walk.

Clients and staff grew used to the little dog padding about the office when she wasn't sleeping in the basket under Euphemia's desk. She became the darling of the business world after starring on the Sage and Sage Christmas calendar. Quite independently, Nicky and Kezia complained to their friends that since Petal's arrival, their mother was less interested in them and more interested in the dog.

Incredibly friendly and well-behaved, Petal charmed everyone she came in contact with, everyone except Alison at reception. It was clear their dislike was mutual and they gave each other a wide berth.

In the fuss that accompanied Petal's arrival, Euphemia forgot about Maree's last letter. It wasn't until she started using her tote bag again after she turned 51 that she found it. This was the shortest letter of all, but with it, in the envelope, wrapped in tissue paper, was a key.

Dear Euphemia,

I know you're opening this letter late, but a year doesn't make much difference, especially if you haven't been through it yet. I mean 'the change', as some of us called it. Sounds so much gentler and less clinical than 'menopause'.

I had hot flushes for years until I took HRT and felt instantly better. But you don't have this option, not if you want your powers to develop.

It's completely up to you, but I was told by the others when I asked them what I must tell you. They were, to a woman, insistent that the powers only come as you harness the energy of each surge or flush. Take away the surges that activate the changes and nothing happens.

Be thankful you don't have them yet. There are reasons you have to wait so long.

The powers would not only be wasted on the young but what safeguards would there be, could there be, once they were activated? How tempting would it be for someone young and impatient to use them as a shortcut to love, instant wealth and even, heaven forbid, celebrity? How quickly the powers would corrupt those who haven't yet learned the value and lessons of life.

True self-awareness comes with time, experience, and reflection. The mistakes we make teach us more than our successes but only the truly thoughtful come to understand this once the pain of failure has been absorbed.

The others tell me that you are going to need all the patience and understanding you can muster to use the powers — or not — for real good — the good you know in your soul to be true.

With anything new, you will make mistakes. You will be uncertain and afraid at times. At times you will do too much and other times not enough. All I ask, Euphemia, is for you to know yourself, and use the powers in moderation doing only what you have to. No showing off! But once you commit to something, see it through. Be brave and be strong because you are.

I don't have much more to tell you. Fredericka, who should have been here, failed the tests. You won't.

The key will open the chest that Kenneth carried up to the attic after I died. You will find out more when you look inside.

A warning: if you try to open the chest before you complete the third milestone, the key will break in the lock. Don't be like Fredericka — be patient. Wait for your body to tell you when the time is right.

I will be watching your progress with interest as always.

Good luck

Maree

Chapter Eight

Euphemia thought about that last letter many times over the next two years. It had been more serious than the others and for the first time she let herself consider the possibility that Maree might be telling the truth.

Now and then her imagination would run riot and she would think about superpowers. She saw herself hurdling tall buildings in a single bound, stopping runaway trains with one hand behind her back and flying up to the stratosphere to prevent meteors from destroying Earth. Kenneth didn't understand why he was being dragged along to yet another action-packed movie of comic book heroes brought to life with advanced CGI, but he didn't complain. Anything was better than the Scandinavian art films with subtitles she usually insisted they see.

Common sense had prevailed until Euphemia chanced upon an article about mitochondrial DNA, a type of DNA that could only be passed down through the female line. Scientists had been able to track everyone on the planet back to a single woman, a mother to us all, who they called Eve, using this mtDNA. Perhaps the exclusive daughter-to-daughter switch was possible after all but this didn't answer all her questions. Why, she wondered, would the switch only work in eldest daughters?

As life continued much the same, Euphemia's curiosity intensified. She was dying to know one way or the other, but the flushes didn't come. The frustration of not knowing and having to wait was unbearable, so Euphemia took Maree's message to keep busy to heart and embarked on a series of projects. She undertook teaching projects at the local business school, revamped computers at Sage Consulting and hired Kezia to develop new software. She took the family off on holidays all over the world, ran longer distances than she had ever run before, redecorated the house and built new garden walls. She drew the line at golf. Kenneth could have that to himself. And she waited. She waited for the first sign of menopause.

Initially all she noticed were the flushes and annoyingly hers seemed stronger and more frequent than any her friends reported. She checked herself in the mirror two weeks after the first and to her immense disappointment she looked exactly the same. Creases still marked the corners of her eyes and mouth, her jaw line still sagged more than she liked. Gray hairs still grew through the blonde highlights and she still looked like a fifty-three-year-old woman, albeit one who was fit and healthy.

A month later she felt taller, but when she checked her height against the doorpost she was exactly the same as she had always been. Yet she was sure her back was straighter and stronger because she felt newly energized muscles pulling her spine into alignment and her shoulders lost their roundness. Her joints stopped clicking when she walked upstairs and the right knee, injured in a skiing accident twenty years before, stopped aching after a long run. She convinced herself that her nails had lost their brittleness and her hairdresser said her hair was thicker, but when she was leaving she heard him tell his next client the same thing. None of these changes came close to what she considered might be superpowers.

One Friday night, Kenneth and Euphemia were sitting in a dimly lit restaurant reading menus. While Kenneth was fumbling in his pockets for his glasses, Euphemia had already scanned the offerings and ordered for them both. Looking quizzically at her, his glasses perched on the end of his nose, he raised an eyebrow and was just about to say something when Jane and Justin French stopped to say hello, on their way to a table farther back in the gloom.

When they'd gone and the wine arrived, Kenneth raised his glass and said, "To you. The only fifty-three-year-old woman who can read a menu in the gloom without her glasses."

Euphemia looked at him, unsure what to say. She hadn't noticed that she could see perfectly well without them. In fact when she thought about it, she remembered she'd left them on the kitchen bench at breakfast and had had to work all day without them and she'd coped perfectly well. In fact her eyesight was better than it had ever been. The figures on the spreadsheets leapt off the page and she didn't have her normal screen headache at five o'clock. She picked up the wine list and checked it. Every word was clear, none of the usual fuzzy double vision she had put up with since turning forty-five.

"You're very observant," she said.

"I've heard of people with short-sightedness when they were young, not needing glasses as they got older, but that's not you, is it? Humor me. See the doctor on Monday, make sure nothing's wrong."

Rather than argue the point Euphemia nodded and thankfully before he could say another word, their meals arrived. The hot fug of delicious smells distracted them both. She was starving and the smell of her T-bone steak leaking blood on the plate in front of her was overwhelmingly strong, firing every one of her taste buds into overdrive. She hadn't enjoyed the aroma of steak so much in years.

After their main meal Kenneth excused himself to go to talk to one of his clients on the other side of the restaurant, leaving Euphemia to order dessert if one of the busy waitresses ever returned to take their order. She was fiddling with her napkin when she looked over at the Frenches. They didn't seem happy. In fact Jane looked desperate and was talking nonstop at Justin's bowed head as he methodically ate his way through his risotto.

Euphemia felt awkward and was just about to turn away in case she was caught staring when above the background noise of the restaurant she could hear their conversation, word for word, exactly as if she were sitting at their table. A wave of embarrassment washed over her and she looked away immediately, hoping no one would see her blushing.

It was too late. Jane had seen her watching them and, forcing a smile, lifted her hand to wave. Euphemia waved back. Thankfully right at that moment Kenneth rejoined her, muttering to her to remind him to check such and such account on Monday.

"Ordered dessert?"

"Not yet. The waitress is super busy. Probably just as well."

"Speak for yourself. I've been looking forward to the mint chocolate mousse since we arrived. You know it's the only reason I come here." He called loudly to the waitress, who sighed, and smiling, squeezed her way between the tables to get to them.

After she'd left with two orders for mousse and coffees to follow, Euphemia took Kenneth's hand in hers and ran her finger seductively over his palm. "I didn't know you were going away for the weekend first thing tomorrow morning. Golf with your buddies. You didn't tell me," she whispered softly, a smile in every word.

Kenneth closed his hand over hers. "I was going to."

"When was that?"

"After the mint chocolate mousse, when I knew you would be putty in my hands, that's when. Why? I don't need to ask your permission, do I? I'm a grown man. I can go and play golf with Roger and the boys any time I like, can't I?"

"Of course you can, darling." He winced at the tone in her voice. "It would have been nice if you'd told me sooner, that's all. I would have made my own plans."

"To be fair, nothing was decided till this morning. Old Justin over there got the four of us a great deal at Wairakei. Wonderful course, brilliant pub and there's a tournament that Roger and I have a chance of winning. Anyway," he said, "how did you know?"

"Jane told me, just now."

"I didn't see you talking to her."

"How else would I know? But that doesn't matter, does it? Actually it works out well. I need some time to myself anyway."

"Not more garden walls, I hope?"

"How rude? I thought you liked the last one," said Euphemia.

"I do. I do."

The mint chocolate mousses arrived and Euphemia was so engrossed savoring the subtle flavors in each mouthful that when she looked up, the Frenches' table was empty. They'd left without saying goodbye or a tip, judging by the look on the waitress's face as she cleared away their glasses.

Chapter Nine

Outside the restaurant it was raining and cold. A southerly front had come off the sea and caught the city unawares. People were shivering under shop verandas, not dressed for the weather, jiggling up and down to stay warm and waiting for transport home. Cars edged past each other slowly on the narrow street, their headlights reflected up into the shop windows from the wet tarmac.

Euphemia had parked her black hatchback in a nearby parking lot and she and Kenneth ran to it, coats over their heads, feet sloshing through puddles, eager to get to the car and get warm. She started the engine while Kenneth turned the heater on full blast. Instantly the windows fogged up, blurring the world outside.

She wound down her window to check the way was clear when to her side, a black Mercedes sedan backed slowly but resolutely towards her and it wasn't stopping. It loomed closer, obstructing her view of everything else. Surely his backing cameras would be bleeping by now, alerting him that he was about to hit something. Why hadn't he stopped?

A millisecond before impact, a surge of heat washed over her. Euphemia put out her arm and feeling the cold wet metal under her hand, she also felt the car halt a hair's breadth from her door. The noisy heater meant Kenneth hadn't noticed what was happening as he fiddled with the search button to find the radio station he liked. He looked up just in time to see the Mercedes backing towards them, and yelling, he reached across and hit the horn.

Euphemia knew the driver of the Mercedes had felt his car stop and, without looking in his rear-view mirror, had revved his engine. His tires spun pointlessly on the tarmac, spattering Euphemia's face and hair with muddy street water. Euphemia pushed back harder and the car moved away another an inch. Kenneth, his hand still on the horn, his face white with fear and anger, was starting to sweat.

People emerged from under the verandas and nearby bars to see what was happening. Several ran over to the Mercedes and banged on the driver's window, gesticulating wildly, yelling at him that there was a car behind him and to go forwards. A few who came around the back saw Euphemia holding the big car to a standstill and started whispering and pointing.

Without any warning, the Mercedes pulled forward, swung quickly out of the car park and turned into a line of traffic, forcing several cars to brake on the slippery road, then it drove off down the street and into the night.

Someone knocked on the passenger window mouthing the words, "Are you all right?"

Kenneth gave the man a thumbs-up and wound down his window. Another man arrived and, leaning close enough to breathe beer fumes into the car, yelled more loudly than necessary, "Hey, mate, your wife is amazing. One and a half tons of car she was pushing off."

Kenneth, smelling the beer and having no idea what he was talking about, nodded, said 'Thanks' and wound his window back up. The man stepped back into the crowd and telling anyone who would listen tried to explain what he had just seen, pointing at Euphemia and mimicking how she held the car at bay.

Euphemia grabbed her handbag and rustled around in the bottom for tissues to wipe the water and mud off her face, the cold night air welcome against her skin. The rain started again in earnest and the crowd quickly dispersed.

Later that night when they were snuggled up in bed, Kenneth said, "That bastard wasn't going to stop. Shouldn't be driving. Lucky I hit the horn when I did."

"Very lucky. I didn't think of it. Goodness knows what would have happened if you hadn't."

"Get some sleep. Love you," he said and kissed her again before turning over and going to sleep.

In the dark, Euphemia stretched out her right arm. She could feel a slight ache around her shoulder but otherwise it felt completely normal, exactly the same as her left arm.

Chapter Ten

The next morning dawned bright and clear. It was as if the storm and last night's events had been a dream. The tuis were in fine form and woke Euphemia and Kenneth with a more melodic song than usual. There was already some heat in the sunshine pouring through a gap in the curtains. Kenneth leapt out of bed and bustled around packing and organizing his gear, trying as hard as he could to pretend that he wasn't excited he was going away with the boys for a weekend purely devoted to golf and maybe a little drinking.

Euphemia, in turn, was trying hard not to look pleased he was leaving.

The street was quiet when she waved him off and she hurried back inside to have her second cup of coffee. Petal roused herself from her bed and, stretching each leg slowly in turn, walked sleepily into the kitchen and plumped down beside Euphemia with an expectant look on her face. "Oh all right," said Euphemia, and poured some dog biscuits into the bowl. Petal couldn't believe her luck. She never got fed in the mornings. Before Euphemia could change her mind, Petal was snuffling up the biscuits, crunching away with a contented look on her face.

Euphemia made the bed and tidied the house. She vacuumed and took a reluctant Petal for a very quick walk around the block. She showered, dressed, and put on her make-up. These weren't delaying tactics. She reasoned that if what Maree had said was true, then she should look her best for whatever was going to happen after she opened the chest. When she finally felt ready to find out one way or the other if there was a Rachel's Switch, she locked the doors to the house, poured herself a fresh mug of black coffee and climbed the stairs to the attic.

The chest sat in the middle of the room where Kenneth had dumped it all those years ago. Covered in dust, junk all around it, it looked very ordinary. Clearing a space, she knelt down in front of it then hesitated. What if she wasn't ready and the key broke in the lock?

Back yourself, she thought. Milestone one, two, and three, tick, tick, tick. And you've held off a reversing Mercedes with one hand. You must be ready. The question you should be asking yourself, Euphemia Sage, is what are you ready for?

She took another deep breath and exhaled slowly and steadily, trying to slow her heart beating fast in her chest. She cleared the cobwebs from around the lock, put in the key and turned it easily. A series of clicks and rumbles followed and the lid popped up. She raised it slowly, letting it fall back on its hinges.

The chest was empty.

She looked again. "It can't be," she said to no one. But it was. Empty. Lined with layers of old newspapers, yellowed and tattered, torn and crusty with age — a musty smell rose from its depths. The chest was completely and totally empty. Nada. Nothing. Zero. Zilch.

Disappointment engulfed her, followed by stunned disbelief. Can't be. Her face wrinkled as she tried to think it through. All the hints, the story about a switch, superpowers, life being more exciting if only she had patience and met the milestones. Nothing. She turned the chest around, praying she had missed something. Maybe whatever it was had got caught and fell out when she opened the lid? She didn't find anything. It really was empty.

"And I believed her," she murmured. "I dared to hope against all rational hope that she was telling the truth."

What a fool. What a sad fool. Feeling ashamed and embarrassed, she looked round the attic to make sure of the obvious — that she was alone and no one was there to see her sag with lost hope for something she had dared to dream. A ray of sunlight poked through a hole in the roof where a nail had come loose and lit up some old pictures stacked against the wall. Must remember to sort those out, she thought, pulling her cardigan around her.

She looked again at the empty chest and sighed. Powers? Rachel's Switch? Having to wait until she reached menopause? All rubbish.

If only I'd trusted my instincts after opening the first letter and not bothered with the others. Silly, silly woman. I really thought that my life, my body, might, no — be honest — *were* going to change. Tears pricked one eye and then the other and she wiped at them, furious with herself. She turned round and sat back, leaning against the chest, cradling the remains of her coffee in her hands.

Then she laughed. Just a shrug to start and then, as the utter ridiculousness of her belief in magic powers and heroes kicked in, she laughed so hard she felt her ribs ache.

What did I expect? A magic wand, a light saber, a cape and golden lasso, an instruction manual for superwomen named Euphemia. Wings would have been nice. Admit it. Flying was always high on the list of wants. An ounce of krypton would have been good too, Maree. I'm not greedy. This last thought made her laugh even more, until she finally had to stop, exhausted.

Sitting up again, Euphemia brushed the dust off her clothes. "This is your reality, Euphemia Sage, an empty chest and dust all over you," she said out loud. In one sleeve she found a tissue and wiped her eyes and blew her nose, then looked at the mess of soggy paper.

Real life is having a tissue, she thought. I'm a middle-aged woman who remembers to always have a tissue. I do not have special powers and special powers do not run in my family.

She could see now, deep inside, how much she had wanted the letters to be true and how she had been willing to accept anything if it meant excitement. Plus who doesn't want to be special — extraordinary? The power of suggestion and a vivid imagination had done the rest. Hot flushes were just that and she was not being energized with each one into some muscle-bound hero in running shoes.

She looked into the chest one last time to make sure but it was just the same. Empty. Wearily she closed the lid, locked it and pushed it away. Let the bloody thing rot. The sheer disappointment welled up in her chest and stomach again as if she'd been hit. Pull yourself together, Euphemia. I'm not that bad, she thought. Life is not that bad. I don't need to be a super-heroine, or super-anything. I am a very lucky woman and at least now... I can get some HRT for these bloody hot flushes.

Downstairs, Euphemia could hear Petal snuffling happily in the bag of dog biscuits. The pantry door squeaked as the fat little tummy brushed against it. Petal, ever the greedy opportunist, was in pug heaven. At least someone was happy. Wait, she thought, the attic door is shut and I'm three floors up. I know I shut the kitchen door.

She paused and listened again and there it was, as clear as if she were in the kitchen itself. The sounds of Petal sneakily stealing dog biscuits, accompanied by her snuffling wheeze, were not only unmistakable but they were very loud.

Euphemia turned back to the chest and unlocked it. Still empty. She made herself stop and think back, to read the last letter again in her mind. And there it was in black and white. Her aunt had said to 'look inside'. So Euphemia did as she was told and this time she looked. She looked hard. Headlines from the tatty pieces of newspaper lining the walls of the chest, which she had ignored before, leapt at her, clamoring for her attention, fighting to be in focus in the center of her vision.

At random she stopped the jostling and chose a headline from 1910.

LOST BOY FOUND ALIVE.

Little Phillip Smith, aged eight, was reunited with his parents yesterday, having been missing on the moors for two days. He reported he had fallen over a cliff and had landed on a ledge high above the sea with no way up or down. His parents were frantic with worry. The police had set up search parties, all to no avail.

On the third day, when despair had set in, a local gentlewoman, Mrs. Georgiana Bathgate, carried Phillip into the police station and placed him in the arms of his distraught mother.

Mrs. Bathgate told the police she had been out walking her dog, and hearing the child's cries for help, had looked over the cliff where she could see him on the ledge below. She managed to attract the attention of a young man who climbed down and carried the now unconscious boy back up to her. She told this reporter that the young man did not want thanks and had hurried away before she could get his name.

The boy's parents were enormously grateful to Mrs. Bathgate but have also asked that the young man come forward as he is the real hero — climbing down a dangerous cliff face to carry their son back up to safety.

The headline from a second article, dated two days after the first, loomed into view.

HERO ASKED TO COME FORWARD.

This reporter asks that the hero who saved Phillip Smith please come forward as further information would be of assistance.

The ledge where Phillip was reported to have been lying is not easily visible from the top of the cliff. This reporter, who visited the spot yesterday, could hear nothing over the sound of the sea pounding on the rocks below.

This reporter was also only able to find one set of footprints in the muddy cliff edge and these were consistent with a lady's hiking shoe.

Later when this reporter visited Mrs. Bathgate at her home in the hope she could provide more information, he noted that her dog was unwell and recovering from surgery carried out on the day of the rescue.

Mrs. Bathgate, when approached for comment, said she could offer no more information and hoped the little boy was doing well. She referred again to the heroism of the passerby and suggested he should make himself known.

This humble reporter reluctantly concedes that until this man does exactly that, some of the mystery surrounding the little boy's rescue will remain unresolved.

Chapter Eleven

Euphemia was just about to read the next article, entitled *Famous Author, Charles Dickens, Saved from Certain Death in Railway Accident*, when the high-pitched whining of a small car driving down the street distracted her. There was a squeal of tires as a car made a sharp turn into her driveway, the engine was turned off and then silence. A car door slammed shut then someone ran up the path and banged loudly on the front door.

"Help, Effie, help! Open up — hurry!"

The banging on the door stopped for a second then started again in earnest. "Effie, open up, hurry! Please be here... please, Effie."

Euphemia winced. Being called Effie felt like someone was running fingernails down her personal blackboard. She had always hated this version of her name. She hated it when she was a little girl and she hated it now. The only person who persisted in calling her Effie, despite repeated requests not to, was Jane French.

So what was Jane doing beating her door down, disturbing the peace and quiet of Saturday morning?

Thoughts of Kenneth and the golf trip flashed through her mind. She'd been in the attic for over an hour and without her phone. Had something happened? An accident? Heart racing, she slammed the chest shut and taking the stairs two at a time landed with a thud before the front door, unlocked it and yanked it open to an empty porch.

Jane's hurried footsteps were now at the back of the house. Petal's warning barks meant she had opened the gate into the back garden and there was loud banging again, this time on the kitchen door and again, entreaties. Jane was whispering, hissing to be let in.

As Euphemia opened the back door, another car braked to a halt in front of the house, followed by the slamming of more doors. At least two people this time, their heavy footsteps on the front path.

A disheveled Jane pushed past her and stumbled inside, closing the door behind her and scrabbling to lock it. Petal, always delighted to see visitors, sniffed around her legs, her curly tail flipping from side to side in excitement.

Jane looked terrible. Her hair was sticking out as if she had just got out of bed, which seemed the most likely explanation because she was wearing a ratty jersey over what looked like pajamas and gumboots. Pale, eyes wildly darting, she barely looked at Euphemia then putting her fingers to her lips, Jane tiptoed into the kitchen and finding the pantry door, opened it and stepped inside, pulling it closed behind her. Unable to shut it, the only clue she was there was a whitened finger curled, shaking with effort, around the edge. Petal stopped barking and sat down, looking from the finger to Euphemia and back to the finger.

Euphemia was about to ask Jane what on earth she was doing, when the doorbell rang several times, each ring more insistent and longer than the one before. She deduced that someone who had come with bad news about husbands would not be hiding in her pantry, so whoever was ringing the doorbell must have something to do with why Jane was hiding in her pantry.

Petal, excited by the prospect of yet more visitors, got up and started running between the front door and the kitchen, sniffing loudly, uncertain which visitor should claim her attention.

At the front door, Euphemia could hear two men talking.

"That silly bitch has to be here and she knows we know she is. Whose place is this anyway?"

"Dunno. Doesn't matter. The boss said we had to get her. Ring again and if there's no answer, go round the back and look for a way in."

Just as one of the men reached up to press the bell again, Euphemia opened the door.

"Can I help you, gentlemen?" she asked, trying not to sound flustered.

Two thick-necked men, cheap suits straining across broad shoulders, stood on her doorstep looking down at her. Broken noses and scars marked both faces but most noticeable was the missing top half of the left ear sported by the larger of the two. Euphemia found it difficult not to stare.

"Sorry to disturb you, ma'am, but we're looking for Jane French. Police. She's needed down at the station. We understand that's her car in your driveway."

"Police? Then you'll have ID, won't you?"

"Sorry, ma'am, left mine in the car," said the man with half an ear. "Mark, you got yours?"

Mark shrugged and shook his head. Half-ear smirked. "Sorry, ma'am. You're more than welcome to ring the station while we come in and look around." Saying this he stepped over the threshold and into the house. Petal backed away, hackles raised, growling.

"Cute dog," said Half-ear stepping over her and pushing past Euphemia.

Euphemia, infuriated by his presumption, walked around him and stood squarely in front of him, feet wide apart, hands on her hips. "I think that's far enough, don't you?" she said. Half-ear took no notice of her and was instead looking over her head checking the layout of the house, searching for any sign of Jane.

The one called Mark went into the living room on his left, while Half-ear proceeded to open and shut the door to the downstairs loo before heading for the kitchen. Euphemia heard a shallow intake of breath from behind the pantry door. She couldn't let him get that far.

A surge of heat flowed through her, her skin tingled and her heart slowed in her chest. She stepped in front of the men again just as they walked into the kitchen proper.

"I said that's far enough."

The tone of her voice was nothing she'd ever used before. It was a tone that brooked no argument, which connected deep into their brains, a tone that triggered memories of when they were little boys and they had to do as they were told or suffer the consequences. The men stopped and looked at their feet, shuffling awkwardly. Petal sat down.

"I am going to count to three," announced Euphemia. "If you have not turned around and left my home by the time I get to three, there will be consequences — consequences you will not like."

"One..." She paused. The men stopped shuffling and chins down, exchanged nervous glances.

Euphemia folded her arms and looked at them expectantly.

"Two..."

She walked calmly back to the front door and held it open.

Just as she was about to say 'Three', Mark buckled, turned on his heels and scuttled out the door, followed two seconds later by Half-ear, looking sullen and churlish.

"We'll be back, won't we, Grant?" called Mark from the driveway.

Half-ear looked Euphemia up then down. He put both hands on his hips and stared defiantly at her, willing her to look him in the eye.

"You may think you can tell us what to do, Mrs., but you can't. We know she's here. We're only going now because Mark wants to, but we'll be back."

By the time they reached their car, the two men were stretching and shaking their heads.

"What just happened?"

"Weird — really weird. Her voice, it reminded me of Mum," said Mark, "just before she used to get the dog collar out."

Half-ear looked back at the house, searching the windows for the telltale curtain flick that meant they were being watched. There was none.

"Do you know what else, Grant? That lady, she wasn't scared."

Chapter Twelve

Euphemia leaned against the door and listened to them talking out in the street. Her hearing was now so acute, she only had to think of the person talking and their words were amplified in her ears.

They were right, she wasn't scared although every sensible bone in her body told her she should have been — especially of Half-ear. There was something about him she couldn't put her finger on. She was surprised he'd left so quietly until she heard Mark talking about their mother. She figured Half-ear was the older of the two and that he'd spent his life looking out for his younger sibling.

Waiting until she heard their car turn the corner at the end of the street, she went back into the kitchen. Petal padded after her and sniffed the pantry door.

"You can come out now, Jane. It's safe," said Euphemia, filling the kettle for a cup of tea.

The pantry door swung open slowly and Jane looked up at her from where she sat huddled against the bag of dog food.

"Effie, what have I done?" she groaned.

Petal nudged her legs and wagging her tail in sympathy, licked her hands. Jane pulled the little dog into her lap, cuddling her tightly. Petal looked uncertainly from one to the other.

Jane nicked a biscuit from the bag and gave it to Petal, who scoffed it gratefully, black eyes looking adoringly at her new friend.

"You've got her undying loyalty now," said Euphemia putting her hand out.

Jane took it and pulled herself up, then rearranged her pajamas and ran her fingers through her hair. "I look awful, I know," she said going round to sit on a stool and with her elbows on the bench, her head sank into her hands.

"Let's have a cup of tea and then you can tell me who those men were and what they wanted. They said they're coming back."

"They're not very nice, are they? They barged into the house as soon as Justin had gone, yelling at me that they were going to break my legs. They would have done it too, if I hadn't said I needed to pee and got out the bathroom window and come here. You were amazing by the way. Counting to three like that."

"Break your legs? For goodness' sake, Jane."

Euphemia made the tea and took the milk out of the fridge. Jane milked her tea and picking up the mug, cradled it in her hands, blowing on the hot liquid to cool it, considering what she was going to say next.

"Effie," she said quietly, "you know Justin lost his job ages ago."

"Yes, and I'm sorry but please don't call me Effie. You know how much I hate it."

"Do you? Really? It's what I've always called you."

"I know. Stop it, would you? Anyway, I thought Justin had found a job and it was all OK."

"That's what we wanted people to think, but my poor darling tried and tried. No one wants a fifty-something man who doesn't understand computers. And you know he has a bad back. Not that I'd let him do any physical work. He's a businessman with skills and connections. And so good with people."

Euphemia nodded for Jane to go on.

"Anyway, with no job, we ran out of money. The house has two mortgages and the credit cards are maxed out. We went to Bali two months ago. We were both stressed out with the worry, so we needed a break. Unfortunately it was quite expensive. Justin said something would turn up but it didn't."

"You should have said."

"And have people pity us?" asked Jane. "I couldn't do that and before you say another word, we are selling the house. We have to. The bank is selling it for us. The mortgagee sale notice is in next Saturday's paper. People will talk, of course. And we have to advertise. Advertise and then auction it quickly before too many buyers get cold feet when they read the building report, the bank tells us."

"It was your mother's house, wasn't it?"

Jane nodded. "She would be turning in her grave if she knew, Effie. You knew her, didn't you, so proud."

"You'll get a great price. It's a big piece of land and in the best part of town, just ripe for turning into apartments if the buyer doesn't want to live there. I have clients who are building a retirement village nearby and I know how much they paid for their land."

"They approached us, but Justin said we could do better, price wise. We only had one mortgage then."

Euphemia got up and filled the Bialetti for coffee. She needed something stronger than tea.

"This is confidential, isn't it? You won't tell anyone?" asked Jane.

Euphemia shook her head.

"The problem is," she said, "we haven't done anything to the house since Mummy was alive and Justine was born. Big old wood and brick houses like that, they need so much maintenance. You wouldn't understand, living modestly as you do, but family estates cost a fortune to keep up. Justin said we would do it one day and wasn't it better to go on holiday than spend money on boring things like piles and roofing?"

"How much does the bank think you'll get?"

"Around the value of the land if the auction goes well. That will just about cover the mortgages. So you can see why I had to borrow money from 'other sources'."

"Wouldn't it have been easier to find a job or maybe not go to Bali? Because I'm presuming you borrowed money from loan sharks?"

"I prefer the term finance company, Effie. And I did try to say that to Justin but he wouldn't have it. Oh God, Effie, Mummy would be so ashamed."

The coffee bubbled up into the pot and the harsh aroma tickled her nostrils, flavors vying for attention, swamping any ability to separate and identify them. If only she was alone, she could concentrate. Instead, Euphemia busied herself getting clean cups, all the while finding it easier to avoid eye contact while she digested Jane's story. "Does Justine know?"

"No, and I can't tell her. She graduates soon and is doing an internship in New York. Justin promised to pay for it because he says you can't invest enough in networking. Some of the money I borrowed we used to pay for her tickets and accommodation. New York is so expensive, Effie."

"How much have you borrowed?" Euphemia poured the coffee and handed Jane a cup.

"I know I've been stupid. After this morning I really know. I just couldn't bear to let them down, so I told Justin I had sold a painting I found on the top of a wardrobe. We'd already sold most of the good antiques years ago but I'm sure you know that. Everyone else does. I gave him the last of the money to go away this weekend. He deserves time away with the boys, Effie, he does."

"So, today, right now you have nothing? I don't understand. We saw you at the restaurant last night."

"Don't scold. Justin suggested it and I didn't have the heart to refuse. He wanted to treat me."

Euphemia spluttered on a mouthful of hot coffee. "How much did you borrow?"

"Twenty thousand dollars. No. I have to tell the truth, a hundred thousand. Effie, I can't believe it... they say I owe a hundred and fifty thousand dollars. They say that includes interest and I need to pay up because next week it'll be two hundred thousand!"

"You've got to be joking."

"I know, I know, I know." Jane hesitated. "Effie, you don't have any money you could lend me, do you? I promise I'd pay it back. I only need ten thousand dollars to get them off my back until the house sells. You and Kenneth live in such a small place but I know your business is doing well, and I wouldn't ask but I'm desperate, Effie, and we are old friends. Remember school?"

"Yes, I do remember school." Euphemia was pleased to see that Jane had the good grace to blush.

"I can't give you anything, Jane. Certainly not ten thousand dollars. It's Saturday. The ATMs wouldn't let me have that much. There must be something else you can do. You must have something left from when your mother was alive. She had that amazing jewelry... maybe you could use that."

"I can't. It's all I have left to remind me of her. Anyway, she left it to Justine. I just look after it. She never liked me as much as she did Justine. Plus, I've hidden it. I don't want the bank getting their grubby mitts on my daughter's inheritance."

Euphemia rolled her cup slowly in her hands. "Justine would understand. She understands business. That's what she's been studying all these years, isn't it? You have to do something, Jane, because the alternative is two broken legs."

"They would heal."

"You can't mean that. Not really. Justin and Justine would be horrified if they knew. From the little I know about loan sharks, they break your legs but you still owe the money. One is not a substitute for the other."

"That's so unfair. Their boss was even waiting for me outside the restaurant last night. He sat in this big, black Mercedes and just looked at me. He didn't say anything, just looked."

Euphemia saw again the silhouette of the driver of the Mercedes that had tried to back into her car and shuddered. "Jane, go to the police. They know what to do."

"I did go. They said they'd send patrols past the house. They said it was a legal loan and they couldn't do anything until something happened. Fat lot of good their patrols did me this morning. It'd be more useful if they sent an ambulance round every couple of hours."

"But now those goons know you're here in my house and I'm involved."

"Sorry, Effie, I shouldn't have come. There's no one else. I couldn't cope with our real friends knowing. I know what they'd say. I'll go."

Jane got up and pulled her jersey down over her pajamas. "I didn't know what else to do."

"Aside from giving you money, what did you think I could do?"

"Could I stay here, Effie, with you?" asked Jane hopefully. "You were so good with those men this morning. I couldn't believe it when they left."

Euphemia thought of the chest upstairs and how she desperately wanted time alone to go through it and find out more about the switch. She thought back to Georgiana rescuing the little boy quite by chance when out for a walk. She looked at Jane standing in her kitchen, obviously in terrible trouble. Maybe this was her first test. Maybe it was her job to rescue Jane.

"You can stay," she said finally. "You're right. It will be safer for you here. Even if it's just the two of us against the two of them."

"You're such a good person. Thank you. I promise I'll be as little bother as possible and it's only till Monday, till Justin gets back. But there was one more reason I came to see you, Effie," said Jane. "I need you to talk to Alison."

"Alison?"

"Alison Sinclair, your receptionist at Sage Consulting. She's the one I owe the money to. Well, actually her and her husband, Malcolm. It was Malcolm who sent those men after me. Malcolm Sinclair is the man who was waiting for me outside the restaurant. I thought you knew about Sinclair Finance. Alison finds out who the people are who need money at Sage Consulting. She contacts them, arranges the loans and then when they can't pay back the money... well, enough said. You've met their debt collectors."

Chapter Thirteen

The woman who opened the door to Euphemia was barely recogniz-
able as the same Alison who worked at the office. This Alison was
wearing an expensive black dress and black shoes with high heels
and red soles — very high heels. Her normally mousy, shoulder-
length hair, washed and blow-dried, was caught up at the nape of
her neck by a diamond-studded hair comb. Gold and diamond earrings twinkled beside eyes darkened with too much eyeliner, a look,
Euphemia thought in passing, only a much younger woman should
ever attempt. This Alison was nothing like the drab Alison from
work.

It doesn't matter, thought Euphemia, I'm furious with both of
them. She had listened in amazement and mounting anger as Jane
revealed what Alison had been doing. Preying on the desperation
of the few clients of Sage Consulting who were unable to save their
businesses and who were at their wits' end with worry. It was not
only reprehensible and beyond the bounds of decent behavior, it was
betrayal.

"So unexpected," said Alison as she ushered Euphemia into her
apartment. "Do sit down. Can I get you anything? Tea? Coffee? I
sound like I'm at the office, don't I? Maybe we should have champagne?"

"This isn't a social call, Alison. I've been talking to Jane French, so
you know why I'm here. How could you?"

"How could I what, Mrs. Sage?" drawled Alison sitting down on the opposite sofa and slowly crossing her legs.

"Where do I start? My God, you have terrorized Jane. You sent men to break her legs. *And*, and," she spluttered, "you have preyed on our clients. From our offices. Sage Consulting clients. Using our good name. Our reputation. We trusted you."

Alison uncrossed her legs slowly, stood up and walked to the other side of the room before she turned, her back against an enormous window looking out over Oriental Bay, forcing Euphemia to squint into the light.

"Do you know how ridiculous you sound?' said Alison. "Jane French owes us money. She knew the deal. She's a grown-up and so faces the consequences when, if, she defaults. All the others, they're all grown-ups too. Able to think for themselves. People you and Mr. Sage gave up on. People you advised to plead bankruptcy. Malcolm and I, we merely offered them another way. A way out. So how dare you come into my home and speak to me like I'm a child. You may be someone at the office, Mrs. Sage, but you're no one here. Look at the way you're dressed, for goodness' sake — dowdy middle-aged suburban runner. Surely you could afford to do better."

Euphemia's eyes, now adjusted to the bright backlight, registered the vicious pleasure on Alison's face as she spoke. Writ deep into every line, emphasized by her heavy make-up, her delight in her revenge was displayed in minute detail. Euphemia studied her, filing away the facial expressions, the fine movements around the mouth and eyes as she spoke.

"God, how I hate that office and having to dress like I belong amongst you," said Alison. "I'm a vibrant woman. I have taste and style. Class, Mrs. Sage. Look at my home. As you can see I don't do suburbia. I belong here, not at reception sucking up to people who think they're better than me. Until they need money, that is, and then they change their tune. Thank you for the clothing allowance by the way. I used it to pay for new underwear. Knickers — one pair. I'm wearing them now." She spat the last sentence.

Euphemia picked up muffled sniggers behind her in the depths of the apartment and realized they weren't alone.

"So that's why you suggested I meet you here. To show me the real you before I fired you. Because now that I know what you've been doing, you must know you are no longer welcome at Sage Consulting."

"You think you can do that? Fire me?"

"I just did. You are formally fired. Don't come in on Monday." Euphemia stood up, ready to leave.

"So, Mrs. Sage, you would ruin your business? Ruin your precious Sage Consulting? Ruin what you and your tediously respectable husband have spent so long building up?"

"What do you mean?"

"If I leave, and I mean *if*, because we haven't established that I will yet, if I left, do you seriously think I wouldn't take you, Sage Consulting and the whole damn thing with me? Do you think I won't expose you as the front for Sinclair Finance, won't reveal the bank statements that detail every commission paid to Sage Consulting for every loan taken out? Sage Consulting is, after all, the registered company office for Sinclair Consulting."

Alison had walked slowly back across the room, her eyes fixed on Euphemia, every sentence timed to inflict damage as she reveled in the drama of the moment.

Euphemia stood her ground, hearing, listening, damned if she was going to be the first to break eye contact.

"What do you think I do all day? Write cards and get coffee? You'd be surprised what I've put in the system. I've buried data so deep you won't find it unless I tell you how to get it out. Data that proves you and Kenneth have known all along about Sinclair Finance. Don't you think your clients — our clients — already suspect that you two are on the take? Malcolm, come and tell Mrs. Sage how you talk so warmly about Kenneth, your old school chum, when you and the boys make a collection."

"Boo!" said Malcolm whispering the word in Euphemia's ear. Of course she had known he was there. She'd heard him tiptoeing down the hall while Alison was giving her hateful speech. But Euphemia jumped anyway. Might as well play his silly game, she thought, and was gratified to catch the flash of annoyance on Alison's face.

Moving to his wife's side and draping a heavy arm casually across her shoulders, only to have it shrugged off, Malcolm asked, "How is my old school buddy Kenneth, by the way? Sending his wife to do a man's job. Not very chivalrous for an ex-rugby god, methinks."

"Kenneth's playing golf with Justin and old mates from school. People he likes. Which is probably why you weren't invited, Malcolm. School bully is the way he talks about you, by the way. And from what I've heard today, you're still a bully, but this time on command. Easy to see who has the brains in the operation."

Malcolm reddened, the veins on his neck filled. He stepped forward, only to be restrained by a hand on his arm.

"As I was saying before my husband came into the room," purred Alison, "I don't consider you're in a position to sack me now. Do you?"

Malcolm tittered. Euphemia registered the distaste on Alison's face.

"In fact," said Alison, "I'll be coming to the office as usual on Monday. As will you. We will carry on normally. You will say nothing to Kenneth or Kezia. Sage Consulting and Sinclair Finance work well together, don't you agree, Malcolm?"

"I've always thought so, my love."

Euphemia looked from one to the other. There was nothing she could say other than to ask, "What about Jane?"

"Jane is her own worst enemy. We both know she's stashed her mother's jewelry somewhere. It would easily cover the loan and if she coughs it up, she may even get to keep a piece to pass on to her precious Justine." Alison frowned. "Jane does not have my sympathy and she does not have our patience. She can pay. Run along and talk to her, Euphemia. Tell her to meet us on the third floor of the parking building in Wakefield Street at 1 pm tomorrow. Tell her, if she doesn't bring the jewelry, we will break her legs — both of them. And tell her she has annoyed me so much that we will find that daughter of hers and break her legs too. No New York internship for her this year. No wonderful networks setting her up for life. And if she doesn't do exactly what we say, that old family mansion of hers — that goes. Fire. Tomorrow. Have I left anything out? Malcolm?"

Euphemia could see Alison meant every word.

"Oh yes, there was something," said Alison inspecting the rings on her fingers. "Tell anyone, Euphemia — Nicky, the police, Kenneth, anyone — and not only will I ruin you and your family but I have contacts who are always on the lookout for fresh talent. How do you think your precious Petal would fare against a real dog, a pit bull, for instance?"

Chapter Fourteen

Jane was sound asleep on the sofa when Euphemia got back. Petal, who was snuggled into the sleeping woman, broke into her doggy smile of welcome before jumping over Jane to circle Euphemia's legs, her corkscrew tail wagging wildly. Jane woke slowly, rubbed her eyes and stretched, then looked at Euphemia hopefully.

"You've got till 1 pm tomorrow. That's as long as Alison will give you. She knows about the jewelry."

"You didn't tell her?"

"Of course I didn't, but she's done her homework and seems to know a lot about you. She knows the jewelry is stashed somewhere. She knows how much it's worth. She said you could keep a piece to give to Justine and she knows Justine is going to New York."

"I've only met her once. How could she possibly know private family stuff?"

"Don't look at me. I was as surprised as you. Maybe Malcolm has been talking to Justin. They know each other, don't they?"

"Yes, but Justin doesn't know I hid Mummy's jewelry. I told him I'd sold it after he lost the first job. The court only awarded him a few thousand for unfair dismissal and I knew he wanted the money then. It kept him quiet for a while, thinking I'd sold it."

"Doesn't matter now, does it? You have to give it to them at one o'clock tomorrow, or else."

"Or else what?"

"Or else they will find you and those goons will break your legs."

Jane looked thoughtful.

"Not just your legs, Jane. Alison said she would find Justine and break hers too. But before that, they would burn your house down. Tomorrow afternoon, if she doesn't get her money."

"The house is insured. At least that's what Justin told me. That would solve all our problems — get the bank off our backs and I could pay the loan back and have money left over. Maybe that's the answer — let them burn down the house."

"Before or after they break your legs?"

"Oh God!" said Jane and immediately burst into tears. "What a bloody mess. And all for a measly hundred thousand dollars."

Euphemia had had enough. Jane clearly had the means to get herself out of the trouble she was in. Why didn't she just get on with it and leave her be? If only she could call Kenneth and tell him about the trouble they were in. Together, they might find a solution. She'd heard of other firms being blackmailed by employees, but nothing on this scale. Alison seemed to have her bases covered. Euphemia realized there was every reason for her to be feeling as scared as Jane — more so. She bent down and picked Petal up and buried her nose in the soft neck wrinkles, her fur smelling only of goodness and innocence, and vowed to keep her safe.

Euphemia needed coffee.

She put Petal down, walked into the kitchen and ran the tap, lost in thought. Petal snuffled around in her bowl but found nothing she liked, and collapsed onto the floor, big goldfish eyes looking up expectantly at Euphemia to do something about this sad state of affairs. Jane came in and sat down.

"I'll have to go to the police, won't I? They'll have to send someone to guard me. I have no pride now. I've told you, so who cares if anyone else finds out?"

"I really don't think the police work like that. Nicky says they're very short-staffed."

"Who?"

"My younger daughter, Jane. She passed her Detective exams before Christmas. Nicky, my daughter, is in the police."

"Why didn't you tell me that before? That's perfect. She'll put in a good word for me. Problem solved."

"It doesn't work like that either. It really doesn't. Besides, Alison told me we can't go to the police. It's not only you she's threatening now. My family too and I believe her. Give her the jewelry as security until the house sells and you can pay her back. At least it'll be safe with her. That will buy us enough time to figure out what to do."

"I wish I'd never told you."

"Well, you did. They aren't just threatening you and Justine any more. I have to say it again, don't I? Alison also threatened me and my family. What she has been doing at the office will destroy us if it gets out. I, we, need time."

"And what if I don't give in to her."

"Then you and I are done. Go home now. Alone. Take what's coming to you. Or go to the police and probably still take the consequences, or Justine will. Where is she, by the way?"

"At a spa. Her treat for passing her exams."

"I'm surprised she's not in an old people's home, it's taken her so long," said Euphemia, bending low over the sink so Jane couldn't hear her. Taking a deep breath, she tried again.

"Judging by how much Alison knows about you and your family, I bet she knows exactly which spa it is."

Euphemia watched Jane slowly digest her last sentence.

"So I have no choice. That bitch gets my jewelry or she'll punish my baby. But you would help get it back for me... later, wouldn't you? Because I would be helping you too, wouldn't I?"

"Promise."

"And I can stay with you tonight?"

"You can stay with me but go and get the jewelry first, just in case they burn the house down today and not tomorrow."

Jane didn't need to be told twice and was out the door in a flash, driving down the quiet suburban street as if her life depended on it.

"Which it does really," said Euphemia to a very puzzled Petal.

Chapter Fifteen

Kezia was at the office when Euphemia called. Usually she despaired that her eldest was spending her youth at work, in front of a computer, but today she could not have been more grateful. She knew men found her daughter attractive, and yet Kezia preferred algorithms to a social life. After this is over, thought Euphemia, the Sage family is going on a long holiday — somewhere with no internet and lots of eligible bachelors.

"I can't believe Alison would do this," said Kezia after Euphemia explained what had happened. "She's so nice, so inoffensive. Frankly, Mum, I didn't think she could tell the back end of a program from the front."

"Neither did I. I can hear admiration in your voice, Kezia. Stop it. She's a criminal. Remember that when she pops into the office later today, which she will. She'll try to find out what you know, so act normally."

"OK. This is going to be very interesting. It's fantastic to have a real problem to solve for a change. Not just Kevin in HR forgetting his log-in password for the umpteenth time. This is exciting."

No, it's not, thought Euphemia after she ended the call. It's terrifying. But there was nothing she could do now, but wait for Kezia to work her magic. She couldn't let herself think about the hard work and sacrifice that had gone into building Sage Consulting only for it to end up at the mercy of that bitch. She remembered back to the morning and what she was supposed to be doing today. For over twenty years she had been looking forward to finding out whether Rachel's Switch actually existed. To have everything hijacked, first by Jane, and now Alison, was such a letdown. She'd had time to read so little of what was in the chest.

Did it confirm the switch? Did it mean she had superpowers? Georgiana's story did seem to back up her own impression that she could see and hear better. She also recognized each day was an improvement on the day before. The way her nose reacted to smell had changed entirely. It was frustrating not to have the time to analyze each and every layer of the flavors and perfumes that invaded her nostrils. So much information flooded her brain, Euphemia felt overwhelmed — and it kept coming.

She felt like she was in a room into which every sort of stuff was being packed, some of which she knew she needed to keep and some she had to get rid of. But which was which? The overload of her senses was creating chaos and she was the only one who could put it into any sort of order.

But when? She needed time alone to focus and reorganize her thoughts. Jane should be away for an hour at least, hopefully longer. That would give her time for a quick visit to the attic.

"Sorry, Petal," she said locking the flap on the dog door. "You have to use the litter box in the laundry. You're under house arrest for your own good." She checked that the rest of the doors and windows were locked, and went upstairs.

The chest had been empty when Euphemia opened it earlier. The newspaper articles fluttered in the draft when she lifted the lid again and a musty smell rose up and tickled her nostrils. Now, however, sitting on the bottom was a ring, which she was certain hadn't been there earlier. It was a simple band of thick gold and set in the middle was a dark oval stone. She picked it up, feeling its weight out of proportion to its size. It fitted perfectly when she slid it onto her finger. Looking old but ordinary, it didn't seem remarkable apart from the fact it had appeared from nowhere inside a box she was certain she had locked earlier that day.

Euphemia rubbed it, pressed the stone to see if it would move, and twisted it around her finger. Nothing. Just in case, and more as a result of the recent movies she had dragged Kenneth to, she extended her fist aiming the ring at one of the pictures stacked on the other side of the room. Nothing. She raised her arm above her head, hopefully. "To infinity and beyond," she called out dramatically, memories of a family trip to see *Toy Story*. Nothing.

It was early afternoon and the sun had moved on, no shaft of light piercing the roof now. In a far corner of the attic a spider was pulling a dead mosquito across its web, its legs grating against the silk. Despite the gloom, Euphemia could see every filament of the dead insect's wings. She could see the mosquito's legs tangled in the strands of silk and the spider's struggle to free them. She could see the effort on the face of the spider, the strain in its eyes, all eight of them, focused on her before it decided she wasn't a threat.

She looked around the attic again. No matter how dark the corner, she could see everything in the finest detail. Cobwebs, rusty nails, buttons on forgotten clothes, old pictures leaning against a far wall, their glass thick with dust, sprang into focus. And judging by the deafening noise, the place was alive with insects going about their business. So much sound, so many images crowding over and into her, one on top of the other, jostling for attention and interpretation.

Cowering before the onslaught, she covered her ears and shut her eyes. Breathe, breathe, she told herself. One thing at once for now, then later, you can work out how to manage this, how to control it and presumably harness it. Right now, she thought as she closed the chest again, go downstairs and cook dinner. The thought of Jane's return stilled her, stopped her mind racing in so many directions at once. It was calming having to think about someone else.

Chapter Sixteen

Jane was no ordinary snorer. Her snores echoed around the darkened house, ricocheting off every hard surface before revving up for a second circuit then slowly dying away. She would stop for a few minutes and just as Euphemia was drifting off to sleep, she would start over. Choking sounds followed by great snorting breaths, soft regular snores, louder and louder, building to a crescendo, and then silence. The silence was the worst. Each time, alarming. Had she choked? Was she dead? Then the cycle would start again. Jane's snores were so loud they rattled the windows in their frames and pinged the fillings in Euphemia's teeth. Even the normally somnolent Petal could be heard padding restlessly around the laundry downstairs.

How on earth does Justin cope? I've only had to listen to her for a few hours, not the years that Justin has had to contend with, Euphemia thought. Visions of creeping in and strangling Jane quickly and efficiently provided only temporary satisfaction. Reading didn't help either. The snoring broke her concentration, so she lay in the dark, willing herself to relax, to try to ignore the noise and not give in to her murderous fantasies.

It was two-thirty when she heard a different noise. She focused and picked up the sound of footsteps at the back door. A quiet snick then the sound of metal brushing against metal. She felt a change in air pressure as the door swung open downstairs and then heard rubber footfalls on wood. Something little and light clattered on the kitchen floor.

Euphemia heard Petal's squeak of greedy pleasure and claws retreating to a rug where the pug liked to sit and chew her bones. *Et tu*, Petal, thought Euphemia, relieved the men had chosen to bribe her dog into submission rather than the alternative. She hoped they'd brought enough of whatever Petal was clearly enjoying because that dog was a fast eater.

Someone whispered, "He wasn't joking when he said she was a snorer. Incredible, I'd have put a pillow over her head long ago."

Silence. No footsteps. No movement — just the sounds of Petal's happy crunching and Jane's snores.

Euphemia eased slowly out of bed. Waiting for her vision to adjust, she noticed a cobweb high in one corner of the bedroom, swinging backwards and forwards in time to Jane's snores. Tomorrow morning, she thought, I'll clean it then.

Euphemia had gone to bed knowing there would be visitors. Trusting Alison wasn't an option. She'd seen the greed on her face when she'd been talking about the jewelry and knew she couldn't wait to get her hands on it. Her thugs were here to collect tonight and tomorrow she'd no doubt deny all knowledge and insist the debt was still owed.

Euphemia had dressed in her winter running clothes: black leggings and a black fitted long-sleeved top, both plain, without any brandings which might catch light and give her away. Looking at herself in the mirror she'd turned this way and that, examining her body. She liked the new definition in her muscles. The saggy bits had found their way back to where they belonged. I look like a middle-aged Catwoman, she'd thought, but without the leather and ears.

The whispering started again downstairs. There were three of them, three men sent to do Alison's dirty work. Two of the voices she recognized as Half-ear and his brother, Mark. The other man seemed to be there only as back-up as he kept asking questions that Half-ear chose to ignore as he ordered Mark to go upstairs and follow the snoring.

Euphemia tugged a black balaclava down over her short blonde hair. She pulled on a pair of black rubber-soled reef shoes she'd found in the garage in a pile of junk she'd asked Kenneth to take to the dump weeks ago. Moving quietly out of her bedroom and across to an alcove at the top of the stairs, she pressed herself back against the wall and waited.

The bottom step creaked. Another job she had asked Kenneth to do. Darkness was irrelevant to her. She looked down and clearly saw Mark's scarred face as he moved slowly but confidently up the stairs towards her, carrying a baseball bat at his side. Paws skittered on the wooden floor in the kitchen, Petal sniffing out another treat flung at her. She heard the others chatting below, the men seemingly relaxed and taking it for granted two middle-aged women would be a walkover in the middle of the night. Mark only needed to find the jewelry and they could all go. No problem.

Mark reached the top of the stairs and looked around towards the door where the snoring was coming from. Standing beside her, within touching distance, oblivious to her presence, Mark stepped forwards. Euphemia slowed her breathing and concentrated on staying absolutely still. She watched a flicker of annoyance cross his face, as the noise of the gossiping men downstairs got louder.

Looking around again, he walked past her, past Jane's room and pushed open the door to the main bedroom. Her bedroom was darker than the hall and it took his eyes time to adjust before he realized the bed was empty. Seconds later he was back in the hall, puzzled, this time moving more cautiously than before. He lifted the baseball bat and, holding it ready, started to quietly open the other doors, searching not for Jane but for her.

Stepping out of the alcove she fell into step behind him and when she was ready she reached up and tapped him on the shoulder. Startled, he turned and tried to raise the bat higher, but she was too close.

There was no room unless he stepped back, which he did. Euphemia, taking advantage of his momentum, pushed.

Mark hit the wall at the end of the hall so hard, the breath gushed out of his lungs with an audible whump. He slumped to the floor, gasping painfully and desperately for air. Euphemia stepped over him, calmly took the bat and waited. As soon as she saw him take his first breath, she dropped all her weight through one knee onto his tummy. His eyes struggled to understand. Euphemia shrugged and picking him up by the back of his T-shirt, half carried, half dragged him back to the top of the stairs and threw him down. Still unable to breathe, he landed helplessly, splayed on the floor, knocking one leg of her hall table. Her favorite bowl, a wedding present, hit the floor and shattered beside his head.

The thugs in the kitchen, alerted by the noise, rushed out to see a woman dressed from head to toe in black standing at the top of the stairs holding Mark's baseball bat in one hand while Mark — purple, struggling to breathe — lay on the floor in front of them. Jane's snores filled the silence.

Euphemia raised the bat over her head, and watched as the men flinched. They looked at each other, before the back-up knelt down beside Mark. It was left to Half-ear to come up the stairs. He didn't look happy but he came anyway. Warily.

Euphemia hurled the bat at the head of the man kneeling beside Mark. Bull's-eye. It bounced with a hollow thunk off his skull immediately knocking him out so that he fell heavily across Mark, just as he was getting his breath back, winding him for the third time. Half-ear turned and saw both colleagues lying helpless at the foot of the stairs. Sensibly he hesitated. Euphemia pounced. She braced her outstretched arms between the wall and the railing and, swinging forward, kicked Half-ear hard under his chin, flipping him backwards down the stairs to land on the two men at the bottom.

Euphemia stayed where she was, adrenalin charging every active synapse in her body. She saw Mark, the only one fully conscious, examining her through his tears of pain, trying to work out what had happened. She folded her arms and leaned casually back against the wall. Slowly the others came round and the pile of tangled arms and legs started to move. Petal, sensing an opportunity, emerged from the kitchen and sniffed pockets for more treats. The little dog looked up and seeing Euphemia, climbed the stairs looking suitably guilty, and sat at Euphemia's feet panting, her pink tongue visible in the dark against the black leggings.

Mark, finally able to breathe, roused the others and hurried them to their feet. He opened the front door and pushed them out into the night, the cool air reviving them. He turned to look back at the still figure on the stairs.

"We'll be back. We won't be bringing any doggie treats next time." He banged the door shut and stumped away into the night, muttering at the other two who were staggering down the path.

Euphemia picked up Petal. "Traitor," she breathed into the warm folds around Petal's neck. Upstairs, Jane was still snoring.

Chapter Seventeen

Euphemia was rigid with fear. The heat was winning, sucking energy out of her body, turning her breath to ash in her mouth. Every time she lifted her head, it was like shoving it into a furnace. Keeping low, seeing almost nothing in the dark, she felt her way forward. She had to keep moving, had to keep pulling herself, fingernail by fingernail towards what she prayed was safety and Kenneth. His voice called her name over and over again, softly at first but if she focused, if she just focused, his voice grew stronger. She wasn't alone. She had someone to go to, someone who loved her.

The phone rang beside her head. Paralyzed, her body couldn't, wouldn't respond. The ringing went on and on, the sound lifting her to the surface, to the morning and the realization that she had been dreaming. Relief replaced fear — almost. Groggily she found it and answered.

Before she could say anything, she heard Kenneth's cheerful voice.

"Good morning, my sweet. I hope you slept well. I can't chat," his voice dropped to a whisper. "You can tell me tomorrow why Jane is staying with you."

"How's the golf?" yawned Euphemia, unwilling to open her eyes quite yet.

"That's why I'm calling. You'll never believe this but Roger and I are top of the board. We not only made the cut but we're coming first."

Euphemia heard Roger's voice singing an off-key version of 'We are the Champions' in the background. "I take it you and Roger are sharing a room."

"All four of us are in the same unit. The tight four, we call ourselves, but Roger and I are winning."

Euphemia smiled. Kenneth sounded more excited than she had heard him in years.

"And because we're winning," he said, "we have to stay another day. It totally depends on how well we play this afternoon and if we're in the top four, the final round is tomorrow morning. I checked and I don't have any meetings organized. You can hold the fort at the office without me, can't you?"

Euphemia thought for a moment about how good it would have been to have him home tonight, to have him hold her in his arms and tell her it would all be all right. That together, they'd see off Alison and her threats to their business. But he was so excited and, in reality, what could he do that she wasn't doing already?

"Hi, Euphemia," she heard Roger's voice again in the background.

"Tell Roger, hi back."

"I will... look, honey. We gotta go. Talk to you later with good news, I hope." The phone went dead.

Euphemia lay back against the pillows, eyes closed, still not ready to start the day. Her thoughts turned to the middle of night and she wondered how Mark and his brother were feeling. Better than the other guy, no doubt. The memory of what she'd done, how she'd ruthlessly dispatched that poor man, came back in graphic detail. And Mark, the feel of his soft tummy when she'd dropped onto it, winding him for the second time — the look of helpless horror on his face made her squirm. What sort of woman are you, Euphemia Sage?

The sort of woman who defends herself against a man stealing into her home in the dead of night with a baseball bat, that's who. That's who I am. Good grief. That is who I am. The realization of what she'd done crept over her. And it didn't take superhuman powers, she thought. All I did was stay calm. The element of surprise was the key.

Dammit, she thought. That's gone now. They know I'm not a pushover, that I'm not some helpless woman who panics and collapses with fear. Maybe I should have...

"Wake up, sleepyhead," called Jane breezing into the bedroom carrying a mug of tea, which she put down on the bedside table. "Goodness me, you sleep late. I've been up for ages. It's a beautiful day outside," said Jane bustling across the room to fling back the curtains and reveal a bright blue sky and sunshine. "I know I should be worried, Effie, but thanks to you, I slept like a baby last night."

"You were lucky to wake up," muttered Euphemia.

"What did you say? I missed it. Happens with Justin. I can see he's said something but I don't hear it. Maybe I do need to get my hearing tested. He keeps telling me I'm deaf. But it's only in the mornings and I assumed it was only him I can't hear. Did I hear you talking to someone as I was coming up the stairs?"

"Kenneth," said Euphemia. "He's playing well, some sort of tournament and he won't be home till tomorrow probably."

"Justin called too. Same story. Probably just as well. He'd only get in the way. I told him I was staying with you and he was surprised. I had to remind him what great chums we were at school. Silly man." Jane sat down on the side of the bed and patted Euphemia's leg companionably.

Euphemia reached for her tea.

"What on earth are you wearing?" asked Jane.

Euphemia was still dressed in the black top and leggings from last night, minus the balaclava and reef shoes, thank goodness. No wonder she'd felt hot.

"Running. I was going to go running this morning but must have slept through the alarm."

"I never sleep through the alarm. Justin does, but then I'm a morning person. Have been since I was a little girl."

"You would be."

"The strangest thing, Effie. There was a baseball bat and a broken bowl on the floor downstairs. I've cleaned up the pieces of the bowl for you. It didn't look valuable so it's in the rubbish. And I let Petal out. She was scratching at the doggie door. It was locked. Poor thing."

"You did what? Don't ever do that again!" yelled Euphemia leaping out of bed and over Jane. Racing downstairs she skidded past the baseball bat, kicking herself for not getting rid of it last night. She ran to the back door terrified, but there was Petal pottering about outside in the vegetable garden. The little dog trotted over the lawn to her call, came in and sat down expectantly in front of her dish. Euphemia relocked the dog flap and the back door, before feeding the little glutton.

"You obviously didn't have enough to eat last night, did you?" Petal, oblivious to sarcasm, started crunching.

Jane appeared with the half-empty mug and put it in the dishwasher.

"I'm sorry if I did the wrong thing again, Effie, I mean Euphemia. I didn't know the dog door wasn't for the dog to actually use. And I never get your name right. Silly me."

Her bottom lip quivered and she gripped the edge of the bench. "I always get everything wrong. Justin tells me I'm useless, Mummy does, I mean did too. Justine doesn't need to tell me. She doesn't say anything, she just looks at me like I'm useless."

Tears ran down her face, streaking her make-up. "I've got you into my mess. And today, I have to give Mummy's jewels, which she told me never, ever to let out of my sight, to Alison bloody Sinclair. And to top it all off, I unlocked your dog door."

She walked over to the table and, sitting down, put her head in her hands and sobbed.

Euphemia took a deep breath. "You're not useless, Jane. I'm sorry I yelled. The stress is clearly getting to both of us," she said walking over and putting her arm around Jane's shoulders. "At least," she said, "you don't have to give it to Alison forever. It's only until you get the money from the house and pay her back."

Jane's sobbing dribbled away to a sniff. She looked around for a tissue. Euphemia gave her the clean one she had in her sleeve and Jane blew her nose loudly enough to make Petal look up from her bowl.

"She's my receptionist. So I'm not blameless. I should have known what she was doing."

Jane stopped still and thought. "I suppose you're right. If Alison hadn't been operating out of Sage Consulting then I wouldn't have borrowed the money from her, would I?"

"No, I don't suppose you would," Euphemia said, gritting her teeth and forcing a smile.

"What are we going to do, Effie?"

"We are going to do whatever is necessary and we are going to stop Alison and her husband from ever doing this to anyone again. I promise."

"You sound so sure but what can two women, middle-aged women, do? Those men yesterday terrified me. And the way Malcolm looks sometimes." Jane shuddered.

Euphemia remembered last night and the pile of men at the bottom of the stairs. She remembered how calm and confident she'd felt looking down at them. How easy it had been and how she had sent them back into the night, licking their wounds. She also heard the anger in Mark's voice when he vowed to be back and his threat to Petal.

"Let's worry about what happens when it happens. I need to get out of these sticky clothes and have a shower. Then we can plan what you're going to do at the parking building."

Jane got up and smoothed down her shirt just as the doorbell rang. Euphemia put her finger to her lips. It rang again.

"It's not fair, they said twenty-four hours," hissed Jane, as she disappeared into the pantry.

Euphemia picked up the baseball bat and cautiously opened the front door.

Nicky looked startled to see her mother dressed head to toe in black and holding a baseball bat, but shrugging, breezed past her and into the kitchen.

"Left my key at the flat. Sorry. I need to get something. Been for a run? I won't ask about that," she said pointing to the bat. "Mum, why is there someone in the pantry? Are you playing hide and seek while Dad's away? You naughty thing."

"Don't be silly," said Euphemia, putting the bat in the laundry before ushering Jane out of the pantry.

"You know Jane French, don't you, Justine's mother?"

"I don't think we've met, but I remember Justine from school," said Nicky, hand outstretched. "Don't suppose you've had breakfast? I'm starving and there's no food at the flat. Brian, my flatmate," she said to Jane, "had a big night and ate the lot when he got home at three this morning. Why were you in the pantry?"

"Checking the size," said Jane stepping in and out of the cupboard somewhat theatrically. "I'm learning kitchen design. Empty nest. Time for a career."

"I've a friend who's a kitchen designer and she loves it," said Nicky opening the fridge and peering inside. "Oh good, there's bacon." She stepped back and there was a yelp. "Oh, hello, sweetheart, sorry. I didn't say hello to you before," said Nicky, picking up Petal who had been bouncing round at her feet since she arrived.

"I'll cook breakfast," said Jane. "It's good for me to try out different kitchens — even old ones like this. Good to know what not to do. Bacon and eggs? Effie, you go and shower and Nicky, you find whatever you came for."

It was a beautiful morning. Still and warm, and they had eaten breakfast at the table in the garden under the trees. Petal was stretched out beside Nicky's feet, her fat belly basking in the sunshine. She loved bacon almost as much as she loved Nicky and Nicky was generous, keeping a steady supply dropping accidentally from her plate. For a few minutes, Euphemia forgot about everything and leaned back in her chair, lifting her face to the warmth.

"Is that a new ring, Mum?"

Euphemia sat up.

"What?"

"This." Nicky reached over and lifted her hand.

"Let me see," said Jane. "I know about jewelry." She took Euphemia's hand from Nicky. "You weren't wearing this yesterday, were you?"

"Did Dad give it to you?"

Euphemia, a little taken aback by the questions, tried to reclaim her hand, but Jane held tight.

"It's a star sapphire, I think. Not a bad one but very dark. You see, Nicky, how the star is buried deep in the blue of the stone... look." She twisted Euphemia's hand so Nicky could see, taking no notice of any discomfort she might be causing.

"Yes, I see. I think. Oh there it is... look how bright the star gets, just for a second. Draws you in, doesn't it?"

Jane let go. Euphemia massaged her fingers.

"I didn't think you liked jewelry, Mum."

"Normally I don't. Gets dirty in the garden. This was in Aunt Maree's chest in the attic. I decided to open it after all these years. Your great-great-grandmother's ring, I think, from the date on the box, but it could be older, who knows?"

"Can I try it on?"

Euphemia tried her best but short of amputating her finger, the ring wouldn't budge.

"Sorry."

"I suppose it could be valuable," sniffed Jane. "As an antique, I mean, certainly not as jewelry. Not like mine anyway. Do you want to see some really good stuff, Nicky?"

"Jane, don't..."

"It's all right, I'd like to. Nicky clearly understands these things and would appreciate my little collection."

"Best not to, don't you think?" Euphemia frowned and shook her head but it was no use.

Jane had already left the table, picking up a few of the plates to take with her into the house on her way. Once Jane decided to do something, it seemed there was little anyone could do to stop her.

A few minutes later, just as Euphemia was asking Nicky about how she was enjoying being on the crime squad and what her new boss was like, Jane emerged, carrying a tooled leather box proudly in front of her.

Sitting down, she cleared a space on the table, then ceremoniously unlocked the box and took out a rolled-up black velvet mat, which she spread out in front of them with a practiced flourish. Nicky looked at her mother and tried not to smile.

One by one, Jane took out the pieces and set them on the black velvet, displaying each item to maximum advantage, turning them this way and that so they caught the sun.

"My great-grandmother started the collection. Or rather my great-grandfather did. Each generation has added to it since. Well, the men did. It was a different world then, wasn't it? In front of you are the results of four generations of work by the dear sweet men in our family."

Euphemia couldn't believe what she was seeing. A sapphire and diamond necklace glistened and sparkled, shown off to perfection against the deep black of the velvet. Beside it, a chunky gold bracelet set with matched emeralds lay heavily on the table. Two drop earrings completed the set, the emeralds the size of bird's eggs. Rubies set in platinum rings, loose diamonds, and in the middle was the largest stone of all, a pale blue Ceylonese sapphire adorned only by what must be a thinly tooled platinum chain.

Nicky couldn't resist and picked up a ring. She looked at Jane for permission to try it on, which Jane, loving the attention, gave with a gracious if not queenly nod.

"Why don't we have fabulous jewels in our family, Mum? Your ring is nice, but nothing like this."

Nicky took off the ring and put it back on the table reluctantly. Amongst the pieces was a gold chain with a simple drop diamond pendant, smaller than the rest by far but still a more valuable necklace than anything Euphemia owned. Nicky picked it up and the little diamond spun in the sunshine, catching the light and sending it out in a rainbow of colors against the greenery.

"That was Justin's present to me when we got married," said Jane. "He promised he would do better on our anniversary, but by then he had different worries so..."

Nicky draped it over her arm, the gold chain running smoothly across her sleeve, then laid it back down. "Jane, this should all be in a bank vault. There should be guards. I don't know anything about jewelry but even I can tell it's worth a lot of money," said Nicky. "Do you always carry this around with you? I know you'll have it insured but the insurance company would have difficulty understanding if any of it went missing. Sorry, Jane. Police. Can't help but be a bit worried."

Nevertheless, Nicky, attracted to its beauty, picked up the emerald bracelet and draped it over her wrist. It looked stunning against her fine bones and young skin.

"Please don't tell anyone," said Jane. "I promised your mother I'd show them to her when Justin was away. He hates me even taking them out of the safe let alone out of the house. He's more attached to them than I am. And of course you're right about the insurance. I could never replace them. One day, it will all be Justine's."

Sensing more tears, Euphemia leaned forward and asked, "Which is the most valuable piece?"

"This one," said Jane, holding up one of the rings. "It's the ring Daddy gave Mummy when he asked her to marry him. He saved every penny for a year and had to borrow money from his father to buy it but he said she deserved the best and he would start the marriage as he meant to go on. Go on, try it."

The square-cut diamond was big but not as big as the sapphire Euphemia really liked. Set simply in white gold between diamond-studded shoulders, the stone was the clearest white, the light it reflected hot and pure, completely different to the tiny diamond on the gold chain.

"Mummy was heartbroken when Daddy died. He was so young

and there were debts. Neither side of the family could help out. Well, not really. Luckily Mummy was young enough to marry again and we kept the house. My stepfather was very cruel, you know, especially when he'd been drinking. She used to say, when he was at his worst, 'Needs must. Needs must, Jane. Smile.'"

"I'm not sure he knew about all this," she said sweeping her hand over the table. "Mummy said it was the only thing she could give me that would mean something later."

Nicky, who had tried on the heavy diamond, took it off and gave it back to Jane, who slipped it onto her ring finger beside her thin gold wedding band.

"Then I met Justin and we moved in with Mummy. Frank, my step-father, had died by then. Thank goodness. Justin and I could look after her properly, the way she deserved. She got on so well with him. They used to spend hours polishing the different pieces, talking about how Justine would inherit everything. He loves the collection. He promised he would do better than the pendant one day. Funny how we take on other people's traditions when we marry."

Jane ran her hands over the stones, smoothing and caressing them in turn, setting out the pieces neatly and in an order she must have perfected over the years.

Nicky looked at Euphemia and raised an eyebrow.

"Will I get your ring, Mum?" asked Nicky.

"You could wait till I am dead, darling."

"I could, but Kezia will see it and she'll want it. I saw it first. Remember."

Nicky stood up, stretched, and walked over and kissed Euphemia on the top of her head. "I'd better be off, duty this afternoon."

"Justine is one lucky girl, Jane. I'll tell her that when I see her next."

Jane leapt up and grabbed Nicky by the arm. "Please don't. She'll know I took it out of the house. She'd tell Justin."

Euphemia saw the panic in Jane's face. What did Justin have over this woman that she was so scared of him? Standing up, she picked up the rest of the plates.

"Wait, Nicky, I'll come with you." They walked into the house together, leaving Jane to gather up her collection.

"What was that all about?" asked Nicky at the front door. "She seemed scared, didn't she? Justin always seemed a bit of a weed."

"Things aren't going so well for them. I'm giving her a place to stay and some company for a few days. Best not to say anything to Justine or anyone else. Keep this between us?"

"I hadn't realized you were her friend, but well done, Mum. The world needs more heroes, or should I say, heroines."

Chapter Eighteen

They'd just finished the breakfast dishes when Jane's phone blared out the William Tell Overture. She picked it up and looking at the screen almost dropped it in fright. It was Alison. She pressed answer.

"Go into another room," said Alison. "I don't want anyone else to hear what I have to say. Hurry up. There are people watching the house so I know you're in the kitchen."

Jane gulped. Anyone watching the house could have seen her showing off her treasures in the garden. She scuttled through to the living room, shooing Euphemia away from her.

Euphemia went upstairs to her bedroom and looked down onto the street, knowing she'd be spotted. She'd brought a cloth and after she flicked away last night's cobweb she started wiping the windowsill. It took only a few moments to find Mark standing behind a tree on one corner and Half-Ear with his head under the hood of a car at the other. Mark, wearing dark glasses that didn't quite cover his bruised face, was muttering into a mouthpiece. At the other end of the street, Half-Ear was also watching. She couldn't see or hear the third man.

Focusing on Mark, she heard him tell Alison, "Sage is upstairs."

A woman with two small children on tricycles walked past the trees and looked at him, before herding her kids away in a hurry. Mark poked out his tongue after she'd gone.

Euphemia stayed in view while she fussed about the window, but turned her attention to the conversation downstairs.

"Jane, after everything we told you," said Alison, "after everything we did for you, you went to the only person in the entire city who will cause us problems. We've added an extra ten thousand dollars penalty payment to your account."

"You can't do that."

"Yes I can. Penalty payments were in the contract you signed, Jane. Fine print."

Jane gasped and was about to say something but Alison stopped her. "Sage has no doubt told you what will happen to you, your precious daughter and your house if you don't do what I say. Not in that order, of course."

"You leave Justine out of this or I'll go to the police, Alison."

"You could do that. But who do you think will get to her first? The police or the ambulance? Justine is at the Alpine Spa, Room 63, and by all accounts having a wonderful time. Money no object, so room service tells us. Likes champagne. Girl after my own heart actually. We'd get along well."

There was silence and then Jane said quietly, "You wouldn't."

"Of course I would, Jane. You know that. There's a man there... waiting. He has a headache after last night, and he's not happy."

"Last night? What's that got to do with me?"

"It's irrelevant. I'm tired of you. Pay the money and if you can't, your stuff better be worth a hundred thousand dollars or the next time you see Justine, she will be in hospital after her... skiing accident."

"But there's no snow."

"Really."

"You wouldn't do this if you had children, Alison."

"Of course I would. Now shut the fuck up. I'm going to say this once. Go to the third floor of the parking building at 1 pm and wait in your car. Alone. If I so much as smell Sage's ordinary little perfume, I will talk to my man at the spa. Do you understand?"

"But..."

"Shut up, Jane. Do you understand?"

"Yes."

The line went dead.

Chapter Nineteen

"Wish me luck."

"Do what they say. Hand over the box. Leave. Simple. Come straight back here and everything will be fine. She only wants the money. Give them the box and leave. Next week you can get it all back."

"Are you sure?"

"I'm sure," said Euphemia. "Now go. You shouldn't be late."

"You promise you'll get it back for me?"

"I promise. Go."

Euphemia waved as Jane drove slowly down the street. She hoped Mark and Half-Ear had seen her and were reporting back. Taking her time she walked casually up the drive and shut her front door loudly enough for half the street to hear. Once inside, she took the stairs two at a time. She figured she had twenty minutes to set up her decoy and get to the parking building before Jane arrived.

Many years ago when money was tight, Euphemia had taught herself to sew. She'd seen her old dressmaker's dummy in the attic yesterday and while Jane was getting ready, had made her own preparations. Her study was on the second floor and could be seen from the street. She positioned the dummy, now dressed in the same clothes she had been wearing outside, at the desk in front of her laptop. She hoped the soccer ball with its old blonde wig and baseball cap would look enough like her from behind to fool the men below. She had to make them think Jane was going to the parking building alone, as promised. All she had to do now was run faster than she had ever run before, taking every short cut she knew, and she could be there before Jane arrived.

Euphemia was a good runner. She knew that but without tapping into the extra energy she had felt surging through her body in the last month, it would be impossible to make it to the middle of town in time. Concentrating hard, she thought only of Jane and how vulnerable she was. Her visions of what might happen came on slowly at first, then faster, building into a flood of feeling. Deep in her brain she could almost see the wash of chemicals being released into pathways she had been oblivious to all her life. Faster and stronger, each chemical triggered the next, recruiting more pathways, linking every nerve to send instructions to every energized fiber of muscle. She looked forward later to finding out what was actually happening, and how, but for the moment, she was just grateful. Outside, Mark and Half-ear had accepted the decoy and had left. She was free.

Blood pumped through her muscles, her heart rate and breathing slowed and she set off, slowly for half a minute and then faster. Vaulting the neighbor's back fence she hit the back lanes, pumping arms lifting her effortlessly with every stride. The freedom and exhilaration almost made her forget what she was running to. Dodging kids on bikes and mothers with pushchairs, she made it to the open space of the park separating the city and the suburbs. Other runners stopped and watched as she passed by, nonplused that a woman, or anyone for that matter, could sustain her pace seemingly effortlessly. The distance fell away.

Once she hit the familiar streets and alleyways of the central city, Euphemia slowed. There were more cars and people around and she didn't want to attract unnecessary attention. She'd made good time and arrived at the side entrance of the parking building early as planned, assuming that everyone else would be at arriving at the front.

Looking up she counted the floors. Six in total and Jane was to meet them on the third. Risking the stairs or the lift might mean she'd be heard and she didn't trust Alison not to have stationed an advance guard or two.

The only way to get to the third floor silently and unseen was to climb up the side of the building. There were plenty of finger holds in the rough concrete walls and it was so much easier than she had anticipated.

I like Rachel's Switch a lot, she thought. The years of waiting now seemed like mere moments. She'd reached the milestones, normal women's milestones, and now this gift was hers. To feel so alive in every cell of her body, to feel so in command of every sense was exhilarating. Thank goodness she'd been forced to wait, she conceded. She could see now that the effects of the switch would have overwhelmed her when she was younger. Youth combined with this wonderful strength in everything she attempted would have thrown her off track. She was sure of it. Mentally she saluted Aunt Maree and reveled in her feelings of invincibility. Bring it on, Alison Sinclair. I can take you and your disgusting husband. And anyone else you might have with you. You don't scare me.

Peering over the half wall to the third floor, Euphemia stood perched on the outside ledge and listened carefully. The floor was empty apart from a few cars scattered about, abandoned for the weekend, no doubt by Friday night revelers. She cocked her head and focused but heard nothing above or below except for the wind blowing across acres of empty floors. For the moment she had the place to herself.

The entry ramp was situated in the middle of the wall opposite her and the exit ramp on the wall to her left. She could see and hear everything from where she was, but she would be seen in return. Taking the risk there was still time, she climbed over the wall and ran crouched low to behind one of the parked cars and knelt behind it, taking care to stay in line with a front wheel.

She didn't have to wait long before she heard the familiar sound of Jane's little car circling its way cautiously up the ramp. It emerged with Jane huddled over the steering wheel looking this way and that.

She turned onto the floor and stopped in the middle of the access lane.

Good girl, you remembered, thought Euphemia.

She could hear the anxiety in Jane's breathing and wanted to reach out and reassure her that she was there, watching over her.

Minutes ticked by. Trust Alison to keep Jane waiting. As her muscles cooled in this awkward position, Euphemia could feel cramp starting to set in. She longed to be able to stretch her legs but didn't dare. Jane was whispering to herself, hands gripping the steering wheel. Over and over she said, "Be strong. Needs must. Be strong. Needs must."

Euphemia remembered what Jane had said about her mother, her courage, and how the jewelry was so important to her. That woman had sacrificed her happiness to ensure an inheritance for her daughter and granddaughter. Jane had been a bloody idiot to put everything at risk, but her real mistake was trusting Justin to make everything right. It wasn't her fault the world had changed and men like him didn't cut it any more. Or was there more to it?

Euphemia knew a little about Justin. He wasn't stupid, so his apparent indifference to their financial situation was puzzling. Worse, he'd done absolutely nothing to help himself, and, according to Jane, hadn't asked any questions when the money arrived out of the blue. A painting worth so much lying undiscovered, till now? Not likely, but he'd accepted it and just kept spending. He'd said nothing to Justine about their difficulties. He'd just kept raising her expectations, seemingly blind to what he must have known was an unsustainable lifestyle. He didn't seem to consider Jane and what she might really want. Strange business all up but as Kenneth always said, the only people who know what's happening in a relationship are the people in it and they only know half the story.

Euphemia thought about her own problems. She was dying to hear that Kezia had found the buried files and that they'd been removed. She wanted to tell Justin what she thought of him, but had to wait until her own vulnerability was resolved. Poor Jane had been carrying the burden of her family for too long. It wasn't fair and Euphemia vowed to help her straighten out the uncaring spendthrift she was married to. No job too small for this superwoman... she thought. Maybe that was it. The story about her ancestor Georgiana had epitomized quiet everyday heroism and service with no fanfare, no amazed adulation from the masses. Was it her turn to step up and help someone in need? Someone with simple problems like Jane?

As if on cue, she recognized the sound of the Mercedes following another car circling up the ramp. It seemed to take forever for them to get to the third floor because the cars detoured around the floors below checking them out before travelling up to the next. She didn't dare look, but listened instead as Jane's breathing became even faster.

Jane's car parked in the middle of the access way meant that the Mercedes had to go around her, and whoever was driving took the narrow side and narrowly missed a parked car, before it arced around and stopped angled across in front of Jane. The second car, a Toyota, stopped behind, effectively trapping Jane's car between them.

The people in the darkened Mercedes didn't get out, their engine idling gently. Two men got out of the Toyota. She recognized Mark and Half-Ear. Did these men get no time to themselves? Mark jogged off to check they were alone on the floor. He was under pressure to be quick because he paid only cursory attention to the car Euphemia was crouched behind. He yelled out to Half-ear and gave him the thumbs up, then took the stairs up to the next floor. Euphemia heard his footsteps jogging each of the three floors above and then he thundered back down the stairs and, puffing, joined Half-Ear.

Only then did the Mercedes engine shut down and one door open. Euphemia heard Malcolm's unmistakable tread walk around and open the other door for his wife. Alison, still in high heels, clicked her way to Jane's car and pulled open her door.

"Get out."

Chapter Twenty

Jane tried but had forgotten to undo her seat belt and was held back. Alison's exasperation was audible.

"I said get out."

Malcolm reached across, unclicked the buckle and stepped back. Jane swung her legs around and eased herself slowly out of the car. Standing with her back against it she was dwarfed by the Sinclairs.

"Your stuff had better be good, Jane," Malcolm whispered.

Jane turned her head from one to the other searching for a glimmer of compassion, and found none.

"How can you do this? Once the house sells, you'll get your money."

"I so don't understand you," said Alison. "On the one hand you're so respectable. You think you're better than me. You think you have dibs on what's right and what's wrong. And on the other hand, you spend money you don't have and then object to paying it back. The fun's over. Time's up."

Malcolm looked around the parking building nervously. A breeze had come up and it was getting cold. "We're wasting time. Get the stuff, Alison, and let's go."

Euphemia couldn't see Jane when she turned and bent back into the car to get the box. She couldn't see Malcolm either, but when Jane was bent low and defenseless in front of him, he must have kicked her and sent her sprawling across the front seat.

Euphemia could hear the sickening crunch as Jane's face hit the handbrake. She heard the sound of a bone or was it a tooth cracking, and then something thick dripping fast onto the bottom of the car. A surge of heat and anger swept through Euphemia, tensing every muscle as she inched forwards, crouched low and ready to sprint across the empty space to reach Jane.

At the car everything was quiet. Jane, stunned, still lay across the front seat. Mark and Half-ear shifted from foot to foot sharing uneasy glances.

"Really, Malcolm? Was that necessary?" said Alison, furious as she pulled him away. Malcolm tittered and looking at the men around him, shrugged.

"You idiot. She was getting it. Look at the blood. It's everywhere."

Jane still hadn't moved. "We don't have all day, Jane, get up. Mark, help her."

Mark, a large man, made things worse when he leaned over Jane in the tight space. Waving him away she picked up the box and pushed herself slowly back across the seat to end up out of the car on her knees. Mark offered her his hand but she batted it away and, using the door for support, hauled herself up as blood dripped in a steady stream down her front and onto the concrete, a thick circle pooling at her feet. She looked terrible. Her nose was swelling fast and already purple. The blood was pouring out of a split in her top lip behind which was a mash of gum where a tooth was hanging by a thread of tissue.

Euphemia inched forward. Such brutality could not go unanswered. She would have the element of surprise but still she hesitated. Could she take so many men at once? Last night she'd had the advantage of home ground and darkness. Today in broad daylight she was a fifty-three-year-old woman and the only things she knew about hand-to-hand combat she'd seen at the movies. Having powers was all very well but she still had no idea how to use them. What if she made things worse?

Jane, standing by the car with all the dignity she could muster,

looked first at Malcolm and then at Alison with undisguised contempt.

"I owe one hundred thousand dollars," she said, her words barely
distinguishable. "That's three or four pieces at most. No more.
You've already got your blood money."

Alison grabbed the box. "It's covered in blood, Malcolm," she said.
"And now it's all over my Louis Vuitton shirt. Ruined."

She flipped the box open and rustled through the contents, select-
ing some pieces, discarding others.

"There isn't much here I really want," she said finally.

Euphemia inched forward again. If she took out Mark first, then
Half-ear, she reckoned Malcolm would run. He was that sort of man,
which only left Alison. Euphemia smiled at the thought of putting
Alison on the ground and keeping her there till the police arrived.
She had to do something, anything. Her phone vibrated in her
pocket and she scrabbled to stop it. Use it, she thought. Call the
police, you idiot. Do it. But what if they heard? She wondered if
you could text the police. Totally and foolishly out of her depth,
Euphemia couldn't believe she'd been so stupid.

"One hundred thousand is a lot of money and maybe this stuff
might cover it," said Alison.

"It's worth more than that and you know it."

"Jane, Jane, Jane. This is business, something you've never had to
worry about, have you? Yes, in theory, the debt is covered, but only if
we could sell it on the open market. Sinclair Finance — we aren't jewelers, are we? We're financiers. Jewelry is an inconvenience. It costs
us. So unless you have cash, let's just say your stuff nearly covers it.
What do you think, darling?"

Malcolm scuffed the floor in front of him with his shoe and
shrugged, not looking up. "You do what you like. Just hurry up."

"You're a thief. A bitch and a thief."

Alison laughed. "I'll let that go. So will my husband and his
friends. For now. But I'm warning you. He doesn't like people insult-

ing his wife. It makes him upset and you wouldn't want to get him upset again. You were quite attractive for a woman your age."

Jane raised her hand automatically to her mouth and touched her lip gingerly. Her mother's diamond engagement ring glinted in the dull light.

"You didn't show me that," said Alison, shoving the box at Malcolm who only just caught it. Grabbing Jane's hand, Alison tugged at the ring.

Jane pulled back. They wrestled and then skidded on the bloody floor. Alison had her hand on Jane's chin forcing it back and up, while she yanked at her hand, desperate to get the ring. Jane, equally desperate to keep it, hugged her hand into her body, the other hand pulling Alison's hair from behind. Mark and Half-ear stepped forward to help, but Malcolm shook his head and arms folded across the box, looked on smirking.

Jane was wearing Nicky's old trainers, which gave her some grip, whereas Alison's stiletto heels combined with her tight pencil skirt meant she had no purchase on the floor whatsoever. In the struggle, one of her heels slid out and she went down, hitting the floor, landing flat on her bottom, legs splayed out in front of her, all dignity gone.

In the silence that followed, Jane's tooth dropped out of her mouth and clattered onto the concrete then rolled under her car. Folding her hand back into her chest, Jane was determined not to hand over the ring. Half-ear stepped from behind Malcolm, and helped Alison up.

"Give me that ring," said Alison.

"No. Take the box and go, or else."

"Or else what, Jane? What will you do?"

Euphemia had started creeping forwards again, keeping as low to the floor as she could, hoping to get close enough to rush the men and send Malcolm packing, when she heard a metallic click. She looked up and saw everyone staring at a pistol that Alison was pointing at Jane's head.

"Give me the ring."

"No. Kill me, Alison. Blow my brains out. I don't care any more. Go on. Kill me. I dare you."

Euphemia froze. What the hell was happening? Nothing had prepared her for this. The only thing she knew about guns was that they killed people. Even if she stood up now and ran at the group full speed, Alison could put a bullet in Jane's head before she reached them.

"Give me the fucking ring, Jane. I'm over this." Alison raised the gun above her head and fired. The bullet embedded in the concrete above, the deafening noise ricocheting around the empty building. Jane's head disappeared into her shoulders, but otherwise she didn't budge. Alison aimed the gun at her again, but still she clung to the ring.

Euphemia felt like slapping her. Give her the ring, Jane. Nothing is worth this.

Mark and Half-ear started backing away, not taking their eyes off Alison or the gun. It was Malcolm who moved first.

"You stupid bitch. It's Sunday, and we're in the middle of town. How long do you reckon it'll be before the police get here?"

Herding the two women before him with outstretched arms, he bundled them into the back of the Mercedes. Euphemia caught one last glimpse of Jane's bloodied face while Alison resolutely held the gun to her head, as Malcolm slammed the door. Tossing the box into the front, he got in and had started the engine before slamming his own door shut. The others didn't need to be told and jumped into the Toyota, which sped down the ramp before the Mercedes, just as sirens sounded in the distance.

Euphemia stood up in time to see the back of the Mercedes disappearing from view.

Chapter Twenty-one

"Mum, what are you doing here?" hissed Nicky, kneeling down beside her.

It had been several hours since the Mercedes had gone. The cool breeze, which had sprung up earlier, had strengthened into a steady wind blowing through the parking building, picking up old fast food wrappers and plastic bags, and spinning them in tight circles in dark corners. The sun had long gone and there had been showers of spotty rain while she waited for the police to finish searching the building.

As soon as she'd heard the sirens she knew there was no point in trying to escape. CCTV footage would have given her away eventually, and there was little to be gained in diverting attention away from the Mercedes to a woman in black leaving the scene after a shooting.

A heavily equipped helmeted officer had been the first to come silently up the ramp, weapon raised to his shoulder, as he scanned the floor and then signaled for the next man to come up after him. As the men arrived and fanned out, Euphemia had stepped forwards, arms high above her head and called out, "I'm unarmed." She didn't know who got the bigger fright.

Next minute they had her surrounded and were yelling at her over and over again to get down and lie face first on the ground, arms and legs spread wide. Which of course, she did.

While one of them was searching her roughly, another was radioing to his commanding officer that an unarmed elderly woman had been taken into custody next to an abandoned car. She bridled at the elderly woman description and raised her head in protest, only to have it pushed back onto the floor and a heavy boot put on the small of her back. There she stayed, uncomfortable and feeling stupid, until the all clear was given and Nicky arrived.

"That's my mother under your boot, officer."

"Sorry, ma'am," said the officer, not sounding in the least bit apologetic. "Your mother is also the elderly woman I spoke to you about," he said, removing his foot slowly.

Euphemia, pride hurt and wanting to prove she was younger than described, popped to her feet with a little jump, dusted off her hands and thanked the officer for his attention. Ignoring her, he nodded at Nicky before jogging off to find the rest of his team.

"Are you all right?" whispered Nicky out of the side of her mouth. "Those boys can be a bit rough."

"Fine," she replied, arching her back.

"Good. Tell me what the hell you're doing here."

The arrival of the forensics team interrupted her response. Dressed in white overalls, they started taping off the area around the car. Kit was unpacked and the photographers got busy, the flashes bright in the dim light. What had been a scene of desolation only minutes before was now a hive of activity.

"I was running past when I heard a woman moaning and another woman yelling, so I came up to see if someone needed help. You know I did that first aid course and I thought I might be useful."

Nicky cocked her head, trying to listen but also watching the team by the car. "And?" she asked, only half paying attention.

"It was Jane, Jane French. Someone was attacking her."

Nicky looked swiftly back at her mother.

"Jane, the woman we had breakfast with this morning?"

"Yes. That's her car."

"And the blood?"

"Jane's. It was terrible. This woman had grabbed her jewelry box and Jane was trying to stop her and then there was a gun and it went off and next minute, I was jumping out of the way as two cars sped off."

"Let's get this straight. A woman you barely see but who for some reason was at our house this morning with her most precious possessions is attacked just as you happen to be running past. You never ever run this way usually, may I add. You hear a fight and decide to investigate, only to find this woman has her jewelry with her in an empty car parking building on a Sunday afternoon and another woman is trying to take it. A gun is fired, two cars drive away, presumably with Jane in one of them, because she isn't here now and neither is the box, is it?"

"That's it," said Euphemia. "Exactly."

"You've got to be kidding me, Mum."

Euphemia, seeing the disbelief on Nicky's face, looked away. Nicky was just about to ask her the obvious question when thankfully she was saved by an interruption from one of the forensics team. Irritated, Nicky indicated she would be there in a moment.

"This is all very odd and frankly unbelievable, Mum. Stay here till I get back and do not, *do not* talk to anyone."

The little car, the driver's door wide open, was swarming with people in white paper overalls. If only Jane had handed over the jewelry straight away, they would be home by now, having a cup of tea and getting dinner ready. Nothing had gone as Euphemia had imagined. Why had Jane been so stupid and why hadn't she done something to save her?

Euphemia was scared. She'd never been as scared as this in her life. Scared for Jane and, truth be told, scared for herself. Why, why hadn't she insisted Jane go back to the police? Why hadn't she called them herself? Why had she been so stupid? To not think things through and consider all the possibilities was unforgiveable. She'd been ridiculously naïve, kidding herself about her powers and how she could use them. Hell, she thought, I don't even know what they are.

Dealing with Alison Sinclair and her vicious husband was light years away from rescuing a little boy down a cliff and she hadn't made the distinction. A gun? She hadn't even considered the possibility there might be weapons involved. How dumb of her. She really was the suburban middle class woman that Alison had ridiculed. This afternoon had proved it.

Maybe she should tell Nicky everything. She looked over at her daughter and resolved to tell her about the Sinclairs as soon as she came back. That way the police could find the car and Jane before Alison did anything, or Malcolm. Euphemia suddenly felt very cold.

Over at the car, Nicky had put on white paper overalls and stepped over the plastic ribbon to look at the ceiling where the bullet was lodged. Euphemia watched as another man took her aside to explain what the scene had revealed so far, pointing out various things on the ground and then in the car. They'd found Jane's handbag and wallet. Another man showed her a diamond on a gold chain, which had been found lying next to the car. Nicky was listening carefully as they pointed out more evidence.

Another squall of rain hit the side of the building sending spatters over one of the balconies. All Euphemia could think about was the sight of Jane's terrified face as she was hustled into the back of the car.

Her phone buzzed in her pocket. Not now Kenneth, dammit, but when she pulled it out and looked at the screen, it wasn't her husband. Unknown number. She turned away from the car and answered.

"Effie, it's me. Alison will kill me if you say anything to the police. She saw you. She says she has nothing to lose by killing me and she will if you say a word."

Jane's voice dropped to a whisper. "I believe her, Effie. She's been horrible. Do what she says. Please."

Nicky, still with the man in overalls, looked over at her mother. Her face crinkled in annoyance to see Euphemia turned away, huddled over her phone, but the man was insisting she crouch down and look under the car to see the tooth. She was about to yell at

Euphemia to put the phone down but she had no choice other than to listen to what the man was saying.

Euphemia was shocked to hear Alison's voice next. "What the hell are you playing at, Sage? What were you doing there? Jane's dead if you say a word. I mean it and by the way we picked up your dog."

There was a pained yelp, which was unmistakably Petal.

"Work tomorrow, nine o'clock." The phone went dead.

"I can't believe you, Mum," said a very angry Nicky. "I told you not to talk to anyone."

"I didn't. I just answered my phone. It was your father." She was surprised at how easily she was able to lie. "He's winning and wanted to tell me." Euphemia shoved her phone deep into her pocket and looked directly at her daughter, daring her to ask to see the phone as proof.

Nicky buckled. "What sort of cars were they?"

"What cars?"

"For goodness' sake, Mum, are you trying to be obstructive?"

"Of course not, sorry. The first car was Japanese, or maybe Korean. Light blue, I think. The second car was a black Mercedes. I'm sure about that because one almost drove into me and your father on Friday night outside the restaurant and I've been thinking about it ever since."

"Mum. Stop it. I don't know why you're twittering on like this but it doesn't suit you. Nothing makes sense. You're the only witness to what looks like a violent crime and I need your help. Sensible help."

"I'm trying my best." Euphemia hated what she was about to do, but she had no choice. She needed to get away; she needed time to think. She put her head in her hands and groaned.

"Mum, this is really, really important. Did you see a number plate or anyone you recognize? How many people were in the car? Think."

"Nicky, I need to go home. This is all too much. I'm not used to it. I work in an office. I only saw people, two, I think, in each car."

"Which car was Jane in?"

"The Mercedes, definitely."

"See, you can be helpful. Just a few more questions, I promise."

"Maybe you could get someone else to come and talk to me at home when I've had some time, but right now, I'm done. I know you're only doing your job and I want to help, I do."

Nicky, frustrated and puzzled, knew her mother wasn't being totally honest and worse, most unlike her, she was upset. Other officers, glancing their way, were muttering under their breaths. It was bad enough your mother was the only witness at your first major crime scene, but to then badger her in front of everyone was not a good look.

Professionally, Nicky knew she had to stand back and have someone more objective interrogate her mother but time was also of the essence. The more she could find out, the sooner they could track down Jane and maybe save her life. She took a deep breath and made herself stand back.

Another man in plain clothes came over and they turned away from Euphemia to talk quietly. Euphemia listened in. "Nicky, we've just checked the CCTV footage. The car number plates have been blocked out, no doubt on purpose."

Nicky's shoulders sagged. "Can't be helped, I suppose," she heard her daughter say. "Right, get a team onto tracking down the owners of all that model Mercedes in the city before checking their owners' movements. Let me know when you have anything."

The rain was getting heavier and the wind was even stronger. Euphemia had been sitting on the edge of the ramp, in her black running clothes, for a couple of hours. Hunched over, her hair bedraggled and her clothes dusty from the floor, she knew how much older and frailer she appeared to them all. The man talking to Nicky muttered something to her about getting her mother into the warmth and Nicky turned and looked at her.

"I'll get one of my men to drive you home and wait with you till Kezia can come over. Sorry about all that before. You remember I told you about Dave Richards, my boss? He will come and talk to you later, when you've had a chance to warm up and have some food."

Without waiting for Euphemia to say anything, Nicky called over a young detective and explained what she wanted him to do. Exhausted as she was, Euphemia noticed a look pass between them; their eye contact was longer than would be normal for colleagues. He was a young man, very good looking, much taller than her daughter and seemed very kind. Nice, thought Euphemia.

Nicky looked up from her laptop when her mother was leaving and waved. She noticed her mother's hair, always resolutely blonde, was graying at the roots. Euphemia's eyes were closed and she looked exhausted as the policeman had to support her on his arm as they walked down the ramp. For the first time, it occurred to Nicky, her mother might be getting old.

Chapter Twenty-two

The house felt cold and unnaturally quiet when they got home. No scatter of claws on the wooden floors, no little dog dancing round her feet, pleased to see her. The most glaring gap was there was no Sunday afternoon Kenneth, slumped in front of the golf on TV, stirring to get up and greet a visitor, trying to look happy about it and failing.

Ben stood awkwardly inside the front door, unsure what to do next. Euphemia was in no mood to talk but she couldn't be rude. It wasn't his fault the afternoon had turned out the way it had — a massive failure of epic proportions.

"Would you like to check upstairs while I put the kettle on?" she suggested.

Ben nodded, grateful to have something to do.

In the kitchen, Euphemia was greeted by a trail of doggy-treat crumbs leading to the broken dog door. The flap lay in pieces where it had been kicked in. Outside in the garden the trail stopped abruptly. Petal had left the building willingly. Euphemia could imagine the pug's utter delight at being given treats for no reason then remembered the uncomprehending yelp of pain. She remembered Jane's bloodied face, raised defiantly in the gloom. A tsunami of horror scenarios hovered in her imagination, threatening to engulf her. Taking a deep breath, she forced the thoughts to stop, and finding the brush and pan quickly swept up the crumbs and the broken dog door and dumped everything in the bin.

Overhead, she could hear Ben methodically opening and closing various doors. Damn. She'd forgotten the decoy in her study.

"Ben!" she screamed. He ran downstairs to find her pointing at a tiny spider high up in a corner of the kitchen.

"Can you please get that? I hate spiders," she said piteously.

Obligingly he reached up, curled his hand around the spider and, opening a window, threw it outside.

"Gone."

"Silly, isn't it? Nicky thinks I'm pathetic. How about you make the coffee, while I have a shower and get changed. My clothes are damp and I'm freezing. You'll find everything in there. Won't be long."

She let the shower run while she tiptoed to the study and tidied away the sewing dummy. Had it fooled them? She doubted it. How amateur it looked now.

Peeling off her clothes she stepped into the shower and let the hot water pour over her head and down her body. Visions of Jane and what she must be doing barged into her mind. She doubted she would be enjoying the luxury of a shower or clean clothes, wherever she was. She saw the greed on Alison's face, and then Malcolm's face, ripe with pleasure, loomed into view as he stood back and surveyed Jane sprawled across the front seat of the car.

I knew evil existed, she thought, in the movies and maybe in other parts of the city. Definitely in other countries where poverty drives desperate people to commit heinous crimes. I'm not a complete idiot. How can it have been here, beside me, all this time and I didn't see it? I don't class myself as naïve, but I never saw any of this. I thought I was aware, on to it. I read the news. I hear what people tell me. I take an interest in the world.

Right beside me, all this time, has been a world of greed and the most disgusting violence and I didn't see it. Did I even look?

She stepped out of the shower and toweled herself dry. Wiping the steam off the mirror she looked at her face and saw the incomprehension in her eyes. Pointless violence is something that happens in movies or on TV, not in my world, not with the people I know.

She straightened up and fiercely brushed the tangles out of her hair, thumping the brush against her scalp over and over again. With each pull of the bristles, she felt the protective walls around her family and what she had thought was civil society, her society, fall away.

I'm on the other side of the mythical white picket fence now, she thought, where there is no decency, no logic and where trust doesn't exist. Where everything has a price. There's no going back. She shuddered. She wanted no part of it. It revolted her. People like Malcolm lived there, people who sneered at a woman covered in her own blood.

Face it, she thought, as she rubbed moisturizer into her face and gave her legs a quick once-over, he and people like him are part of your life now, whether you like it or not. These disgusting people are the ones who hurt others. They're the ones I have to beat to protect the innocent. They deserve no mercy — none.

This is the real change, she realized. Strength, superhuman vision and hearing were all very well, but if I don't use them to beat people like Malcolm and Alison, they're pointless. Standing idly by, too afraid to do anything, like I did this afternoon, was and is pathetic.

"You were useless today — admit it," she said to her reflection in the mirror. "OK, you weren't prepared, but that's not good enough. You have to stop thinking people are nice, that they'll do the right thing, because they won't. Toughen up, Euphemia Sage."

She found some jeans and a polo neck jersey in her bedroom and pulled them on along with a thick pair of Kenneth's socks. She needed to feel his comfort as she confronted what she was going to have to do.

Downstairs she could hear Ben rattling pots on the stove. Thankfully he wasn't useless in the kitchen and by the smell of the coffee, he knew how to use a stove-top.

"Right, you," she said, pointing at herself in the mirror and checking her teeth at the same time. "Focus. Jane, Petal and the business are depending on you. Go to the police only if you're sure Alison won't kill Jane, before they can find her. Are you sure of that? No. Don't go to the police then."

Euphemia brushed her teeth and put on some mascara. I need to find out more about Rachel's Switch, she thought, because next time I won't be playing Lady's Rules. I have to know what I'm capable of. Every success, every failure is a lesson, and for Jane's sake I'd better learn quickly.

When she got downstairs, Ben was sliding two expertly cooked omelets, melted cheese oozing out the sides, onto plates. The coffee was poured and smelled delicious. Euphemia took a seat at one of the places he'd set at the bench.

"I don't know about you, but I'm starving," he said, and pushed the plate towards her.

Chapter Twenty-three

Nicky's boss was much younger than Euphemia had thought he would be, and much tougher. She estimated Detective Inspector Dave Richards was probably only five years older than Nicky, but judging by his rank he was clearly very good at his job. He didn't fall for the poor little old lady routine and made this abundantly clear in their first minutes of meeting. He asked the same questions over and over again, nicely at first, but each time couched slightly differently hoping to expose any inconsistencies in her story of the afternoon's events.

Part of her wanted to come clean and hand the whole mess over to him so she could be done with it, but remembering the sound of Jane's voice on the phone and Petal's piteous yelp, she couldn't bring herself to do it. Getting changed, she'd decided she had to wait until she heard what Alison would say in the morning, at the office. Then and only then could she decide whether it was safe to involve the police.

The Sinclairs wouldn't get any more money from Jane so maybe she was next. God knows she'd happily pay if money was all they wanted. Why Alison was carrying on with the charade of work mystified her and she wasn't ready to put Jane or Petal at risk until she knew the reason. Alison and Malcolm were each as unpredictable and dangerous as the other, but they wanted something more, otherwise why hang around? They had the jewelry. Why not dump Jane and make a run for it?

Dave Richards was getting exasperated. "So, Mrs. Sage, you were running past when you heard someone yelling for help?"

"It was quite loud yelling."

"I don't doubt that, otherwise how would you have heard it? We tested it after you'd gone. We couldn't hear anyone yelling until they were literally hanging out over the side of the building. We're impressed your hearing is so acute."

"Why else would I have gone up, inspector?"

"Indeed," he said, "so, what did you see?"

"You mean after I got to the third floor?"

"I don't mean to be rude, Mrs. Sage, but you do realize a woman's life is as stake? Time is running out and so playing circular question games with you is not the best use of my time."

"I am trying to help, truly."

"So tell me, what did you see... after you got to the third floor?"

"I crept up the ramp because I didn't know what I was going to find. The yelling didn't stop. They were arguing."

"Who was arguing?"

"I didn't see till I got up there." Euphemia saw the irritation on Dave's face and hurried on. "There were cars and two women fighting and men standing around watching, two, no, three."

"Did you recognize any of them?"

"Yes, I was surprised because one of the women was Jane French. We were at school together. She stayed here last night. My husband and her husband have gone away for the weekend to play golf with Roger, who was our best man. Kenneth's and mine. Neville went too. He was our groomsman. Roger and Neville used to play rugby with Kenneth when we were all at university. Not Justin. I don't think he ever played. Rugby. Of course he plays golf because..."

Dave Richards stood up, walked over to Euphemia and bent down so his head was right beside hers. "Nicky told me how smart you were. I know your business reputation. I know you're purposely not helping me or this investigation, Mrs. Sage," he said quietly. "I just don't know why you are not helping me." He turned and walked back to where he had been sitting before and sat down again. No one in the room moved.

"But I will find out. I promise you," he said and then smiled.

Euphemia stared back and shrugged her shoulders. "I am doing my best, inspector. Really."

"Right. You saw the people you saw. And Jane. Did you know Jane, Mrs. French, was going to be there? Is that why you were running past?"

"Not at all. I was as surprised to see her as no doubt she was to see me. Then the gun went off and they all left."

"Just like that. How come there was so much blood on the floor?"

"When I got there, Jane was bleeding. Her face, it looked like it'd been bashed in. She looked terrible and very scared. I wanted to help her but the gun..."

"Yes, you said. Now tell me..." The house phone rang and kept ringing. The inspector motioned to Ben to answer it, which he did and then after a moment, handed it to Euphemia.

"It's your husband."

Dave Richards let out a long sigh, shook his head and flipped open his laptop to check his messages.

Kenneth spoke so loudly everyone in the room could hear. "I've heard about Jane. It's awful. Justin isn't taking it well," said Kenneth. "We won, by the way. Blitzed the round, Roger and me. Final's tomorrow. I could come home, Euphemia, but there's one problem."

"I think I can guess."

"Really? How?"

"You're slurring your words, you sound completely pissed."

"Yes, Euphemia. You're right," he said and then hiccupped. "We'd already had a few to celebrate before Nicky called. Justin's had lots more because he and Neville got knocked out early. So the problem is, and I told Nicky too," he said merrily, "none of us can drive. Doubt we'll be fit to drive till the morning — late morning. I'm worried, of course, but you're strong. The girls are there. And the police. Truly, winning the tournament tomorrow means nothing. Roger doesn't mind my leaving him in the lurch, if you don't want me to play."

This last statement was accompanied with yelling in the background. "Nooooooooo," said Roger shouting into the phone. "I don't mind. Hi, Euphemia."

"Hi, Roger."

By the sounds in the background, they were in a pub, a very crowded pub. Music was blaring and people were shouting orders for more drinks. Dave Richards sat on the sofa, eyebrows raised, unable to believe what he was hearing. Euphemia could hear Justin's voice leading the singing and calling for more wine.

"It's up to you, Euphemia. Roger doesn't mind, do you, buddy?" A sound of glass breaking was followed by catcalls.

"Noooooooo," called Roger again, before he joined in a chorus of 'Desperado'. Dave Richards slammed his laptop shut and stood up.

Kenneth wasn't a big drinker usually. For that matter neither was Roger. It was an easy decision. "Don't worry. Play your round tomorrow. There's nothing you can do anyway. The police are here. They're taking care of it."

"Yeeessssss!" yelled Roger triumphantly.

"Detective Inspector Richards, he's Nicky's boss, Kenneth, he wants to talk to you. Try to sound sober." She handed the phone over.

"Mr. Sage? Justin French is with you. You all know his wife has been kidnapped at gunpoint, don't you?"

"We do and we're very worried but we have complete faith in the police, don't we, Roger?"

"Yeeesssss. We love the police."

"Mr. Sage, listen. I tried to talk to Mr. French before but he's not in much of a state to understand. We're sending a car. It'll get there very early tomorrow morning, but he's no good to us drunk."

"Bit late now, sorry. You're that detective Nicky talks about. She says veeeery nice things about you. I think she fancies you."

Dave Richards' face colored. "Thank you. Please stop Justin from drinking any more tonight, and you boys might want an early night too? You do understand how serious this is. We need him here to help us to find his wife and he's useless to us drunk or hung over."

"Done!"

"Over and outtttt..." yelled Roger. A thump and another crash of glasses was followed by more apologies to an annoyed barmaid.

Euphemia didn't fancy their chances of winning tomorrow. None of this made sense. Kenneth was too competitive to start celebrating before he actually won. And neither he nor Roger were really drinkers, even on boys' weekends. Two beers or a glass of wine was usually their limit. God help their heads in the morning.

Dave Richards and Ben started talking amongst themselves on the other side of the room when it became obvious Kenneth was now determined to send a sentimental message and sloppy kiss good night to Euphemia.

When she finally extracted herself from the call, Dave realized there was no point in continuing. He'd got nothing from Euphemia before they were interrupted and he doubted he'd get anything now. Either she was not as smart as her reputation had led him to believe, or she was not cooperating. Whatever, he was tired. He had a long night ahead and there were better avenues of investigation. He was also very worried. There'd been no word from the kidnappers. Usually by now contact had been made and negotiations had started. Silence did not bode well for Jane.

"Does Ben really have to stay with me, detective inspector?" Euphemia asked as he got ready to leave.

"Yes, Mrs. Sage. You're the only witness to an armed kidnapping. You're important to us obviously. I don't want to scare you but you're important to them, whoever they are. You haven't told us anything useful but they don't know that. So there will be a police officer with you at all times until we find Mrs. French. Is that clear?"

A few minutes after he'd gone, Nicky called. She too sounded exhausted and Euphemia ached to give her a hug and tell her it would be all right, as she used to when she was little. This time, though, Euphemia couldn't be sure it would be all right.

"Ben has to stay with me so Kezia doesn't need to come. I don't need two babysitters and she has better things to do."

"OK, fair enough." Euphemia winced as the tone in her daughter's voice shifted. "Dave told me how unhelpful you were, Mum. I don't get it. You're not stupid. Why aren't you helping us?"

Euphemia hadn't felt this much hostility from Nicky since she had caught her sneaking out the window when she was fifteen and had grounded her for six weeks.

"Shock?" she suggested knowing how lame this sounded. "Maybe I'll remember more tomorrow?"

"No, Mum, you're tough. We'll get to the bottom of this helpless woman act. And if I find out you're involved, Mum, I can't save you. Understand?"

"Yes. There's nothing more I can tell you. Honest."

"You play it that way. You've met my boss. He doesn't believe you either and he doesn't stop till he gets results. Woe betide anyone who gets in his way."

"I honestly can't tell you any more."

"Can't? Or won't?"

"Nicky..."

The phone went dead.

Chapter Twenty-four

Euphemia was left holding the phone. Ben shifted uneasily in the chair opposite, trying to pretend he hadn't heard the terse mother-daughter exchange.

"Nicky was top in our class at Police College," he said.

"I know."

"Top in every subject except IT. She was second in that and we never heard the end of it. She doesn't like losing."

"Never did."

"What was she like when she was little?" he asked.

"A dynamo. Never gave me a moment's peace. Kezia was quietly bright. Nicky was the opposite, bright but out there. Hated being inside. She wasn't still for a moment."

"I don't know if I could keep up with her."

"Not many people can."

"They probably haven't tried hard enough."

Euphemia walked into the kitchen to put the kettle on for the hundredth time that day. She got out the dog biscuits and filled Petal's bowl before she remembered and tipped the biscuits back into the bag and returned it to the pantry.

Ben's gentle questions had distracted her temporarily. Lying to Nicky was not something she enjoyed.

"Don't look so worried, Mrs. Sage," said Ben following her into the kitchen. "It'll be all right. Dave is good — really good. You look exhausted, you go to bed. I'll make sure everything's locked up."

Euphemia got a packet of herb teabags from the pantry and lifted it up for Ben to see. He nodded. She poured hot water over the bags and watched quietly as it turned a swirling bright pink in the mugs.

"You like my daughter, don't you, Ben? I don't mean just as a colleague."

He had the maturity to answer her seriously. "I do, but I'm not sure she thinks of me the same way."

"I saw the way she looked at you at the car park. You might have a chance. Just don't rush her. Make her think it was her idea. She likes to be in charge."

"Doesn't she just?"

"You don't mind? Most men would run a mile from a bossy woman."

"I don't mind and I'm not a pushover. Who do you think beat her in IT?"

"Good, because she can be unthinkingly cruel to doormats. She gets impatient with people who can't stand up for themselves."

"No worries there, but I'm not into the alpha male thing."

Euphemia sipped her tea enjoying the tang of the fruit in the hot liquid. "You must have nice parents."

"One left and you're right, he's nice. Mum died when I was nine. Cancer. She'd been sick for years before that. Dad was in the SAS and was overseas when she was diagnosed. Came straight home. Gave up everything to look after us. When she died, a bit of him died with her. Something I didn't understand till I grew up."

"I'm so sorry. My mother died as well but that was years after she left me with my aunt. I never knew her. My aunt brought me up. I knew she loved me but she wasn't my mother. It feels strange, doesn't it, grieving for someone as important as a parent, but never knowing them as a person? The curiosity doesn't go away. Never knew my father but that doesn't bother me. Not sure why."

"It hasn't stopped you, has it?"

"Stopped me?"

"From being happy. Nicky's always talking about you and her

father and how amazing you both are. It is possible to be happy, isn't it? You need one person who believes in you. I have Dad, and you had your aunt."

"Your father must be very proud of you."

"He says he is, not often, but enough."

Ben fussed about with his cup in the sink, then walked over to check the lock on the back door.

"What happened?" he asked, looking at the gaping hole where the flap was missing.

"Petal, my dog. She's a pug. Very greedy."

"The famous Petal; I wondered where she was. Nicky talks about her all the time too."

"She's a glutton. Got stuck and I had to dismantle it to get her out. Broke it. No one can get through it so I didn't think it would matter."

"Where is she?"

"At the vet's. Got a nasty cut when she got stuck. It's been that sort of day."

Euphemia was horrified at how suddenly she could tell so many lies and how easily they came to her.

"You go to bed. I'll put something over it. Don't want the neighbor's cat taking advantage. It was lurking around the compost bins when I looked."

Euphemia was grateful. It was comfortable with him there. Ben was more like a guest than a policeman. He wasn't trying to wheedle information out of her when she let her guard down. More importantly, he liked Nicky. Most men were scared off by her, but he didn't seem fazed at all.

"I know you're supposed to stay awake in case the bad guys come, but I'll get you a pillow and some blankets. I'm told the sofa is comfortable." She showed him the downstairs bathroom and where he could find fresh towels. She was pointing out things in the kitchen he might need when he interrupted her.

"Don't worry, Mrs. Sage. You go to bed. I'll be fine. Call out if you need me."

Bed had never looked so good. She'd had so little sleep the night before. Still dressed, she lay down for just a moment and closed her eyes. She was sprawled face down when her phone buzzed beside her. She fumbled for it and wiping a thread of saliva away from her mouth, looked at the screen. It was 11 pm. She'd been asleep for three hours.

"Sage? At work tomorrow, act normally."

Instantly alert, she asked, "Alison? Is Jane OK?"

There was a long pause. She heard steps on metal and a door swing shut.

"Effie. We're fine, Petal and me. Keeping each other company. Do whatever she says, Effie. Please."

There was the sound of a scuffle and Alison was back.

"Remember, act normally. I meant it about your pug. Nothing would make me happier than to hand it over and see how it copes against real dogs."

The phone went dead.

Sage? thought Euphemia. When has Alison ever called me Sage?

She sat up, wiped her mouth again and ran her fingers through her hair. The light was still on and downstairs she could hear the shopping channel on television, turned low. Soft snoring told her Ben was asleep.

Putting aside Alison's hoodlum speak, Euphemia went over the conversation, replaying every sound in her mind.

Jane and Petal were alive. Jane sounding scared, was lisping no doubt because of the missing tooth and swollen lip. Alison was there. Just Alison. She hadn't heard anyone else in the background, but she had heard a low hum followed by a long squeal of what might be brakes. It wasn't a car because the sound was too long. A truck maybe? Then a whish of air and a dull thump.

Where had she heard that combination before? They weren't at the apartment. That was well and truly insulated from traffic noise. Plus she gave Alison more credit. It would have been stupid to go there. If she had talked to the police that would be the first place they'd look.

Tomorrow Alison would be at work acting as if nothing had happened. Euphemia was supposed to do the same. Which meant either someone else would be with Jane and Petal, or they'd be alone.

If Half-Ear and Mark were there, they would be OK. The brothers were thugs but she'd seen how they looked when they saw the gun. They'd snatched Petal with bribes, not brute force. They were happy enough to give someone a good kicking but murder and kidnapping were out of their league. Euphemia doubted the Sinclairs would be paying them enough to cover the risk of prison.

Hopefully tomorrow Malcolm wouldn't be left in charge. Alison was mad but she wasn't stupid. Malcolm, on the other hand, was an idiot, which made him unpredictable and therefore exceptionally dangerous.

How long had the Sinclairs been targeting her clients? she wondered. Judging by the performance this afternoon they weren't professionals. What self-respecting criminal takes a pug dog hostage? They were seriously out of their depth. Legal loan sharking might be immoral but wouldn't land them in prison. Kidnapping and grievous bodily harm meant prison for sure, and for a long time.

Would they really go as far as murdering Jane to keep her quiet? Alison must only now be starting to understand how much trouble she was in. Malcolm would never get it. Could she keep him on track or would she panic?

The unknown is sometimes worse than anything, thought Euphemia. She needed information about herself before tomorrow and whatever the Sinclairs might do then.

Chapter Twenty-five

The neighborhood was Sunday night quiet. There were no cars, no sounds. Even the cat next door had given up his rat patrol and was curled up underneath the agapanthus by the compost bins. The wind had disappeared taking the rain clouds with it, leaving the moon and stars in the night sky to compete with the lights of the city.

In the attic, the spider looked at Euphemia as she sat down and unlocked the chest. Eight eyes ranged across its knobby head like lights on a truck, all of them pointed at her. She stared back wondering who would blink first. She let her gaze wander and saw an addition to the web — an egg sac hung off one side, shifting slightly in the attic drafts.

"You're a girl," said Euphemia. "There must be a boy spider I haven't seen yet."

The spider said nothing and Euphemia thought it better not to inquire further. She blinked. The spider turned and scrabbled away to the far side of her web.

Euphemia had come back to the chest for help. She had no idea what she was looking for but where else could she go? She needed to find out as much as she could about herself, her family and just what exactly Rachel's Switch entailed.

Ben's rhythmic snores floated up the stairs from the living room. She was pleased because he'd looked exhausted. Her few hours of sleep had been sufficient to recharge and completely re-energize her. Maybe that too was the switch at work, reducing her downtime.

Peering deep inside the chest again, Euphemia scanned the bottom and walls for anything, any clue. This time headlines weren't looming into view, vying for attention. There was no ring, nothing else had arrived mysteriously inside the chest in the interim. Feeling deep into the corners and cracks, all she came up with were dirty fingernails and dusty hands. What she needed had to be here, and she knew it would be obvious once she saw it.

She shut the lid and turned the chest around. She was examining the outside when she knocked the ring against the front of the lid. It sounded hollow. She turned the chest and knocked the next side — solid. She turned it and knocked the other side — solid again. When she turned the chest round to face her again, a tiny button set into a mitered corner caught her eye. She pressed it. A panel slid smartly back to reveal a screen. A screen made of white material, like a movie screen but much smaller. Two spindles were at each end, one full and the other empty.

Feeling across the top of the lid, she found two wheels set flush where the edges joined together. Hats off to whomever the cabinet-maker was who built this, she thought, admiring the intricacy of the mechanism.

Euphemia made herself comfortable on the hard floor and gently, because she didn't want to rip the paper, started turning the wheel on her left. As if it had been made yesterday, the paper moved from one spindle to the other and as it unrolled she learned the story of Rachel's Switch.

There was a picture of a village and a date... 1624, *Coldfham, Warwickfhire*. Once she remembered the old lettering and replaced 'f' with 's', it made sense. A church, small but with a respectable enough steeple, was surrounded by houses, nothing grand, thatched roofs and fenced gardens. A cow, a couple of goats and several large geese were drawn standing on the green beside a large pond.

Euphemia felt her blood go cold. This had to be the same village, Coldsham, the same pond where her mother had run off the road and drowned. But that was thirty-seven years ago and this picture said 1624.

The fine ink drawings had been done by a skilled artist. Lines feathered and bold, dense and intricate brought the old village to life, drawing her in.

She turned the wheel. The next scene was of a woman surrounded by other women, babies on their hips. One woman taller and more carefully drawn than the others stood out. She had regular features, large eyes and thick hair, most of it tucked under a cap, but some escaped down her back. The artist had captured the smile on the woman's face and the intelligence in her eyes. She was carrying a basket loaded with eggs, a corked jug, bunches of herbs and books. At the bottom of the picture was written the words *Rachel — midwyfe and healer.*

Euphemia studied her face carefully. This had to be her relation, her something-something-great-great-great-grandmother visiting her from 1624, the original Rachel. Euphemia could see something of Kezia in her. There was a clarity that resonated and she reached out and softly touched the drawing.

She turned the wheel. The same woman was now bound by thick ropes, her clothes torn, her hair tangled and a crowd surrounded her, jeering and throwing missiles of vegetables and dung. The mob was beside the pond and in the foreground a man in black was standing over them holding a Bible, a white collar at his throat. Euphemia could feel the thin cold of winter, there were no leaves on the trees and everyone except Rachel was warmly clothed. Clouds bunched on the horizon behind them threatening rain. The artist had even drawn wheel ruts and animal tracks in the mud beside the pond.

'*Behold, Rachel the witch. Punish her for her sins — curdling the milk of her neighbor's cow, disobeying her guardian, refusing to name the father of her child and daring to seek knowledge — all signs of the devil. She must be tested.*'

Euphemia's heart twisted in her chest to see the wretched fear drawn so skillfully on Rachel's face, the gloating faces of the mob and the sanctimony of the parson. Rachel was to be ducked.

At school she'd read all about ducking stools used in old England to torture women accused of witchcraft. Ducking was how intelligent women were punished for speaking out, so her teacher had said. If the woman lived, she was possessed by the devil, and if she drowned, she had been innocent all along. The cruel logic had sent shivers of fear down their schoolgirl spines.

The picture in front of her had no stool, but she remembered they weren't always necessary. All a village needed was a deep pond, a willing mob and rope.

In the next scene, Rachel was wearing a loose shift, which barely covered her nakedness, and she was trussed tightly like a chicken, each thumb tied to the opposite foot. She was on her back on the muddy beach and the artist had taken particular care to include her advanced state of pregnancy in the drawing. Men were preparing to heave her, helpless, far out into the water.

Euphemia rolled the wheel and the next picture was as she expected. It showed Rachel flying out above the pond, hair and ropes streaming behind her, the raised hand of the minister holding a cross high above the proceedings while the villagers looked keenly on.

She turned the wheel quickly but the paper was blank and stayed blank. This couldn't be all there was. Had the story ended there, she wouldn't be alive — there had to be more.

The surface of the pond, drawn flat and undisturbed, appeared. Some in the crowd were scanning the water, searching, while others, heads down, looking ashamed, were trudging back to their homes. Some accusing looks were directed at the parson, who was striding off down the road, a thin black figure receding into the distance. Below in capital letters and framed with speech marks was written 'RACHEL' and a swoop of wind leading to the next picture.

Euphemia saw the face of a man on horseback, searching and hopeful. Well-dressed, he was standing up in his stirrups to see farther out across the pond, his horse exhausted with sweat foaming at its mouth and spotting its flanks.

Turning the wheel again she saw a rope floating on the water, the man now off his horse, hauling on the rope, his feet braced against a log in the mud, calling to others for help.

Next the weed-bedraggled body of the woman lay on the water's edge. Her gown stuck to her body, her belly full with child, eyes closed and mouth slack, while the man now knelt beside her and looked up to the heavens imploringly. 'Mercy.'

Euphemia turned the wheel and felt the paper go taut as it reached the end of the scroll. She saw the woman sitting up, her hand on her belly, her eyes staring ahead, sure and certain, while the man hugged her to his chest, tears of joy coursing down his cheeks.

Rachel had lived, when her neighbors thought her dead. She had been pulled from the water and saved.

That was it. There was no more.

Chapter Twenty-six

All well and good, thought Euphemia, but what does it mean? There was nothing on the scroll to show her what she could do, nothing about her strengths, or weaknesses for that matter, nothing which told her how to beat Alison. Maybe I can hold my breath. Great, she thought, I can see how that might be useful at the office in the morning. Not.

Fredericka should have been here. My mother should have been here to show me what the switch means, to teach me. She was the one who was supposed to do it but like everything else, she stuffed up. Memories of photographs of her mother at parties, drunk, men leering at her, flashed across her brain. Anger and rage at her mother's selfishness, the woman's utter foolishness, rose up, as drops of sweat slid down her body. She felt the blow of each heartbeat battering against her ribs, getting faster and faster. What if I can't do this? What if I can't save Jane? Or Petal? Or the business? Catastrophe built upon catastrophe, each worse than the one before, each one making it harder and harder to breathe so that the attic swam before her. Euphemia fell to the floor paralyzed as the room went black.

"But wait, there's more. Buy one knife set and you get not one, not two but three, all for the price of one. But this is a limited offer; call this number now or miss out. This offer won't be repeated."

She woke to the sound of the TV from downstairs and opened her eyes. She saw the spider unmoving in the middle of her web, staring at her. A nail in one of the floorboards was pressed hard into her cheek and she was cold. Her clothes were damp but she could breathe and her heart was behaving itself. Music drifted up from below. She looked at her watch. It was 4 am. Nothing had changed. The day stretched ahead of her. Sitting up, she ran her hands through her hair and scratched her scalp, which felt amazingly good. The panic was gone.

She had a couple of hours left. Best not to waste it. After locking the chest and saying goodbye to the spider, she tiptoed downstairs past the sleeping Ben and reheated the coffee in the microwave, scared the ping would wake Ben. It didn't and the hot bitter liquid was the jolt she needed. She took her cup upstairs and opened her laptop.

Google.

'Female only inheritance'. Press Search.

Why is it, she thought, computers are faster at night than during the day? On the screen was a long list of scientific references to mito-chondrial DNA (mtDNA), interspersed with articles from newspa-pers about the mother of us all, Eve, and how all humans living today could be traced back to one woman. Other articles, newer research, debunked the Eve theory noting the timelines between the fossil record and the DNA were out of sync. She looked down the list for something more detailed she could read without having to do a PhD in genetics first and found something understandable, as usual, in Wikipedia.

MtDNA is found outside the nucleus in the mitochondria, she read; while the nucleus holds the DNA we inherit from both parents. MtDNA, though, is only passed on by the mother in the vast major-ity of people. It controls how fast our body processes energy and pro-teins. Most of those with mtDNA abnormalities have difficulty mak-ing energy available and this causes problems in the heart, eye move-ments and muscle function which is how we know what mtDNA does in the body- it regulates how we use energy. New studies are being done into how mtDNA affects aging and how these genes could hasten or slow the aging process.

Mutations in mtDNA can be passed from mother to daughter. Mutations can result from random events or changes occurring in the uterine environment if stress is induced at critical times of fetal development.

It didn't take much for Euphemia to make the connection between the stress caused to Rachel's unborn child by the near drowning and the changes in mtDNA. Hormonal surges somehow then triggered the activation of the mutation known in the family as Rachel's Switch. Her energy levels had zoomed since the menopause. She could see better, and run so much faster. Her muscles were stronger and more responsive. The switch was like a youth drug but better.

Once the switch in the mtDNA was there, then of course, it would be passed on. What didn't make sense was why only to the eldest daughter? Why not all the daughters? What if the eldest daughter died, or didn't have a daughter of her own? Surely that would mean the switch should have died out? She remembered Maree talking about the others in her letters. She had to assume that meant there were others with the switch who had the same changes in their DNA, but how could that be when it was one daughter to one daughter inheritance. Irritatingly Wikipedia did not have all the answers to her questions, but more irritatingly she was running out of time.

Outside in the distance she could hear the early-morning delivery trucks making their way along the motorway into the city. She closed the laptop, stood up, and stretched, relishing the elasticity in her muscles and the flexibility in her spine. Her body felt great, lithe and strong. Every part of her felt charged with life. The light had shifted; the hills behind the city, merged with the darkness earlier, now stood in silhouette against the sky. Opening the window, Euphemia breathed in the cool morning air.

The temptation was too strong. She changed into her running gear and slipping past the comatose Ben, eased quietly out the front door and took off. Running hard was easy. She sprinted to the end of the street and round the corner, reaching the end of the block, frustrated at having to stop at lights. The morning traffic was thicker now. Drivers, still sleepy, ties askew on the men and make-up only half done on the women, were listening to radios blaring morning jollity. They took no notice of her as she jogged impatiently on the spot waiting for the lights to change.

She heard it from over a block away. The squeal, the whishing sound, and then the thump as the doors closed behind passengers. The lights changed in her favor but she stayed where she was watching the bus as it pulled up beside her at the intersection. Last night when Alison called, she had to have been near a bus stop. Nothing else could make those sounds, in that order. It wasn't much of a clue but it was better than nothing, she thought.

Unwilling to postpone her run any longer, Euphemia ran out into the traffic, dodging and weaving amongst the cars, judging distances and speeds so no one had time to react, let alone slow down. Without looking back, Euphemia Sage kept on running.

Chapter Twenty-seven

Kenneth woke and immediately wished it was tomorrow. Pain pounded the backs of his eyes with the precision and strength of a sledgehammer wielded by a blind blacksmith. His mouth felt as though he had spent the night before licking an ashtray. Who in God's name had brought out the cigars and why, why had he thought he could smoke? He'd never smoked. He'd never wanted to smoke but for some mysterious reason, which totally eluded him this morning, last night it seemed like a good idea. He turned and slowly opened one eye to look at the clock ticking too loudly beside the bed.

The lump under the duvet snoring quietly on the other bed could only be Roger. Kenneth stretched out his leg and prodded the lump with his foot.

"We have half an hour to make the tournament or we get disqualified, Roger."

"What tournament?"

"The one we thought we could win."

"Really?"

There was a loud groan and Roger sat up. After a second of silence he leapt up from the bed and made a dash for the bathroom, where he vomited loudly into the loo.

"You could have shut the door," said Kenneth, feeling queasy himself.

"I didn't know we had curry last night," said Roger wiping his mouth, wandering back into the bedroom.

"Did we?"

"Pretty sure that's what it was."

"Justin must have ordered it." Roger started rummaging around in his bag. "He made a hell of a racket leaving at whatever hour he did this morning. Dropped something heavy right on top of me on his way out." Roger stripped off and put on a clean T-shirt and pants.

Kenneth's mission for the next five minutes was to stay as still as possible. "He woke me when he fell on my bed on his way to the bathroom."

"He's a strange one, isn't he, old Justin? Did he say anything to you about Jane? I tried to talk to him but he shut me down. Said he would sort it out when he got back. I don't think I would have been that cool if I'd just been told Lisa had been kidnapped at gunpoint."

Kenneth opened both eyes. "Same if it was Euphemia," he said, easing himself to a sitting position and pulling his bag towards him. He searched for the aspirin, which Euphemia always packed — just in case. Tearing open the packet, he popped three out of the foil and swilled them back with a glass of water.

"Want some?"

"I plan to take my punishment like a man, so yes, I do."

"I need to lie down again," said Kenneth slumping back onto the bed.

"We could win this tournament, you know."

"We could have won it, you mean, if we hadn't got so drunk last night. I never get that drunk."

"Neither do I, old mate, but what can you expect when Justin had us drinking jugs of rum and god knows what else, at lunch, for Chrissakes. And we did it."

"Maybe he was paid by the opposition to take us out?"

"Consenting adults, Kenneth. No excuses. On the other hand, you might be right. I heard he's hard up, and that pair are pretty desperate."

"Whoever suggested the cigars needs to be shot."

"That would be you."

"And you didn't stop me?"

"You're a big boy. Now get up."

Kenneth sat up again, one eye open, testing his balance.

"Do you really think we can win this? I mean honestly. Tell me, because if we can't, I'd rather go home. I had a horrible dream. Euphemia was in trouble and she needed me, or she will need me, or she's in trouble. You know how everything gets fuddled when you wake up."

"Euphemia Sage is the least needy woman I know. We can win but we've got five minutes to get to the clubhouse."

"If you're sure?"

"Of course I'm not. But no one ever won a golf tournament driving home."

Kenneth moved his head from side to side. No pain. "You're right. She'd call if she really needed me. How come you don't feel as terrible as I do?"

"I didn't smoke."

"Did Justin?"

"Nope, just you."

Chapter Twenty-eight

The cold woke Jane. Shivering under the thin blanket, she hugged Petal into her body, curling round the little dog to try to warm up. The pain in her mouth had kept her awake most of the night but mercifully in the last few hours it had eased, and she felt as though she had slept for a few hours at least. She had no idea of the time, but presumed it was morning because that was what her bladder was telling her. Alison had taken her watch and the windowless room was pitch black.

Last night, flanked by Malcolm and the man with half an ear, she'd been pulled out of the car and hustled down several flights of metal stairs to this place. Cold and very quiet, thick concrete walls muffled any sounds from outside. She could tell there would be no point in screaming.

Alison had thrown her the blanket and pointed at a pile of flattened cardboard boxes in one corner where she could sleep. In the other corner, Malcolm was hard at work blowing up an air mattress, while Alison unrolled a thick sleeping bag. Jane refused to complain. She'd got this far and she was damned if she was going to give them the satisfaction of hearing how miserable she felt.

She moved Petal away from her to take the pressure off her bladder. Heaven knows when she would be able to use the bathroom in the corridor outside and she didn't want to risk Alison's wrath by waking her.

Yesterday, she'd seen how disorganized the Sinclairs were. After changing cars, they'd spent the whole afternoon driving aimlessly around town. Malcolm drove, wearing a cap low over his eyes, while Alison sat in the back, the gun pointed at Jane who was made to lie on the floor. Every jolt and bump of the car had sent a new wave of pain through her empty tooth socket, but she refused to wince or show any weakness. She knew she could survive this, but only if she didn't irritate them.

When it was almost dark, Malcolm finally agreed to Alison's plan. His idea had been simple. Dump Jane somewhere far out of town and the two of them make a run for it with the jewelry. Jane liked his idea because she too saw how dumb it was. Alison had explained over and over again the flaws in his plan. It was only after she slowly explained for the tenth time that they needed to make sure the jewelry wasn't fake that he agreed to her idea. With the gun jammed harder against her head as Alison grew increasingly impatient with Malcolm, Jane had had to lie as still as possible. Every muscle ached as she lay on the floor, squashed between the seats. She would have given anything for something to eat or drink and a couple of hundred aspirins for the pain. She made herself think about the house sale and made a list of everything she had to do to get it ready — anything to take her mind off her predicament.

As she listened to them arguing about which one was going to stay with her, Jane realized they were complete amateurs. How had they run their 'finance company' all this time if they were so useless at making decisions? By the time they'd finally sorted out that it was Alison who would stay with her, Jane had stopped caring. Each was as bad as the other.

This morning Petal was in pug heaven. She'd finally found someone who didn't make her sleep in the laundry. Cuddled into Jane's warm tummy, her nose twitched and her paws flickered as she dreamed about chasing the cat next door out from under the agapanthus and in front of a passing car. A small bark escaped mid-dream, just loud enough to disturb the other woman in the room, the woman from the office who smelt bad. The only human Petal hated.

The little dog sat up and looked across at horrible Alison and snarled until Jane wrapped her hand around her snout, muffling her.

Alison, snuggled inside her warm sleeping bag, looked across at her hostages and stretched. She was in a foul mood. She'd been kept awake by Jane's snoring the whole night. It was incomprehensible that one person, and not a very big person, could make so much noise and not wake up. If Malcolm hadn't taken the bullets, Jane would be dead by now. Shot in the name of sleep. Alison looked at her new watch, a vintage Rolex given to Jane on her 21st birthday.

06.30. Where was Malcolm? He was supposed to have been here half an hour ago. She needed to shower and get to work before Sage if their plan was going to work. She'd known this would happen when she drew the short straw to stay with Jane. He was probably still asleep in the king-sized bed in his hotel room. Or maybe he'd reverted to form and was awake but lying transfixed by the cartoon channel he watched every morning while she got ready for work.

At least she hoped that's where he was. There was nothing to stop him making a run for it. It was precisely what she would have done if she'd been him. It was also the reason she'd kept the jewelry with her. She looked at her watch again. Jane's mother had good taste. When all this was over, she'd get the engraving on the back, ground off and her own name etched into it. Good grief, it was 6.45. Malcolm was really late. She wanted to call him but there was no reception in the basement, only on the stairwell outside. She pushed the sleeping bag off and stood up shakily on the air mattress.

She thought of a hot shower and clean clothes — and then remembered they would be Office Alison clothes. Knowing she would be putting on her disgusting cardigan and saggy leggings, tying back her hair without washing it, albeit for the last time, was only mute consolation. Her shoulders sagged. She looked over at Jane and found her staring back at her.

"What?"

"You should be ashamed of yourself, Alison Sinclair," said Jane sitting up, the blanket pulled around her shoulders and Petal panting in her lap.

"But I'm not, Jane. Your problem, not mine. In fact all the problems today are your problems. I wouldn't get me annoyed if I were you. You never know what I might do." Alison reached down, picked up the gun and, aiming it at Jane, pulled the trigger. The click echoed in the cold concrete room.

Chapter Twenty-nine

There's something heart-warming about a young man so deeply asleep that life can carry on around him and he still doesn't wake up, thought Euphemia as she walked past Ben, showered, dressed and ready for work. She was wearing a dark navy trouser suit she often wore to the office, a white pussy bow shirt and flat ankle boots, nothing that would make Alison suspicious but which left her free to move easily.

Ben woke when the smell of fresh coffee percolated through to the living room and tapped him on the nose. He sat up, taking a moment to register where he was, before realizing he was supposed to be guarding the woman in the kitchen. The TV was still on and a woman was pitching a machine guaranteed to take inches off your thighs and which if you ordered two you'd get a third free. He found the remote wedged down the back of the sofa and switched the TV off. The light on his phone blinked steadily for his attention, and he was accessing his voice messages when Euphemia handed him a cup of black coffee. He took a quick slurp and burnt the roof of his mouth, but kept listening as Nicky asked why he wasn't picking up and warning him Dave Richards was on the warpath.

"I am going to work with you, Mrs. Sage," he said when he returned his empty cup to the kitchen "All day. Just in case one of the kidnappers tries to make contact, you understand."

"Fine with me, Ben, but I'm leaving. I have a client meeting in thirty minutes."

This wasn't exactly true but Euphemia needed time alone at the office and Ben was still wearing his rumpled suit and hadn't shaved.

"You're going to have to freshen up and meet me there. We run a business consultancy and you can't spend the day at the office looking like you spent the night on a park bench after a big night out. Anyone watching would know straight away you were there for other reasons. Uber down when you're ready. I promise I won't tell Nicky, or Detective Inspector Richards. I really have to go. By the way, you're a business student sitting in with me as part of a work experience program, got it? Alison, the receptionist, means well but she's nosy, so don't get caught in the tearoom with her or she will know the name of your pet lamb you had when you were six before you've had time to boil the water."

Sage Consulting was situated in one of the newer office buildings in the middle of town. Starting out as a husband and wife team in the suburbs, when the girls were small, Kenneth and Euphemia had worked from home. Their first customers were other start-ups, initially suburban retailers and sole traders operating in their area. As their reputation as business and financial consultants had grown, they'd needed more space. They moved into an older building close by but quickly outgrew this and decided to take the risk and sign the lease on two floors of a building being constructed by one of their clients.

Sage Consulting never looked back. The firm now employed over fifty people and they were considering taking over the floor below them when it became vacant.

What drew clients to Sage Consulting was not only the teamwork but also their practicality and excellent communication skills. Kenneth got on with everyone and his sense of humor and tolerance made him a popular member of the local Chamber of Commerce. Euphemia, slightly less diplomatic, was trusted to call a spade a spade, which meant clients knew they were getting real advice and not just a glossy overview designed to reassure all was well when they should be taking action.

Euphemia and Kenneth understood how stressful owning and running a business could be, especially at the beginning. Both were skilled in steering people through good times and bad. Their clients remembered and returned sometimes years later when they again needed advice.

Euphemia loved the work and the people they met. Business was such an all-encompassing term for enterprises as diverse as tech start-ups to home care for the elderly. She was never bored and it was rewarding to see businesses thrive and prosper in the community. Working together had also helped Euphemia's insecurity, something Kenneth understood but made a point of never mentioning.

In the early days, when they were both working long hours, seven days a week from home, the girls had grown up first in a playpen, and then doing their homework on a spare desk while Kenneth and Euphemia worked beside them. Kezia had loved it but Nicky hated being kept indoors against her will in the confines of the office. Both girls liked playing on the computers but only Kezia was truly fascinated by them. Nicky, the tomboy, would nag her parents relentlessly to be let out to play, dragging one or both of them down to the park or to the tennis club whenever she could. It was a relief to everyone when the business could afford to take on more staff and one of them was able to be with the girls after school, until they were old enough to look after themselves.

Euphemia turned her car into her building and thought about how Alison was putting everything they had worked for at risk. Not only that but the damage she was doing to their clients was incalculable and would have to be put right.

She was relieved to see the basement car park was empty. The traffic had been light and the new flyover around a local park had made a difference to how quickly she could get across town to the office. She added a mental note to congratulate the Mayor on how well it worked when she next saw him. The town had made a lot of progress under his administration after years of nothing being done while the previous mayor dithered trying to please too many people and satisfying none.

Work on improvements was happening on almost every street. She'd had to dodge signs and roadworks on the way into the building. On the pavement, the sound of jackhammers amidst a parade of small trucks and diggers was deafening, and it was a relief to get into the quiet of the lift. Having better hearing was wonderful but the sound of machinery scraping against concrete was not something she wanted to listen to for too long.

The lift doors opened and her heart sank. Sitting at the front desk as if this was just a normal Monday was Alison. Dressed in her usual cardigan and leggings, neat enough to be sure but dowdy, she wore no jewelry apart from a wedding ring, her hair unwashed and tied back in a ponytail. Make-up free, she looked awful, as if she hadn't slept for days, the stilettos replaced with flat ballet shoes which reversed the height advantage of yesterday when she stood up to glare at Euphemia. She might look like Office Alison again but the malice in her voice was unmistakable.

"I came early," she said. "We need to talk."

"Tell Malcolm to come out and we will," said Euphemia briskly.

"How did you know he was here?"

"I must have heard him cough, or probably I just realized you can't make a decision without him."

Taking the lead, Euphemia marched down the carpeted corridor to the boardroom, walked in and sat in her usual seat at the head of the table. Alison and Malcolm were left to follow. Malcolm moved to his position of choice, standing as close as possible to Euphemia, looming over her attempting to intimidate her. Why did dumb men think this worked? She looked up at him and raised her eyebrows. He shuffled awkwardly before finally deciding to sit. Alison chose the seat at the other end of the long table, Kenneth's seat. They stared at each other, waiting for Malcolm to settle.

"We have Jane and your dog," said Malcolm importantly.

"She knows that."

"I was just setting out the position, Alison, if you don't mind. It is important to emphasize exactly what is at stake." He paused. "Jane's life and your dog's life." He paused for effect.

"Oh, do get on with it, Malcolm."

"Which means, Euphemia, you have to do exactly what we tell you to do, when we tell you to do it. Thanks to my lovely wife, things have got rather out of hand and now we have to make it right so we can leave with as little fuss as possible. That depends on you."

Euphemia listened to Malcolm but looked at Alison, searching her face for clues. Alison stared back, the hate sparkling in her eyes as her husband pompously restated the obvious. Examining Alison's face for minute muscle movements around her eyes and mouth, Euphemia could see the woman's exhaustion. Without make-up to disguise the saggy bags under her eyes and the slackness around the jaw, Alison looked older but not defeated. She was also dehydrated and hungry, the dank hair another clue she had had to hurry to get to the office. Euphemia reached for the jug of water and slowly poured herself a glass, drinking the water without taking her eyes off Alison's, enjoying the discomfort on Alison's face.

Malcolm droned on and by now both women had tuned out. Euphemia could see that any intelligence in this relationship was Alison's. For the moment, and for whatever reason, she seemed prepared to let her husband have his moment in the spotlight.

Euphemia focused again on Alison's mouth and the complex group of muscles that reveal so much about a person's thoughts and feelings. Fine movements betrayed the fixed expression of wifely support as contempt, even hatred, for her husband. And there was something else, something Euphemia hadn't expected. Alison was thinking about someone or something else. Her mind was wandering to something happier, something she was looking forward to, something completely unrelated to her husband.

"So are we agreed?" asked Malcolm

"I'm sorry, Malcolm, I missed that," said Euphemia, making him repeat himself.

"I'm going to get the jewelry assessed this morning. Once we know it's kosher, the old girl and I are off to fresh fields, to places new and exciting."

He looked to Alison for agreement but she just stared at Euphemia.

Unabashed he carried on: "After a suitable interval, we will contact you and let you know where you can find Jane and your dog. Go to the police, do anything at all before that, and we tell you nothing. You won't find them and they'll starve to death. Simple. This morning Alison will be watching every move you make."

"How do I know they're still alive? How can I trust either of you?"

Alison spoke for the first time that morning. Her words, snaking their way into the silence, were menacing and cruel.

"Think of it this way, Euphemia. What choice do you have? And just in case you think we don't mean what we say, have a souvenir."

Alison reached into the pocket of her cardigan and pulled out a wad of tissue, which she tossed down the table to Euphemia.

"Go on, open it."

Euphemia peeled back layers of pink soggy tissue paper and found a curved thick black toenail, the fleshy lump at the base still oozing fluid. She knew instantly where it had come from and the pain Petal must have gone through. Her gut heaved with the cruelty of what they had done, tears pouring down her cheeks.

"I see we really do have your attention now."

"How could you?"

"Well, obviously it was mainly Malcolm, but he had help."

"You bastards."

"Do you think I care? Understand this. We leave today, with our money, and if you get in our way... then your dog losing a toenail won't be the worst thing we do."

Chapter Thirty

Euphemia stayed in the boardroom after the Sinclairs left. Cruelty mystified and nauseated her. What makes people capable of inflicting pain on another being, human or animal? What sort of person puts money ahead of everything and everyone else?

Alison had been right — seeing the bloody nail on the tissue paper had finally made her realize how malevolent they were. Kicking Jane when she was most vulnerable hadn't been a schoolboy impulse but the action of a psychopath. Both of them were beyond redemption, beyond any forgiveness.

For the rest of the morning she knew she had to mask her disgust and do whatever they said. The urge to wipe her hands of them and call the police, if only to have the satisfaction of watching them being hauled away, was getting stronger. Almost as strong as the urge to march out to reception and beat the living daylights out of that cruel bitch. In her mind's eye, Euphemia saw Alison's bloody face, her finger held aloft after she'd had a nail ripped out, begging for mercy.

Soon, she thought. Now she had to muster every inch of self-control. She promised herself the beating could wait and just as she was visualizing how she would do it, Kezia popped her head around the door.

"Got a minute, Mum?"

Euphemia thought of something pleasant so she was smiling before she swiveled around in her chair to greet her eldest daughter. It was the first time she'd seen Kezia since opening the chest and it felt strange knowing that she was next in line to inherit the switch. Kezia's similarity to Rachel was unnerving. They had only been line drawings but if they were accurate, then Kezia had Rachel's eyes, and the same intelligent forehead. The likeness made Euphemia want to get up and throw her arms around her.

"Mum, you look awful."

"Do I?"

"Has something happened?"

"Nothing." Euphemia thought about pummeling Alison to a pulp and her smile broadened. "Is that better?"

"Not really," said Kezia, but ever practical, she moved on. "I've got good news and bad news. The good news is I've found the planted files. They're buried deep in something I've only just heard about in a chat group. It's something new called a stealth drive, and it's been illegally downloaded into the system. My guess is that Alison got the access codes somehow and this let whoever in to insert the drive without too much bother."

"Never heard of a stealth drive."

"They're cunning little beasts, and they're the latest security threat. They have no footprint. They mimic normal code with a few minor differences, which is how data like bank records can be so easily corrupted. One of the guys likened it to DNA, vast chains of the same patterns. You insert or swap one or two different base pairs and there's a whole new creature. Once loaded, they're only accessible with a series of encrypted passwords that are changed every ten minutes according to a preset algorithm. Supposedly, only the one who wrote the code knows the correct step at which to interrupt the algorithm. I have to find that step and then shadow my way through behind it till I get to the rogue sequence to rewrite it back to the system code, which effectively disables it. If I try anything before everything is exactly lined up, byte for byte, then the system implodes. The whole system gone — kaput. Totally ingenious."

"I'm glad you think so, but it sounds diabolical. You have backed up, haven't you, in multiple formats? Just in case." She saw the withering look on Kezia's face. "How can we maintain security against something we can't detect? I mean after this is over. Anyone could plant a stealth drive and we wouldn't know until it's too late and our client information is taken, or worse, as in this case, corrupted."

"Give me time, Mum, because I think I have found the answer. Let me disable this one first. Alison must know some very smart people. My group thought stealth drives were still in the development phase."

"OK, so that was the good news. I hate to ask about the bad news?"

"Sorry but it's all going to take a couple of hours. I don't want to rush it. Back-up is all very well."

"If that's all, then please take all the time you need. It's not Alison I'm worried about now. It's the mastermind who set her and us up. We have to make Sage Consulting as safe as we possibly can before he or she does something worse."

"You still haven't told me what this is about. What's Alison got against us? I mean look at her... she's so..." Kezia broke off searching for a suitable description and finally blurted out, "ordinary."

"Ordinary? Not now — just the opposite."

"I know you'll tell me later, but I can see you're in trouble, Mum. I brought you a new app I've been working on. It's not perfect but it's something I found by mistake and it's probably illegal. OK, it is illegal but we can sort that out later. It's a close-range hack app. It allows you to track conversations on any phone number you enter but you have to be close to the hacked phone to use it — around two hundred meters. Won't work further away."

Euphemia watched in awe as her daughter downloaded the app into her phone. "You constantly amaze me, Kezia. And I will tell you everything soon. This is just what I need — seriously, you don't know how helpful this is."

Kezia looked up and smiled... just the way Rachel, her forebear, had smiled in the drawing. Euphemia's heart lurched a few beats as the generations across the centuries connected for a split second.

"I'd better get back. Time is money, Mum."

"Your father taught you that, not me."

"And where is he?"

They answered together. "On the golf course!"

Chapter Thirty-one

Jane had run out of tears and still she couldn't forget Petal's howls. The little dog lay shivering, curled into a tight ball against her stomach, head buried in her paws. Jane reached for her watch, then remembered Alison had snatched it from her last night. She guessed the Sinclairs had left a few hours ago but she couldn't be sure. She would never be sure of anything again.

Her stepfather at his worst had punched her mother once or twice when he was drunk, immediately dissolving into sobs of pathetic self-pity. Losing her tooth had been excruciating but it had happened so suddenly it somehow made it more bearable. But being forced to stand and watch what Malcolm and Half-ear had done to Petal, the premeditation involved, made her sick. Literally. She had vomited up the meager breakfast Malcolm had tossed at her when he'd arrived. If they meant to frighten her, to terrify her into submission, they'd succeeded.

That was when Alison started asking her questions about the jewelry, when Petal was lying bleeding and limp, on the floor, Malcolm standing over her with the pliers in his hand. She'd had no choice but to tell them what they wanted to know. Wanted to hear.

Alison had spread her sleeping bag out on the floor, opened the box and tumbled her jewelry onto it, the diamonds and precious metals gleaming incongruously in the dull light. "How much is this one worth?" she'd demanded. She'd held up piece after piece expecting a value and while this went on, Malcolm tapped the numbers into his phone. Jane told them everything and at the end, Malcolm had leaned over and whispered the total amount to Alison.

"You've been very helpful, Jane. Finally. We still need an assessment but you've helped." Alison saw the look on Jane's face. "Oh all right, pick the dog up." Taking care not to bump the bloody paw, Jane had reached down and picked up Petal's limp body and stroked her gently.

"Why can't we just take the stuff and get out of here?" asked Malcolm petulantly.

"Because I said so," hissed Alison. "For God's sake, you're such a child. It won't take long. It'll be better later."

"Look at her, Alison, she's telling the truth. She's too scared not to."

"Stop whining, Malcolm. You know how much I hate it."

"But Alison, listen."

"Enough. Get Sammy to check it and if he says it's OK, it'll be just like we planned. You've got the easy part. I'm the one who has to take care of Sage. Big mistake to get her involved, Jane. Look what's happened because you couldn't keep your mouth shut. Malcolm, Grant, find that toenail."

While Malcolm and Grant were searching for the toenail, Alison changed her clothes and brushed her hair. She rubbed moisturizer into her face and flicked on some mascara, following it with a swish of lip gloss.

"See how I've had to look all these years, Jane? Life isn't fair, is it? You've never had to work, have you? You left that to your husband, didn't you? Nice for some."

"Found it," called Malcolm triumphantly. "Who would have thought it would be so hard to get something so small out of that dog. They're buried deep, toenails."

Jane turned and bracing herself against the wall with one hand, leaned over and vomited again, strings of saliva dangling from her mouth.

"Charming. Your mother would be so proud of you," Alison said, laughing. "We're leaving you here. The room's soundproof, if you hadn't already worked that out."

The door shut behind them and once more she was in darkness but she could feel the rumbling vibrations of traffic through her feet. She had to be somewhere in the city. Someone must come soon, even if only by accident.

Petal was beginning to rouse in her arms. The paw had stopped bleeding but Jane could feel it swelling and didn't want to think about how painful it must be. Jane felt her way over to the sleeping bag thinking the warmth would help them both, but Petal, even in her weakened state, struggled violently in her arms, crying piteously as soon as she detected Alison's smell.

"OK. I understand."

Jane went back to the pile of cardboard and wrapped them both in the thin blanket.

"We will get out of here, Petal, I know we will. Euphemia will save us. She has to."

Chapter Thirty-two

Alison grabbed Euphemia by the arm and hustled her into the tea-room.

"Who is he? Why is he here today?"

Euphemia looked round the corner into the waiting area and was relieved to see Ben. Shaved and wearing a fresh suit, he looked more like a nervous schoolboy waiting outside the headmaster's office than a police officer there to look after her. She waved to him before Alison physically pulled her back into the tearoom.

"He says he has an appointment. I don't have him in the system. Is he police?"

"Relax would you, and let go of my arm. You're creasing my suit. He's a student here to learn what a business consultant does in real life. It was arranged last week and I forgot to put it in the diary. Believe me, Alison, I want him here as much as you. You said I had to act normally and that's what I'm doing."

They were interrupted when Alistair, one of the admin staff, clattered his way into the tearoom to get his morning coffee. Dressed in lycra and still wearing his helmet and bike shoes, Alistair, overweight and saggy, was a poor advertisement for the sport of cycling.

"Morning, ladies," he said cheerfully. They nodded without looking at him and he took the hint. "Better get on. Things to do," he said, taking his coffee and hobbling off to the men's room.

"Ben, come and meet Alison, our receptionist." Just as Ben was shaking her hand, the lift opened and a man, reeking of alcohol, fell through the doors and lurched to the reception desk.

"You fucking bitch..." he said lunging at Alison, who was already backing away before she turned tail, ran down the corridor and disappeared.

It took a few moments for Euphemia to recognize Chris Turner, one of their oldest clients. Disheveled and unshaven, Chris lent over the desk and picked up papers and envelopes and started dropping them one by one onto the floor. He plucked the flowers out of the vase and scattered them in front of reception. His eyes never left Euphemia as next he slowly poured the water from the vase all over Alison's keyboard.

Ben grabbed his arm, which steadied him. Euphemia had an idea why he was here and put her arm around his shoulders and led him down the hall to her office. She looked back at Ben indicating he should stay at reception in the meantime and he raised an eyebrow. She nodded she would be OK.

Chris stunk. His hair was greasy and smelled as badly as his clothes, which reeked of stale cigarette smoke and whisky. She fought the urge to gag, opening her windows only to be greeted by the noise of the jackhammers digging up the road below. As much as the noise offended her ears, the smell was worse and she left the windows as wide open as was possible.

Chris had been a client from their early days. He was a plumber who had started out clearing blocked drains and fitting domestic bathrooms. He was a good tradesman and made a reasonable living but he was ambitious. Shelley, his wife, used to say, when anyone would listen, that he was 'driven'. It wasn't long before he'd won major commercial contracts installing bathrooms and plumbing in the burgeoning numbers of multi-story apartment buildings and hotels in the city.

Alan, his first apprentice, was equally ambitious and within a couple of years, Chris had made him a partner. Together they worked long hours and the firm inevitably prospered. Chris became a successful go-to man in the community. Coming from a poor back-ground, he could always be relied upon to donate to good causes and mentor young people on their way to success.

It had all come crashing down three months ago when Shelley told him about her relationship with Alan. They'd been having the affair for ten years and, to add insult to injury, Shelley had also told him that the youngest of their four children was Alan's son, not his. She wanted a divorce.

Alan had told his wife a month earlier. Sarah didn't mind as much as Chris, having suspected her husband hadn't loved her for years. She was delighted to take the cash Alan had given her in exchange for her share of the business. She also recognized the guilt compo-nent in his offer and realized the generosity would not last if she held out for more. It was unfortunate that Alan had paid Sarah with money from the firm's accounts unbeknownst to Chris.

Chris was destroyed. His life crashed down around him and in that first week after the revelations, he'd holed up in a room at the city's best hotel and drunk himself into a stupor. He'd been happy and had assumed Shelley was too. Everything he'd worked for, everything he thought was good, had been ruined and not by strangers, but by the two people he loved and trusted most.

He was still drunk when the creditors found him, demanding their money for work done and materials supplied. The contracts he had with two hotel chains were declared null and void because the firm hadn't met completion targets. Other firms had come in to finish pro-jects and his company was liable. Worse, Alan and Shelley had disap-peared with the kids and were unreachable. Holiday in the Bahamas, his PA told him when he sobered up and returned to the office.

Chris knew his firm was good for the money but he needed time to sort through the mess. Time when his shattered heart was reeling from the betrayals by those he most cared about. Misery alternated with rage. He couldn't believe that 'good old Chris' had been left to cope and make everything right.

Euphemia had found out when Alan and Shelley had asked to

meet her before they left. Sage Consulting was instructed to get the plumbing firm's accounts up to date so the business could be divided up for the inevitable property settlement. Alan and Shelley had been planning this move for almost a year and so had grown used to the idea. It didn't occur to either of them that Chris would react this way. After all, Sarah had been great and was already moving on with her life. Later they told Euphemia it was best if they got out of his way for a few weeks. In the meantime, "Could Euphemia and Kenneth please do the necessary?"

Alan and Shelley now owned seventy-five percent of the business and so once the books were in order, Sage Consulting was to put the business up for sale to the highest bidder and as soon as possible.

Euphemia and Kenneth were delegated to inform Chris of these events after the couple had left.

However, much as she and Kenneth disliked this, it was not their place to comment on the lives of their clients.

As expected, Chris had been irate. It was unlikely he would be left with much after everyone was paid out. Missing the deadlines had almost destroyed the firm's credibility amongst his customers and there were plenty of other firms more than willing to step in and take his business.

Chris had left their first meeting utterly dejected, a beaten man. They hadn't expected four days later to see him in the business news, happily shaking hands with a Chinese consortium currently constructing two office towers in the CBD, having just signed a deal to manage their plumbing and electrical work.

Chapter Thirty-three

Today, Chris stumbled across the room and sat in the chair facing her desk. "I'm surprised you have the cheek to have that fucking woman sitting out there."

"You mean Alison?"

"Of course I mean her, your loan shark buddy, the one you feed your clients to when they have nowhere else to go."

"I don't. She's not..."

"Of course she is, Euphemia. Do you think I'm stupid? Or let me rephrase that... do you *still* think I'm stupid?"

"The Sinclairs have nothing to do with Sage Consulting. Alison is a receptionist — that's all. And not for much longer."

"I trusted you," said Chris, the bitter anger oozing out of his voice. "And Kenneth. After all these years, I thought I was more than a bank account to be milked for fees. I thought we were friends. Where is he, by the way?"

"Playing golf," she said softly.

Chris looked up. "Of course he bloody is. He's earned his time on the golf course, hasn't he, living off the sweat of those of us who do the real work. People who graft for a living, working in other people's shit, year after year to put food on the family table, clothes on their kids' backs. People who trust that when someone offers them money, a way out of a hole so deep it goes all the way to bloody China, that that person can be trusted because they work for the Sages."

"We didn't know what Alison was doing, I swear. Chris, we'll make it up to you. Trust me."

"You don't know the meaning of the word trust! It's worth nothing. It's a word that people use to distract you while they stab you in the back, take everything you own and love. I don't believe you're as innocent as you say. There's a bit of talk about you round town."

Chris stood up, leaned forward, his knuckles on her desk. "Euphemia Sage, hear this loud and clear. *I don't trust you! I don't trust any of you bastards!*"

His face twisted, his eyes blazing, he was almost beyond reason. She could hear people gathering in the corridor outside murmuring, and just had time to see Ben's worried face before Chris raced across the office, slammed the door and locked it.

"Call the police and I'll kill her before they get here!" he yelled through the door. "I've got a knife. And I don't care — about anything any more!"

"I'm all right, Ben... do as he says. Don't call the police. Chris and I are old friends. We're going to talk this through like sensible adults."

She could hear Ben telling others what to do in quiet whispers. She heard Kezia arrive, then Ben telling her to stay calm. To Kezia, being told to stay calm by a complete stranger was like a red rag to a bull. She ignored him.

"Mum, are you OK? Chris, she's telling the truth. It's Kezia, Chris, open up."

Chris hesitated when he heard her daughter's voice. Euphemia remembered how his firm had supported Kezia's tech team at school and how he'd been delighted when they'd won the championship. He'd always had a soft spot for both her daughters, admiring the computer skills of one and the touch rugby skills of the other.

Chris shook himself. "You Sages are all alike... we're not old friends! You just used me like everybody else, so no, Kezia, I'm not opening the door. You're a pack of crooks and it's time the rest of this town knew it. How many other people have you conned? How many other poor suckers are out there bleeding their hard work into your pockets?"

Outside there was a collective intake of breath and then the murmurings started again in earnest, getting louder until Kezia turned on them. "It's not true. You know that. Sage is solid and Chris is just upset about something else. Go back to work and let Mum and me deal with this. Chris, open the door."

"Why don't you just fuck off, Kezia?"

Chris pulled a large kitchen knife out from under his clothes and motioned with it to Euphemia to sit down.

"Tell her, Euphemia. Tell Kezia I have a knife and if she wants to see you again, she will shut the fuck up."

Chris's voice was getting louder with each word till he was almost screaming at the end. Spit flew across the desk and landed on Euphemia's cheek. His face straining with rage, he rounded her desk and standing over her, thrust the knife within inches of her face.

"It's true, Kezia," she called, "just give us a few minutes will you. I'm fine and Chris doesn't need the drama of the police."

"You mean you and your scumbag receptionist don't want the police. I'd have to tell them about the thugs you sent round to my house this morning. Her husband. My. Home. Euphemia. Taking anything they thought might be valuable. Going through Shelley's stuff, the kids' stuff. Me, waking up to some guy with half an ear holding a baseball bat in my face. Of course you don't want the police. You don't want anyone finding out that's how Sage Consulting really does business."

The whispers grew louder and she heard Kezia try again in vain to reassure everyone. The only voice she couldn't hear was Alison's. Where was she? Had she fled back to Malcolm and Jane? What the hell was Malcolm doing at Chris's house today of all days? And for what? They had the jewelry. For Jane's sake, she had to get Chris under control quickly.

"What do you want, Chris? What can I do?" she said.

"I want my life back," he yelled, jabbing the knife towards her with each syllable. "I want everything back the way it was. I want Shelley to love me. I want my money, my company, my kids back and I want to see fucking Alan die a miserable death in the bottom of a rat-infested sewer. That's what I want. Manage that Superwoman, because I can't."

Exhaustion and desperation were etched deep in his face. Chris Turner, a man who normally would never hurt a fly, was now a man with nothing to lose.

Euphemia thought quickly. She'd never been confronted with a knife-wielding man before. Quickly she worked out the length of the blade, the angles, his state, and she reckoned she could take him. One to one, she knew her speed and reflexes were more than a match for his. She just needed to pick the exact moment when he was at his weakest and take him by surprise. She sympathized with Chris, really she did, but it was Jane who was in danger, not him. His problems could wait. Besides, he was starting to grate. How dare he come here and threaten her with a knife, no matter what he thought she might have done. Trust works both ways and he needed to get his facts straight. The reality was, there was nothing he could do except tidy up the chaos. Holding a knife to the throat of one of the few people who would help him do that was pointless.

"Here's what you do," he said. "Call Shelley. Don't tell me you don't know where she is. Tell her to come back, but she has to come back today. Then, transfer Sage funds into my account so I can get the Chinese off my back."

"No. Can't. And won't."

"Yes, you bloody can."

"Chris, it won't work. Shelley... is... not... coming... back." She said each word slowly and distinctly.

A terrible sound, a sound from deep in the man's shattered soul, reverberated around the office. The people outside hushed.

Chris looked at her but didn't see her. She could have been any woman standing in front of him, hurting him, belittling him. She tensed, waiting.

Chris moved the knife down so the point rested against the skin of her neck and then stepped behind her, gripping her round the head with his free hand. She relaxed.

"You're wrong," he hissed. "You and that other bitch think you can get away with it, don't you?"

Chris, his stinking breath washing over her, pulled her head back then lightly and slowly drew the knife across her throat. She detected the pleasure in his restraint before she felt her blood trickling down her neck. There was no pain. She could feel his tension building as he started to focus on gathering the courage for his next sweep across her neck. She had one opportunity and just a split second to stop him.

He had no chance of seeing her hand as it moved and clamped his wrist, immobilizing him. She tightened her grip and he whimpered with pain before she twisted his arm backwards and away forcing him to drop his other arm from around her head. She saw his look of surprise as she stood and twisted around to face him. He was in agony but was smart enough to understand how easily his bones would snap if he moved. Euphemia twisted his hand back further, forcing him to let go of the knife, which fell to a soft thud on the carpet. Changing the angle of her grip, she pushed him onto his knees in front of her.

"Is this really how you want things to go, Chris?"

"It's all gone," he sobbed. With that, Chris slumped back, his dead weight pulling Euphemia off balance, down onto the floor beside him. Her grip gone, he scrabbled across the carpet for his knife. She rolled sideways but he got it first and stood up. Reaching down, he grabbed her by the hair and hauled her to feet pushing her back against the wall in one movement. All reason gone, hatred blazing in his eyes, she knew he was going to kill her.

Euphemia, her back against the wall, brought up one knee and connected with Chris's scrotum so hard and fast it lifted him off his feet and sent him flying backwards across the room hitting the window with such force that it buckled with the impact. The wind knocked out of him, his testicles on fire, Chris's mouth opened and closed as he fought to find air. He couldn't move and couldn't breathe. His eyes followed her as she picked up the knife and put it in a drawer. When he finally took his first shallow painful breath, he rolled onto his side, cradling his groin and started to cry.

Euphemia pulled her clothes into order and unlocked the door. Kezia tumbled through first, straight into her arms and hugged her, then she saw Chris slumped against the wall. Seeing he was now harmless, she ignored him and looked at her mother.

"You're bleeding," she said. "Mum, your neck, he cut you."

"I'm OK."

"Really? He's just cut your throat and you say you're OK? Use this." She took off her scarf ,rolled it into a rope and padded it against the wound. Euphemia closed her jacket over her bloodstained shirt.

"I said I'm fine and I am. There's a lot to do, Kezia. He won't be the last unless you can isolate that drive and remove the false data. Don't worry about me, just bring me those files."

Ben had come in behind them and was kneeling beside Chris checking him out before helping him to his feet. The staff waited respectfully in the corridor, most with heartwarming concern, but there were a few who were clearly unsettled by what they'd heard.

"Ben's going to call an ambulance," she told them. "He's a student who's here for the day. Sorry about the lack of introductions. Chris, who most of you do know, is not himself. He's had some personal problems, which have nothing to do with this firm. Despite what you might have heard, Sage Consulting is not involved."

She could feel blood seeping through Kezia's scarf and saw the look of horror on their faces.

"You need to get that looked at, Mrs. Sage... it looks as though he cut you. You'll need stitches for sure."

"Thank you, Olivia, but I'll be fine. It doesn't hurt, honestly." She pressed the scarf more firmly against the wound and felt the bleeding slow and stop. "Has anyone seen Alison? I'm sure she must be very frightened after the way Chris went for her earlier."

There was a mass shrug. No one had seen her.

It was the worst news Euphemia had had all day.

Chapter Thirty-four

"I thought you'd be happier."

"I am. It's great but hurry up..."

"We need to stay for the photos at least."

"Really?"

"Yes," said Roger. "And please look happy. We won, and look at the size of that trophy. I want photos for Lisa and the kids of us on the podium, not a rushed selfie taken later. So cooperate."

"Just don't hang around talking. I have this terrible feeling I'm needed at home, now or soon, I don't know."

"Exactly. You don't know."

Kenneth reluctantly took his position on the podium next to Roger who was doing the honors and shaking hands with the club president. The second placed pair looked very grumpy and almost refused to do the decent thing and congratulate the winners.

They'd been assured by Justin that their investment would pay off and Kenneth and Roger would be so hung over this morning, neither would be able to play to the flags, let alone the holes.

To be beaten by Kenneth's last lucky putt on the eighteenth had been bad enough. Having to watch Roger's victory dance was worse, but having to pose for photos was the ultimate humiliation. Knowing Justin French had got five hundred dollars out of them plus expenses to sabotage the competition added insult to injury. And where was he now? Gone. They agreed it wasn't the money that galled them. Five hundred dollars was chump change to both men, who were partners in a large multinational law firm. It was the principle. Damn it, Justin French was not honorable. He was certainly untrustworthy and most definitely not someone they would ever play golf with again. Like Kenneth, they couldn't wait for the ceremony to be over.

Roger was still posing for photos when Kenneth raced back to the motel. Throwing their belongings into the car, he noticed a bag which he'd seen Justin carrying the day before. It was an overnight bag — good quality and locked. The odd thing was the tag. It had two initials on it: Mr. and Mrs. J. and A. French. Not J. and J. French — definitely 'A'. Kenneth looked at it again, but urged on by a feeling he couldn't place, threw it in the back of the car with everything else and checking there was nothing left behind, slammed the motel door behind him. Roger just got back in time to leap into the car as Kenneth drove out of the hotel grounds. Any longer and he would have been left behind.

The atmosphere in the car was understandably fraught. After thirty minutes Roger was first to break the silence.

"I'm not like you. I don't have cupboards of trophies at home. This is the first thing I've ever won. Not counting the egg and spoon swimming race at school when I was fourteen, which, incidentally, was not as easy to win as it sounds. No lack of competition in that race and very choppy water. What I'm saying, Kenneth, is that it would have been nice to enjoy the moment. Instead, all my stuff, at least I hope it's all there, has been thrown in the car without a by-your-leave and you were just about to go without me."

"I wouldn't have left you."

"Sure? You won't even give me time to take off my golf shoes. Really, sometimes I wonder why we're friends."

They drove on in silence for another fifteen minutes, until Roger had finally had enough of holding the awkwardly large trophy on his knee and demanded that Kenneth stop so he could put the bloody thing in the back and also change his shoes.

"Sorry, Roger. Should be more patient. You keep the trophy when we get back."

"Should think so. Normally, Kenneth, you're one of the most laid-back guys around. You're known for it — cool calm Kenneth Sage on the rugby field — and the way you handled the pressure today and sank that putt was amazing. I don't understand."

"You'll think I've lost it, if I tell you."

"Try me."

"OK, you remember when Euphemia and I first got married and her Aunt Maree lived with us?"

"Yes, nice old thing. Quite witty, I remember, in a quiet, surprising sort of way."

"That's Maree, or was. She died before Kezia was born. We got on like a house on fire — it made Euphemia nervous. Lots of reasons, can't explain. Anyway, Maree liked me and told me stuff about Euphemia's family. She didn't know details because she wasn't one of them, but Euphemia is. And she wasn't then but I think she is now. She hasn't told me because she doesn't know I know. How she'd think I wouldn't notice beats me, but I guess she's got a lot on her mind. It's why I came away this weekend, to give her time. And that's why I have to get back."

"Right. Obvious. What are you talking about?"

"Euphemia and the... you know."

"What?"

"She's going through menopause."

"Christ, you can't be serious. All this for that. Lisa did it two years ago and it's not a biggie, Kenneth. She'll live."

"No, Roger. Euphemia is different... she's got special powers now."

There was silence in the car.

"This is sounding awfully weird."

"That's what I said when Maree told me. But she said it was true and Maree wasn't a fantasist any more than I am, Roger. Something happens to them as they get older. They become powerful."

"Now you're really talking rubbish."

"OK, I'll shut up. But it's why I have to get home."

"You know they've invented the telephone. We can even carry

them around with us now. If Euphemia-the-powerful needed you, wouldn't she call? Or better, she could beam you a message using her powers?"

"All right, don't believe me."

"As amazing as Euphemia Sage is, Kenneth, and we all take our hats off to your very impressive wife, I'm not sure even I would believe she's more powerful than your average menopausal woman. Why would she be different to everyone else?"

"To do good, according to Maree."

"You mean like saving small children from speeding trains and cities from meteors?"

"Something like that. Yes. All right, all right. It sounds ridiculous when I tell you."

"It is ridiculous. And if it was anyone else telling me this rubbish, I'd say, stop the car and let me out. I'm going to make an exception for you. But I still want you to stop... for a burger? I'm starving."

The aspirin Kenneth had taken earlier was wearing off. He could feel his headache creeping into the backs of his eyes, along with a sick empty feeling rising up from his stomach. A burger and fries was just what he felt like too. Roger was probably right. Telling his best mate the secret he had been carrying around for years made him realize how stupid it sounded. There was no urgency. Maybe it's because I'm hung over and tired and all I need is food and a good night's sleep.

But he could still hear Maree telling him to be aware, and to follow his instincts when Euphemia reached a certain age — and, rather than wait, he was to act on them. Otherwise, said Maree, he might lose her. The prospect of never seeing the shy, young runner he had fallen in love with years ago and who he loved now more than he ever thought possible, was unthinkable. Losing Euphemia was not something he could bear. If Maree had been telling the truth, if Euphemia truly did need him, then he had to eat, or he would be useless when he got back. A couple more aspirin wouldn't hurt either.

"Next place we see, we'll stop. A burger, fries and banana milkshake with ice cream. And some nuggets with barbecue sauce."

"Now you're talking," said Roger.

"You won't tell Lisa, will you? Or anyone?"

"Wouldn't dream of it. Who'd believe me?"

Chapter Thirty-five

Nicky and Dave arrived at the Frenches' home early on Monday morning and passed two men erecting a Mortgagee Sale sign at the front gate before driving slowly up the drive to the house. Two uniformed PCs, pleased to see them, got out of their car and stretched. Sent to guard the place last night, they'd spent the night eating junk food and trying to keep each other awake with YouTube clips.

The house looked magnificent at a distance, two stories of brick and timber framing encircled by established trees. Close up it was a different story. Nicky was shocked by the neglect. Weeds grew in gaps in the roof where tiles had come away and were now lying in pieces on the ground around the house. Water dripped down tendrils of green slime through holes in the guttering, and windows sagged in unpainted frames. What had once been a grand statement, a house built to impress, had degenerated into an overgrown ruin.

She looked at Dave, the bags under his eyes and his pale waxy skin testament to his exhaustion. She'd been lucky to catch a few hours' sleep in a chair in the back room. The morning crew told her he'd been working all night.

Dave yawned, pleased to be out of the stuffy incident room and in the fresh air. No sleep and lack of progress had not put him in a good mood. The CCTV had revealed nothing that Mrs. Sage hadn't already told them. Jane French had indeed been hustled into a black Mercedes and it had indeed sped out of the building behind a Japanese car, a Toyota, with two men in it. Leaving the parking building, the cars had gone in different and opposite directions and were quickly lost in the Sunday afternoon traffic.

One bright spot was they'd been able to identify the two men in the Toyota. Grant and his brother, Mark Deans, were well known to the police and before them, Social Services. Brought up by a drug-addled and violent mother, the boys had had no chance of a normal life. Grant had lost the top of his ear when his mother, determined to teach him a lesson for throwing out her stash, had sliced it off with her boyfriend's knife, or so one of the stories went, because there were other versions, depending on who you spoke to. The only consistent fact was the violent mother. He'd met her once and even Dave had been afraid of her.

As soon as they escaped the Boys' Home where they'd been sent by the Youth Court as adolescents, they hired themselves out to anyone who would pay. Word on the street was they had no qualms about anything they were asked to do. The apples had not fallen far from the maternal tree. Dave doubted that even if found they would give much in the way of useful information.

CCTV didn't reveal the number plate of the Mercedes, as it had been covered up. Frustrating, but not an insurmountable problem. The local Mercedes dealer had been most cooperative when he was hauled out of bed at 1 am to open his office and go through the sales in the last twelve months of that particular model. The list was surprisingly long but had depressingly few actual names. Family trusts and companies had made most of the purchases. One of his team was now tasked with laboriously going through the registers to identify real people and hopefully amongst them find the person who was driving that car yesterday — a car that had disappeared, in all likelihood dumped in a garage or warehouse.

The other new information had come when they'd searched the Frenches' bank accounts. The statements tallied with the Mortgagee Sale sign they'd driven past this morning confirming the dire financial straits the couple was in. What little evidence Dave had now pointed to either one or both of the Frenches being desperate for money and getting involved with the wrong people.

The one aspect of the case that kept annoying him, and which didn't fit the picture, was Nicky's mother. She hadn't told him anything he didn't already know from the CCTV footage. Why was she there? Dave didn't buy the 'jogging past and heard screams' story. She knew more than she was saying. He sensed Nicky's embarrassment when her mother was mentioned and wondered if he should keep her on the team but they were short-staffed and so for the next twelve hours he didn't have a choice.

Regrettably the laws of the land meant he couldn't beat the information out of Euphemia Sage. He had to hope Justin French would be more helpful when he finally arrived, if he arrived. The PC driving him back from Wairakei must have been on a restricted license, it was taking so long. Dave Richards was tired and insightful enough to recognize he may be a little irritable this morning.

Nicky found the key to the front door under a dilapidated plant pot. She was about to moan to Dave about the lax security of homeowners but seeing his face decided not to. The entrance hall was large enough to accommodate two small vans side by side. The uniformed PCs standing open-mouthed behind her as she walked in weren't used to such grandeur and whistled and nudged each other.

A carved oak staircase led up to a wrap-around balcony on the second floor. Towering over the hall was a magnificent stained-glass window, the light from which lit up the faded stair carpet and scuffed parquet flooring in a myriad of colors.

Thirst getting the better of him, one of the PCs volunteered to make everyone a cup of tea and disappeared down a small corridor set to one side, presumably leading to the kitchen and service areas at the back of the house.

Nicky opened the first door and walked into a large room, at the far end of which was a grand piano. A cavernous stone fireplace big enough to roast several small children simultaneously was filled with blackened logs and a big pile of ash. Full-length windows opening out onto the drive were draped with heavy velvet curtains faded in stripes by the sun. Shabby but comfortable sofas and chairs surrounded the stone fireplace at one end, while smaller arrangements of chairs and sofas defined several more intimate conversation areas in other parts of the room. Old magazines tipped into piles on the floor beside occasional tables. Vases with dead flowers in varying states of desiccation were scattered about and everything was covered in a thick film of dust.

Dave marched over to the windows and drew back the curtains. Shafts of dust-filled sunlight threw the room into patches of light and shade. Try as he might, the windows wouldn't open, stuck fast in their frames, the effort leaving dark smudges on his hands. The PC returned with the tea and Nicky cleared a space on the table beside the fireplace for it. They were drinking their second cup when the car bringing Justin home finally drew up outside.

Justin looked as dilapidated as his home. He was hung over and unshaven, his patchy stubble highlighting his bloodshot eyes and sickly complexion. His hand trembled as he reached for the cup of tea that one of the PCs placed in front of him. The rumpled golf clothes, a bright red sweater, tartan pants and yellow socks contrasted wildly with the faded elegance of the room.

"Have you found my wife yet?" he asked after he had finished his tea and put his cup down for a refill.

"I'm sorry, Mr. French, we haven't but we're working on it. We're so pleased you're here," said Dave. "We need your help. Detective Sage is going to ask you some questions."

"Sage?" said Justin spluttering into his cup. "Kenneth's daughter? The driver told me your mother was there when Jane was taken. What are you doing asking me questions? This isn't right, is it?"

Justin stood up and walked over to Dave, who was typing into his laptop, which he'd put on the piano.

"How can it be right to have the daughter of a witness, the only witness, working on the team looking for Jane? I want to speak to the Commissioner. I know Henry. I'm the president of the golf club.

He wouldn't like this if he knew, which judging by the looks on your faces, he doesn't, does he?"

"My staff are my business, Mr. French," said Dave, who'd stopped typing and was drawing himself up to his full height of six foot two. "The Commissioner is fully aware of this investigation. He called again just before and asked to be kept informed with any progress. Now sit down and answer the questions. We've wasted enough time already."

"Are you saying that's my fault?"

"Not yet," said Dave coldly. "Nicky?"

Nicky, refusing to let either man see how this outburst had unsettled her, flipped open the cover and leafed slowly through a few pages of her notebook.

"Mr. French, when did you last see Jane, Mrs. French?"

"Saturday morning," said Justin petulantly. "She was fast asleep when I left to play golf with your father. This isn't right," he appealed again, but Dave didn't look up.

"Did you know about the jewelry?"

"What jewelry?"

"Your wife's jewelry. We know from the CCTV footage Mrs. French had a box of jewelry with her when she was taken."

Nicky handed him a plastic evidence bag containing the little diamond pendant on the gold chain they'd found at the car park.

"I gave her that," he said. "Where did you get it?"

"The car park where she was taken."

"What was it doing there?"

"That's what we were hoping you could tell us."

"How would I know?"

Dave looked up. "Mr. French, you do want to help us, don't you?"

"I am trying but how would I know what Jane was doing? I was playing golf."

"Let's try this another way, shall we?" asked Nicky. "We've been looking over your bank records."

"What gives you the right to do that? Now I really do want to speak to Henry. This is too much."

"Your wife has been kidnapped. I would've thought you wouldn't mind what we did as long as we found her and brought her home. We don't have much time, so again, please answer the questions."

"I'm not happy, not happy at all."

"Duly noted. Your bank records, or rather your wife's accounts, show a deposit a few months back of $100,000. Do you know where this money might have come from? Did she sell her jewelry, for instance?"

"She'd never sell it although once she pretended she had, but I knew. It was given to her by her mother to keep in trust for our daughter, Justine. Jane would rather die than part with a single piece."

"So where did she get such a large sum of money?"

"I don't know. I can't help you. I was playing golf and all this is a huge shock. Instead of wasting time questioning me, why aren't you out looking for the people who took her?"

Nicky turned the page in her notebook then carried on. "How much was the jewelry worth, Mr. French?"

"I don't know. She never discussed it. She and her mother were as thick as thieves and they didn't tell me anything, other than it was all to go to Justine."

Nicky knew from the conversation with Jane and her mother yesterday that he was lying. But what could she say? Dave would never trust her again if she admitted she knew more than she'd said at this late stage of the investigation. She kicked herself for not being brave enough to tell him what she knew earlier.

"So can you tell us anything? Do you have photographs for insurance purposes maybe?"

"No, Jane took care of that. Said I didn't need to know. She'd left instructions with her lawyer where to find the box if anything happened to her."

"You mean, she hid it and you weren't told where it was?"

"She said, 'It's not that I don't trust you. You don't want to be tempted.' She treated me like a child."

"So you know nothing about the jewelry."

"I said that."

"And the money?"

"I only know one minute we were flat broke and the next, we weren't. She said she'd found a painting in the house and sold it. We needed the money so I didn't ask."

"And you went on holiday."

"Is that a crime, Detective Sage?"

"No, no, it isn't. But we know from your bank statements and the sale sign outside that things aren't good. Financially. You must be very worried. Desperate even?"

"Something will turn up. It always does. The house will clear the debts and when I find work, then we'll be fine. No, I'm not worried and I'm not desperate. And I'm not a guilty husband." He looked up and stared at Nicky daring her to say otherwise. "If you're finished? It's been a long drive after a big night and I'd like to get cleaned up."

Nicky looked over to Dave for guidance. He'd been typing on his laptop throughout her questioning and hadn't looked as though he was paying attention. She waited and he looked up and nodded before walking across to Justin.

"Mr. French, you don't seem to know very much, do you?"

Justin shrugged.

"Your wife doesn't tell you much, does she?"

Justin shifted in his seat, but stayed silent.

"So you wouldn't have known if the jewelry was real?"

"It was real. Definitely real."

"But if you knew nothing about it, and she never let you see it, how could you know that?"

"Why would she have guarded it like she did if it wasn't real?"

"You're her husband. You tell me."

"It's been a long night, detective. I have a headache and I would

like to get cleaned up. I don't need trick questions. The jewelry was...
is real."

"I've just been told on good authority that it's all fake. Good fakes
but..."

"What good authority? I don't believe you. You're trying to trick
me. I don't know what you're trying to imply but it won't work."

"Our inquiries tell us every piece of your wife's jewelry is a copy,
made many years ago by one of the jewelers in town at the request of
your mother-in-law."

If it was possible for Justin to look worse, he started to now. He
swallowed and finding his mouth dry, reached for the cup but it was
empty. He coughed. "All I know is the jewelry was left to her, by
her mother. Jane guarded it like a hellcat. When the time is right
she'll pass it on to Justine. If it's fake then maybe Jane herself doesn't
know."

"So where is the real jewelry?"

"I have no idea," he said pushing up from the chair. He looked
awkward and small as Dave was standing right in front of him. Edg-
ing his way to the side, he said, "I'm going upstairs to shower and get
changed. I might even have a sleep."

"Good idea," said Dave quietly. "You go. You've been more helpful
than you know, hasn't he, Detective Sage?"

"Yes, sir, most helpful."

Justin hopped nervously from foot to foot.

"Just one more thing," said Dave. "You seem very relaxed about
your financial situation. Was your wife? Was she upset about having
to sell this house, which we understand was built by her grandfa-
ther?"

"Great-grandfather," corrected Justin. "Not particularly. We had
enough money for Justine to go to New York, my job prospects were
looking up and she was tired of the place. Too big for one woman to
look after. We went out for dinner on Friday night and talked about
it. Without this house to look after she planned to find a little job
somewhere."

"So she was relaxed about the sale?"

"I've said that, haven't I? Come to think of it, Euphemia and Kenneth Sage were at the same restaurant on Friday night. Getting beyond a coincidence, don't you think? Maybe you should go and talk to Euphemia Sage again, detectives. Unless there's a conflict of interest?" He sneered the last question.

Nicky blushed. Justin saw it and smirked. Dave reached out and put his hand on her arm.

"Now I understand," said Justin triumphantly. "You two are an item. Wait till the Commissioner hears about this. I'd heard the police were corrupt but this takes the cake."

Dave Richards was not a man who was easily riled, which was just as well for Justin, because on the rare occasions when he did lose his temper, he spared no one. He braced himself and stepped towards the shorter man, opened his mouth then thought better of it and turned away in contempt. "PC Taylor, please go upstairs with Mr. French and make sure he has everything he needs."

"That's hardly necessary. This is my house."

"I insist, Mr. French. Your wife has been kidnapped for no reason you can think of. The least we can do is make sure that you are safe. PC Taylor?"

Sulkily, Justin walked out of the room ahead of the uniformed officer. He stopped at the door, turned and was going to say something but when he saw the look on Dave Richards' face, he made the wise decision to stay quiet.

Nicky busied herself with her notes and tried to reassemble her thoughts. Her mother's unexplained involvement as well as knowing that Justin was lying, and now being accused of being in a relationship with her boss made her very uncomfortable and she didn't know where to look when the door shut.

"Don't worry about him," said Dave. "He's a slimeball of the first order. He knows more than he's saying. When you got close to him, what did you notice?"

She forced herself to think. "His clothes stunk but his breath was clean — toothpaste, not alcohol. He can't really have been drinking last night, or at least not as much as he said."

"Good girl. You're on my team for a reason, Nicky. You're a good detective. Nothing more. We'll sort this stuff out with your mother. She's mixed up somehow, but she's not the one I'm interested in. She hasn't got a motive but Mr. French, well, different story."

"How do you know the jewelry is fake? It's with Jane, isn't it?"

"Someone rang round the big jewelers this morning to see if anyone had photos. Most people with important pieces get them assessed regularly and the jewelers know who's got what. We got lucky as one of them remembered the fakes being made for Jane's mother."

"So has Jane got the fakes or the real stuff?"

"My guess is, she got the fakes and she was going to hand them over and hope she'd get away with it."

"So where's the real jewelry?"

"Quite. If we track that down, we'll find Jane and we might get some answers."

He turned back to his laptop.

His hand on her arm, the look in his eyes, might never have happened. But she knew it had and so did someone else, albeit a slime-ball.

Chapter Thirty-six

Sage Consulting occupied the top two floors of a ten-floor building in the middle of town. The ninth floor consisted of a large open plan office, an informal environment where people worked both individually and in teams, providing back office support. This was Kezia's domain. Her contact with the best and brightest in her years as a student then tutor at Victoria University meant she had access to young talent early, before they were picked up by rival firms. Over a few short years she'd built a loyal team who enjoyed the freedom and the resources that Sage Consulting could offer.

The tenth floor was the public face of Sage Consulting and where Kenneth and Euphemia had their offices. The boardroom looked out over Oriental Bay on one side and the Port of Wellington on the other, an impressive view that never failed to draw visitors to stare out the windows to the harbor and the city below. In the distance the Rimataka Hills, graced with unseasonal spring snow, stood as a bulwark between the Wairarapa and the Hutt River Valley. This room was where the firm held large meetings and once a month where they entertained. The kitchen at the end of the boardroom was designed for caterers and also served as a bar when they hosted seminars and functions. A private bathroom was discreetly located down a short corridor next to the bar.

Euphemia had looked everywhere for Alison, all the while brushing off the staff's concerns about her neck. The bleeding had stopped and she wasn't in any pain so, as far as she was concerned, there was no need for fuss. Far more important was finding Alison, her only link to Jane and Petal. Without her, Euphemia only had the sound of a bus to go on. The switch had imbued her with strength, speed, and enhanced senses, but the ability to see vast distances and through buildings would have been quite handy right now. Other superheroes had it way too easy, she thought.

Ben joined her search after seeing Chris into the ambulance. It was lucky the paramedics had brought a plentiful stock of ice packs because the swelling and pain between his legs prevented him from standing up, let alone walk, and he had to be taken away in a wheel-chair. Ben relayed the information while she was searched the board-room and bar. He followed her downstairs where she looked under the desks and behind partitions on the ninth floor, not sure what the urgency was. Euphemia tried to look sorry when she heard about Chris, but she wasn't. If she hadn't kicked him when she did, she'd be dead and he'd be in prison. And no one apart from the police would be looking for Jane. Wins all round as far as she was concerned and if Chris's genitals were casualties in the process, then so be it.

As she searched the floors asking if anyone had seen Alison, she noticed the staff seemed to have recovered their equilibrium. By now Euphemia looked normal, much better than they'd feared, so they were unconcerned and back at their computers. She hadn't had time to take a good look herself but her neck felt fine. All she could feel was some tingling under her scarf, so she did what any normal per-son would do and didn't think about it.

Euphemia was sure Alison was on the ninth floor and was just about to go to recheck the tenth floor when Kezia saw her and beck-oned her over, turning her screen away when she saw Ben.

"I should have everything in less than an hour," she said softly, not wanting to be overheard. "There's something interesting on that app I showed you."

"You've met Ben, haven't you?" asked Euphemia.

"Not officially. It was you I pushed out of the way before, wasn't it?

Sorry, I know you were only trying to help," said Kezia standing up and turning to look at him.

If Euphemia hadn't seen what happened, she told Kenneth later, she would have laughed at anyone who told her.

Kezia was tall but she just reached Ben's shoulders and his standing close to the desk meant she had to put her head back to look up at him. Their eyes met and it was if the world stopped. The attraction was palpable. Kezia, flushed deep and red to the roots of her thick blonde hair, didn't say anything. Ben's gaze was locked on hers and they seemed totally oblivious to their surroundings. Awkward for a mother to see, she told Kenneth later, especially after the talk she'd had with Ben the night before about Nicky.

"Kezia, you had something to tell me?" she prompted.

Kezia looked back at her absently then remembered. Extracting herself from Ben's gaze, she cleared her throat. Ben went over to the water cooler, poured himself a cup and drank it in one gulp.

"It's the app, the one I put on your phone," said Kezia. "I checked and Alison's phone hasn't moved all morning. She can't have it with her. Judging by the number of calls she's had, someone badly wants to talk to her. Find her phone and I bet she won't be far away."

Euphemia ran out of the office and took the stairs back to the tenth floor two at a time. Alison's phone lay half hidden under the morning mail and the day's paper. It was locked and she didn't know the code, so she'd have to wait. Malcolm had said he would call at lunchtime. Alison would emerge sooner or later.

Euphemia decided she had time to clean up while she waited. She picked up the phone and with a little skip went back to her office, got a clean shirt from her cupboard and went into the bathroom in the boardroom knowing she would have more privacy there. She hadn't realized how much blood she'd lost until she undid her jacket and saw her shirt in the mirror. It was bright red from the neck to her waist. She untied the bloodstained scarf and braced herself to cope with whatever was under it.

Her neck looked fine. There was only the thinnest red line stretching around it. The pins and needles she had been ignoring were rapidly subsiding. As she watched in the mirror the red line disappeared, absorbed back into her normal skin, and the tingling stopped. There was no wound, no scar, her neck looked pristine. She had healed perfectly in less than an hour. A wound she'd thought would take over a week to scab up and which she'd been certain would leave some sort of scar, was gone. If she changed her shirt it would be as if nothing had happened.

It was when she was congratulating herself on discovering her powers of super-healing she heard soft breathing behind her. The cubicle door was closed but bending down she didn't see any feet. It wasn't rocket science to figure out she'd found Alison.

"I've got your phone," said Euphemia.

The lock turned, the door swung back and Alison stepped out.

"Give it to me."

Euphemia held it up above her head, out of Alison's reach, and stepped around her.

"Tell me where Jane and Petal are and you can have it."

"You must be joking."

Euphemia edged her way towards the cubicle and held the phone over the toilet bowl.

"Obviously not, Alison. Half or full?"

"Half or full what?

"Flush."

"Don't!"

"Tell me where they are."

"I can't."

"Not good enough."

"OK, Sage, drop it then, because if I can't take the call from Malcolm, he'll kill them. You know he's capable. That's the plan if I don't answer the phone so go ahead. Make my day."

"I don't believe you."

"Again," said Alison, hands raised, "what choice do you have?"

Euphemia pursed her lips. The woman was right. She pocketed the phone, rolled up her old shirt and put it in the rubbish bin.

"Come with me," said Euphemia and she walked back to reception.

Ben, anxiously searching for her and praying he'd not lost her for the second time that morning, sagged with relief when he saw her.

"Tell him to go away," hissed Alison.

"Ben, Kezia has something for me. You couldn't go downstairs and get it, could you?"

Ben didn't need to be asked twice and disappeared.

"I thought you'd been cut, on the neck. Olivia was bawling in the loo earlier about the firm going broke and you having your throat cut by that madman, Turner. There's nothing wrong with you."

"You're right. I'm fine. Fuss over nothing. Where are Jane and Petal? Tell me and I'll let you go. I'll keep quiet and give you and Malcolm time to get away."

"From the way Olivia was talking, you got cut quite badly," continued Alison.

"Let it go, Alison. It's not important. Where is Jane?"

"Right across your neck and there was blood all over you, she said, but now looking at you, there's not even a scratch."

"You know how Olivia exaggerates. Forget it. Where are they? Surely Chris coming here this morning is warning enough for you. You and Malcolm have to leave before more of the people you duped come looking for you. I promise I'll cover for you as long as I can."

"So it's all true."

"What are you talking about?"

"Somehow, a man holds you hostage and cuts your throat and next minute he's the one on the floor unable to move — not you. You've escaped. He's so badly beat up he's in a wheelchair. You. There's not a mark on you. Not a scratch. It was all true."

"What are you talking about?"

"Your mother said one day you'd be a very special person, with some sort of family powers, and look. What's more magical than being cut with a knife, blood everywhere, and less than an hour later, there's nothing to see?"

Euphemia froze. She'd heard the words 'Your mother said' and nothing else.

"My mother?"

"Didn't you know? How silly of me not to mention it earlier." Alison paused for effect. The she said slowly and deliberately, "I knew your mother, the exotic glamorous pain in the backside, Fredericka Marchamp. I was ten when she swept into our lives, and stayed. Stayed far too long. Had eyes only for my father and he stupidly seemed to feel something for her. He kept telling me she was going to be my new mother but I never believed it. She died. Everything was supposed to go back to normal. He promised me it would. But it wasn't the same. He wasn't the same. And it was all your stupid mother's fault."

All Euphemia could hear over and over again were the words 'Your mother said'. She didn't doubt Alison was telling the truth. The tone of her voice, the malicious gloating, it was all there. The shameless delight in finally spilling the secret she must have been saving up for just this moment was all the proof she needed.

The years tumbled into flashes of time and emotions and she couldn't breathe, couldn't think. Alison knew her mother. A wave of heat surged through her, clouding her vision, constricting her. She struggled out of her jacket and let it fall to the floor. Her mother, who should have been with her own daughter, was instead playing stepmother to another girl on the far side of the world, giving this girl all the love and attention she should have had.

Euphemia did what she'd done all her life. She escaped. She ran to the bathroom, locked the door and was violently sick.

Chapter Thirty-seven

Alistair was hot and sweaty in all the wrong places when he clattered his way past the reception desk after his lunchtime bike ride. He was training for the weekend club championship and keen to improve on his performance last year when he'd fallen at the last bend and been disqualified for taking down the entire peloton. It had been a tense year at the club and he badly needed to redeem himself.

"Saw your husband at the airport," he said casually as he passed Alison.

"What?"

"I think it was your husband. Big man? Balding? He recognized me, I think. We met at the Christmas party last year and had a long talk about the Tour de France. Said he'd always wanted to go and watch it. I'm sure it was him."

"You must be mistaken," she said, but seeing the look on his face, Alison waved him away impatiently.

Hah, she thought as she picked up Euphemia's jacket and patted down the pockets before she retrieved her phone. She keyed in the code to unlock it. Euphemia had gone off to cry and left it behind, the stupid cow. Her reaction had just confirmed her father had been telling the truth all these years. Jane and Petal had faded into insignificance as soon as Alison had mentioned her mother. It had felt so good to wipe some of that misplaced pride off her face and watch her run off like a hysterical schoolgirl to the toilets. Payback time. Fredericka had been nice enough when she wasn't drinking but nothing had been the same after she died. Alison had been the one who'd had to bear the burden all these years. What a sook. Euphemia Sage, didn't know the half of it. She keyed in the number.

"Malcolm, where are you?"

"In the car."

"Really, so how come Alistair said he saw you at the airport? Going somewhere?"

"I was just going to call, my love. The jewelry — it's fake. Copies. Sammy says good copies but only worth a couple of grand. You were right to get it checked, my love."

Alison shut her eyes. Her visions of wearing beautiful dresses and magnificent jewelry, going to fabulous parties amongst the great and the good, dissolved into a puddle of nothing. Copies, no matter how good, just weren't the same.

"So what are you doing at the airport?"

"Ah well," he drawled. "No point in staying around, is there, old girl? We gave it a go and it didn't work out. *C'est la vie* and all that."

"So you were going to leave and not tell me? Leave me to deal with the mess downstairs and find my own way out? Is that it?"

"You're a big girl. You can look after yourself. You've got enough stashed away."

"I do not."

"Stop it. I know what you've been doing. You think you're the clever one, the brains, but I'm not as stupid as you think."

"What am I supposed to do with Jane?"

"You'll think of something. You always do. Hey, gotta go, they're calling my flight and I haven't gone through security yet. It's been great, Alison. Loved every minute."

The phone went dead. Alison resisted the temptation to hurl it across the foyer and shoved it instead into her handbag. The little derringer pistol nestling at the bottom clinked against it. Keeping bullets in the bottom of her filing cabinet had been a masterstroke. Fakes? Fucking Jane would pay for this.

Malcolm thumbed the power on his phone to off. He might as well take it with him and get a new SIM card when he arrived. How long his money would last on the island was hard to say, but he'd taken as much as he could find at short notice. Chris Turner had had a surprising stash in one of his children's teddy bears. And he'd extracted as much as he could from Alison's hoard. She'd been cunning where she'd hidden some of it, and he knew he hadn't found it all, but it was enough to last a year or two if he wasn't too flashy.

Malcolm was looking forward to making a new start on his own. In the last few months Alison had changed. She'd pushed him and the boys too hard, too often, ruffled too many feathers.

Even he'd felt sorry for Chris Turner when he visited him this morning. The guy was a mess and was on the bones of his ass. Taking the last of his cash had left him with nothing. If they'd waited until he was back on his feet, they could have milked him for years. Chris would have been a good earner for their off-piste finance business, if only the debt had been allowed to mature. Malcolm didn't understand why Alison was in such a rush. And he didn't want to wait around for the police to tell him in an interview room, because the way she was acting, that's where they were both headed.

Grant appeared out of the mass of people clogging up the concourse and handed him the newspaper he'd asked for. Loyal Grant and his even dumber brother, Mark, had made all this possible. Malcolm would never have got the money out of some of their more stubborn clients without them. They'd done whatever he'd asked, backing him up in some pretty tight corners. He'd miss them. Hell, he might even send for them if things went well on the island. Grant was a great guy, driving him in the Mercedes to the airport, despite the risk.

He wondered how long it would take the police to identify it. Life was nothing without that frisson of risk, thought Malcolm, especially if others end up wearing it.

"Alison's got your money," he said to Grant. "And Mark's. Pick it up from her when you get back to town. Thanks, mate, for everything. Couldn't have done it without you."

Malcolm put his hand out and was surprised when Grant took it and then pulled him close for a hug. A handshake would have been sufficient but if Grant wanted a hug then so be it. Malcolm didn't feel the small plastic bag drop into his jacket pocket.

Grant had already turned away and was walking back through the crowds, his half-ear hidden under a baseball cap he'd picked up this morning at the Turner house. The cap and the plastic bag of meth had made his day worthwhile.

Chapter Thirty-eight

Euphemia turned the tap on full, cupped her hands under the cold water, and gathering it into her mouth swished it around the inside of her cheeks and spat the last bitterness of her vomit into the sink. She was so tired. She was tired of carrying her abandonment around after all these years. The fear that loomed back into her present, unwanted and unbidden, when she least expected it, would barge through her carefully constructed defenses and leave her over-whelmed and confused. She was tired of being whisked back to when she was three, standing on a doorstep in the dark, her mother's footsteps receding in the distance. She was tired of reliving standing on the doorstep, doing her best to be brave, to smile and be nice to the kind lady who would open the door.

Alison's revelations had triggered that scene on the doorstep with every smell, every cold dark detail etched into her soul replaying like a movie in her head. The sensations taking her down that one inevitable pathway to the only solution she had ever understood which could explain her mother's abandonment — that she wasn't good enough, that she was unlovable. Her inadequacy underpinned everything. It had made her study harder, run faster, look better, and be the best mother, the best wife she could be — all to no avail. The memory of the deep loss and the reason for it had never left her.

Until now.

Something was happening inside her brain, deep inside. She felt a rearrangement as new connections searched out and found others.

A new order clicked into place as unexplored neural pathways were opening, revealing other possibilities, different explanations. Euphemia felt the scars she had carried all her life healing, just as her neck had healed. Her memory was the same, but her perspective had changed. The abandonment was not about her. It was not about an unlovable three-year-old any longer. It was not her fault. How could it be?

The words from Maree's last letter came back to her guiding her away from the pain of something which was past, over. Done. Know yourself, do what you have to and once you have started something, finish it. Simple. Why hadn't she heard this before? She smiled. Poor Maree, she thought, she had tried so hard and I was so caught up in feeling sorry for myself, I didn't listen. I didn't want to.

Euphemia dried her hands and looked at her reflection. An attractive blonde woman looked back. A clear-eyed intelligent woman, with a straight back and a strong body standing tall and proud, stared back at her from the mirror. She turned her head this way and that and examined her neck, the neck which a few hours before had been cut by a madman, and which had healed perfectly. She smiled at the woman in the mirror. "I get it. But that's enough for now. You have Jane and a dog to rescue as well as a business to save. There is only you, Euphemia. No one else. "

Chapter Thirty-nine

"What are you doing?" Alison screamed from the doorway.

Petal cowered in Jane's arms, shivering in abject fear when Alison swung back the heavy door.

"Doing what I should have done before. Letting Mrs. French and this poor puppy go. They need help after what you and the boss did to them."

Jane could have kicked herself. She really hadn't believed Grant when he'd arrived a few minutes ago and told her he'd come to help. He'd told her to hurry but, afraid, she'd held back and now it was too late.

Alison pulled the door shut behind her with a loud clang.

"You always were stupid, Grant, but this. I never thought you were disloyal."

"You shouldn't have done it."

"Done what? What are you driveling on about?"

"You shouldn't have hurt little Petal. She never did anything to you."

"Let me get this right," said Alison walking over and standing in front of him. "You and your even dimmer brother have been beating people up whenever Malcolm told you to. For months, I might add. And that's OK? You don't bat an eyelid when Jane loses a tooth. But you object to us taking one small souvenir from a dog. That was wrong and the other stuff wasn't?"

Grant looked around the room, anywhere but at Alison. "You shouldn't have done it," he mumbled again.

"Well, we did," said Alison, poking him hard in the chest to emphasize each word. "You were here. And if I remember rightly, you even held the bloody dog down."

Grant burst into tears. The big man's shoulder shook as he wept uncontrollably, and turning away from her, he fumbled in his jeans for something to wipe his nose on. Jane found a bloody tissue in her sleeve and took it over to him. She reached up tentatively and put her hand on his shoulder, only to have him recoil as if she'd hit him.

"When we were young, Mark and me, we found a kitten. Mum killed it in front of us. Said we were sissies. She threw it over the back fence. How do you think I lost my ear, Mrs. Sinclair?"

"Do I care?"

"Mum had to bash me on the side of the head with a shovel to get the kitten off me. I had to have the top part cut off when it got infected. So what you did to that dog was wrong and you're right, I should've stopped it. I'm to blame too. And you. And Mr. Sinclair. People deserve what they get, mostly. But that kitten didn't do anything wrong and neither did Petal."

"Boo fucking hoo, I'm sure. Grant, I don't care. It's just lucky I got back here when I did."

"Mrs. Sinclair, ma'am, we're leaving."

"Today is going from bad to worse," muttered Alison, digging around in the bottom of her tatty handbag. "First Malcolm. Now you. Not to mention Euphemia bloody Sage. Oh yes, and Jane. I almost forgot. The jewelry's fake, Jane. Worthless copies. You're so proud of it and it's nothing but paste."

"Then let us go like Grant says. We're no use to you. I promise we won't go to the police. You and Malcolm can get away."

"If only it were that simple."

"It is simple. It's over."

Alison laughed. "For one thing, Malcolm's gone. Run out with all the money he could get his hands on. Isn't that right, Grant? You took him to the airport."

"He said you'd pay us. He said you had our wages."

"I'm hardly going to pay you now, am I, after this, even if I did have any money? He's cheated us both."

"He was like a dad to me and Mark."

"Good grief. I don't have time for your father fantasies or the save the animal stunts."

Jane tucked Petal firmly under her arm and started walking towards the door.

"Where do you think you're going?"

"Petal and I are leaving. Grant's right. I need to see a dentist and Petal needs to see a vet. It's over. There's no jewelry, your husband's run off with the money and even your staff have turned on you. Now get out of our way."

Alison looked at Grant and raised an eyebrow. He shook his head and stayed where he was.

There was a loud click.

"Don't think I wouldn't."

"Wouldn't what?" said Jane reaching for the door handle.

"This."

The bullet missed Jane's head by six inches, denting the heavy steel before falling on the floor and rolling away. The noise blew out Jane's left eardrum, leaving behind a loud and very painful ringing on one side of her head. A trickle of blood rolled down her earlobe. She'd dropped Petal but not before the little dog had automatically emptied her bladder in fright.

Alison took a moment then shook her hand before ostentatiously chambering the next bullet, knowing she had her captives' full attention. She waved the pistol at them, indicating they move into the far corner. Petal, her tail between her legs and ears pinned back against her head, was running around the room in circles searching fruitlessly for an escape. Grant picked her up and cuddled her into his bulk, trying to soothe her with soft pats and whispered words, and refused to look at Alison. Jane crawled across the floor before slumping against the wall beside Grant. She had her hand over her ear and looked up at Grant but he shook his head. There they stayed.

Chapter Forty

Dave and Nicky studied Malcolm Sinclair through the one-way mirror. Alone in the room, he was drumming his fingernails on the thin table, trying to look relaxed but not succeeding. Dark patches of sweat looped his armpits, staining his blue shirt. He looked around casually checking the corners for cameras and finding none, tipped a salute and a nervous smile to the mirror. It was clear from his expression, he was not finding his new surroundings to his taste.

"Do you think it's the chair he doesn't like? They're not very comfortable, and certainly not what he's used to."

"Maybe he has claustrophobia?" asked Nicky.

"It's possible, but that's a hiding to nothing. He'll have to get used to small rooms. I can't see him living anywhere else for a while. Can you?"

The phone buzzed in Dave's pocket. He looked at the text and showed it to Nicky.

"Time to go."

Malcolm jumped when the door swung open and seeing a woman automatically got to his feet while she took her seat and introduced herself and Detective Inspector Richards. He sat down again and put his arms on the table.

"I went to school with a Sage. No relation, I suppose?"

"My father."

"Give him my regards, won't you? I'm not sure why I'm here. I have a plane to catch."

"Mr. Sinclair, you were caught trying to leave the country with a large sum of cash, which you hadn't declared. You were also in possession of three ounces of pure methamphetamine."

"The cash I can explain. The meth isn't mine. I can't explain that unless someone planted it when I was being searched. Never touched the stuff. Don't do drugs."

"Nevertheless, Mr. Sinclair, we found it in your pocket. We also have CCTV footage of you being driven to the airport in a black Mercedes sedan. A car we've been looking for in relation to a robbery and kidnapping yesterday. The car has been found outside in the drop-off zone where your driver left it. It's on its way to forensics, as we speak, and if we find blood in this car, and in particular Mrs. Jane French's blood, then you can imagine the conclusions which will be drawn."

Malcolm's face drained of color and he leaned forward.

"Normally, Mr. Sinclair, we would be waiting for your lawyer to arrive. I believe you called one earlier. But right now we don't have time. We need your help. Tell us where we can find Jane French."

Nicky and Dave pretended not to notice the flash of cunning crossing Malcolm's face.

"I could do that... or," he paused, "I could wait for my lawyer to arrive. She's in court. I told her there was no hurry. I've missed the plane. The next one is a couple of hours. So if it's all the same to you, unless you can help me, I don't think I can help you."

"We thought you might say that, so we have decided to drop the parking ticket. There is an automatic two-hundred-dollar fine for leaving a car unattended in the drop-off zone."

"Thank you. Most generous. But I'm sure you can do better than that. After all, a woman's life is at stake as we chit-chat."

"So you do appreciate that. Good. Mr. Sinclair, being a man of the world you must realize this interview is being recorded. Imagine how a jury will react when they hear what you just said. And remember you waived the right to have a lawyer present by talking to us. If I were a juror, any delay on your part might be interpreted as being an accessory to murder, should anything happen, that is."

Malcolm looked guiltily up at the mirror.

"Come on, Malcolm. I'm sure your friends at the golf club would like to hear how eager you were to do the decent thing and help us. Honor and all that," said Nicky.

Malcolm shrugged. "I lost my honor when I married my wife, young lady. It's been gone for so long I don't think I know the meaning of the word. My so-called friends at the golf club barely spoke to me until I started splashing money about. Even then, I had to make a substantial donation to the club. So, honor, much like everything else in this world, is just a commodity. It can be bought and sold for the price of a ticket to Tahiti. The only person who was ever polite to me was Justin French and that was only because he was in the same boat as me — broke. So what do I care what they think? Let's wait for my lawyer."

"We could drop the possession charge. That would take at least four years off your sentence, but only if you tell us where to find Jane — now. Otherwise the deal is off. You can rot in prison for all I care. What with kidnapping, robbery, and grievous bodily harm, currency offences, and anything else I can think of to add to the charge sheet, you are going to prison, Mr. Sinclair. You will spend the next decade of your life in a room smaller than this, with a bucket to shit in and a roommate to watch you do it."

There was a long silence. Malcolm shifted in his chair and ran his fingers over his head, the sweat rings on his shirt under his arms widening visibly.

"You'd better hurry," he said wearily. "Alison isn't one to sit around. But I doubt if she'd be expecting you yet." He laughed quietly. "I'd give anything to see the look on her face when you guys burst through the door. She's in the basement of the building where she works. Sage Consulting — you know where that is, don't you, detective? There's a floor below the car park and a room with a steel door just next to the staircase. That's where you'll find Jane French, your bloody dog and, with any luck, my wife."

"What dog?"

"That smarmy pug dog. Petal. Bit worse for wear, I'm afraid. Actually I don't give a shit. Hate dogs, especially little yappy ones."

Dave Richards was already on his phone as he left the room.

Nicky followed, but turned in the doorway. "Why do you have Petal?"

"To keep your mother quiet. So she wouldn't go blabbing to you lot that it was Alison and me who took Jane. She came to our place yesterday to beg us to let Jane off the hook about the money she owed. We were fine till she found out about us. As soon as Jane told her about Alison running Sinclair Finance out of Sage, we knew it was all over. So Alison got the boys to pick up your dog... to keep your mum quiet till we got the jewelry, which turned out to be worthless shit anyway. And look how it's turned out. Bloody Justin."

Nicky waited, hoping Dave hadn't heard what Malcolm had just said, because she needed time to work out how this was going to run. Her mother had taken it upon herself to interfere in a police investigation. What was she thinking?

Nicky stood back as a slim woman in an expensive suit, carrying a large briefcase, barged officiously past her into the room.

"I hope you haven't said anything, Mr. Sinclair. Remember my instructions, say nothing until I arrive."

Nicky was just about to shut the door when Malcolm called out.

"Alison's got a gun. She'll use it too, mad cow. I think it's that time of the month." His laughter followed Nicky down the hall.

Chapter Forty-one

"Ben, would you mind taking these to Kezia?" asked Euphemia, holding out a folder of papers. "I'm sorry to have to ask you again but Alison has disappeared."

Ben hesitated then against his better judgment he grabbed the proffered folder and hurried away. Love or lust, whatever it was, Euphemia would take advantage of it while she could. Only last night he'd been talking fondly of Nicky. And today, he seemed smitten by Kezia. Either Ben didn't know his own mind, or he did but it had changed. She sensed trouble ahead but filed her maternal concern under problems for another day and tapped up Kezia's app.

She was relieved to see there'd been no calls while she was in the bathroom. Even better, Alison was still somewhere in the building. But there were ten floors, not counting the car park, so where?

The bus, thought Euphemia. Alison would have had to be near street level when she'd called last night. She went back to her office and quickly changed out of her business suit and into the clothes she kept for her lunchtime runs. Pocketing her car keys, phone and headphones she pulled on her running shoes, took the lift downstairs and walked onto the street looking around for more clues.

As luck would have it, the men operating the jackhammer had stopped for lunch and one of the city's new electric buses had just pulled up at the bus stop outside the front door. She instantly recognized the sounds of the door opening and closing. Jane had to be nearby. She took the ramp to the car park and was searching the floor, looking behind pillars and cars, when her phone vibrated in her pocket. The app had activated. Alison was getting a call. She put an earbud in one ear and let the other dangle free.

"How long till you get here?" asked the caller.

"I need to do one last thing, then depending on traffic, we should be there in half an hour," replied Alison. "Not long."

"I heard what you did to Jane."

"You would have done the ..." The call ended abruptly.

Euphemia couldn't place the voice. It wasn't Malcolm, so who was it? She played back voices of men she knew but the identity of the caller eluded her. Obviously well known to Alison, it was someone she felt comfortable with and who was expecting her. Why? Why drag this out? They'd got the jewelry. Surely the Sinclairs needed to get out of town as soon as they could. The jewelry would give them enough to start again, so why take more risks?

The car park was empty so Euphemia opened the door beside the lift shaft, which accessed the utility floor below. She'd been down here only once before when she and Kenneth had been deciding whether to take the lease upstairs. She liked big buildings. There was something about their organization that intrigued her.

The utility floor housed the lift machinery and beside that a pump to get rid of ground water, as well as various control boards. Next to this was a small room where the cleaners stored some of their equipment. The location signal on her phone was stronger after the last call; she knew she was close.

Grateful for the soft rubber of her shoes, soundless on the metal stairs, she put her ear to the door and listened. There was a rustle as someone inside the tiny room moved. She focused and could hear breathing — an animal panting softly — and close by one, no, two people. Closer to the door again was a third person breathing more quietly than the others. She counted off Alison and Jane but who was the third?

She reached down and slowly turned the handle. Nothing happened. The door was locked. It was a solid heavy metal door so there was no way, even with her added strength, that she would get in on the first attempt if she tried to muscle her way through. She looked hopefully at her sapphire ring. It stayed the same, dark and silent. Super-heroine defeated by the oldest trick in the book — a locked door. If only she'd brought a Plan B.

Her phone vibrated again in her pocket.

Two messages. The first was from Kenneth: 'Not far away. See you at the office. Love you.' The second was from Kezia: 'Stealth drive extracted. Data safe. Ben wonders where U R?'

Euphemia smiled with relief. Just Jane to save now and we're done, she thought. Easy! She shoved her phone in her pocket and heard footsteps. Flipping round into the shadows, she pressed back against the door to the pump room hoping to find refuge in there but it too was locked. A bolt slid back and the cupboard door swung open. A warm smell of stale humans mixed with dog shit wafted out into the stairwell.

"You might as well come in, Euphemia. I've been waiting for you," said Alison. I thought you'd be quicker than this. I'm starting to think Fredericka was exaggerating. But just in case she wasn't, don't try anything. You may have your powers but I have a gun and it's aimed at Jane."

Chapter Forty-two

"Yes, I know I was supposed to be watching her, Nicky. But she's gone. Gave me the slip about five, no, ten minutes ago," said Ben.

"Amazing,' said Nicky, talking to Dave in the background. "He's lost her. Doesn't know where she is. We're on our way, Ben. Keep looking."

"She can't have gone far," replied Ben, knowing how pathetic this sounded.

"Have you checked to see if her car is still downstairs?" asked Nicky, "No, wait. Stop. Dave says stay where you are. Keep everyone with you. Don't let anyone leave and certainly don't let anyone go down to the car park. That's where Mrs. French, Jane, is being held. If you see Alison Sinclair, be careful. She's got a gun."

"Alison Sinclair, the receptionist?"

"That's her."

"The receptionist?"

"Don't do anything stupid. Just do what you can."

"The receptionist?"

"For Chrissakes, Ben."

Ben turned to Kezia. "Did you hear? Alison Sinclair has a gun. You make sure everyone on this floor stays put but try not to alarm them. If you see Alison, stay clear. I'm going down to the other floors to make sure they stay put too. The police are on their way."

"I knew you weren't a business student," said Kezia. "Now I know where I've seen you before. With Nicky. You're that policeman she's been talking about? You've been lying to me all morning."

"I'm sorry, Kezia, OK? Right now, we need to make sure everyone stays put. It sounds dramatic but do it. I doubt if Alison will be back but if you see her, text me. Ben opened the door to the stairwell, looked lingeringly at Kezia for longer than he should and smiled ruefully. "Gotta go."

Kezia immediately called her father.

"Mum's in trouble. You need to be here," she said.

"I'm stuck on the motorway. What sort of trouble?" asked Kenneth.

"Alison Sinclair has been blackmailing her, and Mum is looking for her and I think she's armed."

"Your mother's armed? Euphemia has a gun?"

"No. Alison."

"Alison, the receptionist? Malcolm Sinclair's wife?"

"Yes, Dad. Keep up. The police are on their way and no one is allowed in or out of the building."

"Does Nicky know? Why didn't you call me before?"

"Mum said not to. She said she could handle it and I thought she could but I didn't know about the gun then. Nicky knows — she's on her way. She planted a cop with Mum and didn't tell me. He's been here all morning, hanging around pretending to be a business student. The one Nicky likes, Dad, you remember."

"Not really, Kezia. Where's your mother?"

"No idea. I have to go and warn everyone. Half the Wellington police force is on its way."

"What can I do?"

"Be here soon. Please. We can't leave the building. The police told us to wait for them to get here."

"Stay safe. I'm coming as fast as Roger can drive me."

"You need to know Mum's been acting strangely. She had a fight with Chris Turner in her office and her throat got cut but she's better now. Oh ,and the stealth drive has been inactivated."

"Chris Turner, the plumber? Cut her throat? Stealth drive? Kezia, next time Mum tells you not to call me... call me."

Kenneth looked at his phone.

"I told you, Roger," he said. "I told you she needed me."

"Coincidence. Pure coincidence."

"Take this exit. We're going to the office. I thought this was supposed to be a smart motorway but no one's moving."

"It's nearly rush hour so the system breaks down then cos no one follows the instructions. Smart motor way- dumb drivers. I'm trying, Kenneth. I'll get you there."

Chapter Forty-three

Euphemia walked past Alison into the room. The door banged shut and Alison slid the bolt across. Seeing Euphemia, Petal's tail started wagging, albeit weakly as she limped across the room. Euphemia's heart almost broke seeing her brave little pug ignoring pain to get to her. She knelt down and picked her up. A flurry of licking and tail wagging followed, the little body pressing hard against her, Petal's black eyes bulging with pleasure and relief.

Jane smiled at her with almost the same look. "I knew you'd come."

Euphemia smiled back, until she noticed Half-ear standing in a corner at the back of the room and she raised an eyebrow.

"It's OK," yelled Jane. "He came to rescue us, but I wasn't quick enough. Truly. He wanted to save Petal. He's on our side."

Grant locked eyes with Euphemia for a moment but otherwise his face was immobile. He stayed leaning against the wall, his arms folded.

"Much good that will do you," said Alison. "Grant's best with instructions. Aren't you, Grant? Not good at thinking for yourself. Probably brain-damaged when your mother clocked you with that shovel. And stop yelling. Jane, it's really getting on my nerves."

"Why do you have to be such a bitch, Alison?" yelled Jane.

"Brave now, are we, Jane? Now that Euphemia is here? Think she's going to save you, do you? Well, she's not. Even someone with special powers is useless against a gun. I've been waiting for you, Euphemia, because you're the last piece in the puzzle."

"What puzzle? What are you talking about?" On the far side of the room, she watched as Jane leaned forwards, her hand cupping her left ear. "Why is Jane doing that? What have you done to her?"

"Nothing serious."

Jane stepped towards them, her eyes fixed on Alison's mouth, her head cocked to one side.

"Can't you hear, Jane?" yelled Euphemia. "Is that the problem?"

Jane nodded vigorously.

"She wasn't deaf yesterday, Alison."

"It's only one ear. She's making it worse than it is," said Alison.

"Jane's never done anything to you. She made one mistake. Borrowing money from you because she was desperate, and look at her. Look at her face, and now she's deaf. What did you do?"

"Nothing," said Alison. "Oh, all right. She got too close to a bullet. It'll get better and it's only the one ear. She can hear a little bit. Being a drama queen, if you ask me. You don't know how annoying she is. She yells all the time when she's awake and she snores like a mountain lion when she's asleep. There's no rest from her. I'll be glad to see the back of her."

"You're unbelievable."

"Really. Well, you're not the boss now, are you, Ms. Fancy Pants? I am, so get used to it."

"You're not the boss either, are you? You might be holding the gun but there's someone else, someone who's telling you what to do and when to do it. You're just the idiot who has created this mess."

"You think you're so smart, don't you?"

"OK," said Euphemia, "explain how a stealth drive works."

"What's a stealth drive?"

"Exactly. You do what you're told to do. No idea why or what. It's why you and Malcolm haven't just skedaddled. You've got the jewelry and no doubt money from your finance company... so why are you still here, risking the police finding you, if there isn't unfinished business with whoever?"

"The jewelry's fake. Worthless copies. And Malcolm's gone. Left the country."

"Good fakes," yelled Jane, picking up the word jewelry.

Alison and Euphemia turned and looked at her together. "You knew, didn't you? What were you going to do when they found out, Jane?" asked Euphemia.

"The house would have been sold by then. Heaps of money to pay them back, if they only could have waited like we asked," yelled Jane.

"Nevertheless..."

Euphemia's phone vibrated in her pocket.

"Give it to me," demanded Alison.

"No. It doesn't matter who it is. Fake jewelry and no Malcolm, it's over."

"We haven't even started... give me your phone."

"No. Give me the gun."

In a thrice, Euphemia turned and threw Petal to Grant, who caught her neatly. But in that same moment, Alison had shoved her aside, grabbed Jane and put the gun to her head.

"I know you're faster and stronger than me, Euphemia. I know all about your powers. You've proved yourself in the last forty-eight hours. You're the real thing. But are you faster than a bullet to the brain? Can I pull this trigger faster than you can get the gun? Do you want to test it and see? I didn't think so. Take the phone out of your pocket and put it on the floor. No smart moves."

Euphemia read the text as she put the phone down: 'The police are on their way.' She had to keep Alison talking.

"Grant, pick it up and read the message," ordered Alison, yanking Jane's head round, pressing harder than she needed to on the empty tooth socket. Tears of pain rolled down Jane's face.

Grant crouched down, still cuddling Petal into him, and held the phone up to Alison.

"I said read it to me."

"I can't read," said Grant quietly.

"For Chrissakes." She squinted at the screen and moved her head back and forwards. "I haven't got my bloody glasses. You read it, Jane," she said, loosening her grip.

"I can't read it — my glasses are in my car."

"Euphemia?"

"It says 'The police are on their way.'"

Alison paled. The police weren't part of the plan. Suddenly, and obviously to everyone in the room, Alison was at a loss to know what to do next. Euphemia watched her grip on Jane slacken and seized the moment. She stepped forward and swung the other leg to push Jane away with her foot, toppling her backwards and out of harm's way. Alison lunged after her, but Euphemia had already grabbed her wrist and bent her hand backwards, making Alison cry out in pain, forcing her down, tightening her grip so hard that the little pistol clattered to the floor.

From where she lay on the floor, Jane looked up at Euphemia and gave her two triumphant thumbs up. It was over.

Euphemia twisted Alison over onto her stomach and pulled her arm behind her back, forcing it painfully up between her shoulder blades almost lifting her off the floor as she did so. She turned to find the gun just as a loud click sounded beside her ear.

"Pick it up very carefully by the barrel and hand it to me."

Grant was holding another pistol, a bigger one, against her temple. His was the sort of pistol you see in movies. It was a seriously scary gun. Letting go of Alison, Euphemia turned to look at him and what she saw frightened her. Grant was no longer Malcolm Sinclair's dumb thug. His body had hardened, his movements were now precise. And his eyes were different. They were cold eyes, killer's eyes.

"You were right about one thing, Mrs. Sage. This is a mess. A total botch-up from start to finish," said Grant. "Take your dog and give me that." He dumped Petal into her arms and took Alison's pistol and tucked it into the back of his trousers under his jacket. "Jane, Mrs. Sage, over there, please. You too, Alison, and shut up about your arm. Have you heard Jane complaining? Grow a pair, Alison."

"Wait till Malcolm hears about this."

"Malcolm's gone, Alison. You just told us. Be quiet, there's a good girl."

"How dare you speak to me like... Ouch! Get off my foot."

Euphemia complied. "Alison, do as he says and shut up," she hissed.

"I see that you understand the situation perfectly, Mrs. Sage. It's nice to be dealing with an intelligent woman."

Alison bridled and was about to object but feeling the pressure of Euphemia's foot again, she closed her mouth. She folded her arms across her chest and looked at him petulantly, then mouthed the words 'You wait'.

"What did he say? I can't hear a thing," yelled Jane. Euphemia made a shushing gesture to her and smiled. Jane smiled back exposing the gap in her front teeth. "Sorry I got you into this," she whispered loudly.

"Oh please," said Alison. "You still haven't figured this out, have you, Jane?"

"I warned you, Alison."

Grant produced a roll of duct tape from his jacket and proceeded to wrap a length of it around Alison's head, sealing her mouth once and for all. Her eyes blazed in fury but only for the second it took for her to grasp that where Grant was concerned, he just didn't care.

Euphemia heard the sirens first — before Petal, before any of them — but they gave her no joy. Grant had his pistol aimed at them lined up against the far wall and kept it steady while he unbolted the door and swung it open. Fresh air and noise from the jackhammers out on the street flooded in. She counted two cars pull up and doors opening, with more arriving by the second. The jackhammers stopped and there was an eerie silence before she heard footsteps running up and down the street.

"This is Detective Inspector Dave Richards from the Wellington Police. Mrs. Sinclair, we have you surrounded. I would suggest you take the easy option and give yourself up. It's over. We have your husband. Put your weapon down and walk up the ramp with your arms raised. You will see us waiting for you and when you do, kneel with your arms held high above your head. Whatever you do, move slowly and follow our instructions. "

Alison's eyes bulged with indignation and she spluttered behind the tape.

"Should I send you up, Alison?" asked Grant. "You'd make a great decoy." He cocked his head and winked. "I don't think I need a decoy, do you, ladies? I have something much better. I have hostages. Mrs. Sage, I'd be grateful if you'd pick up your phone and call your daughter — Nicky the policewoman daughter, not Kezia the beautiful geek. Kezia is the next in line, I've been told."

Chapter Forty-four

Half an hour later, Nicky watched as her mother drove up the ramp, out of the building, turned left past the waiting police cars and onto Wakefield Street across the intersection while the traffic lights blinked red, and disappeared around the bend on Aotea Quay. Sitting next to her in the passenger seat was Alison Sinclair, her mouth sealed shut with duct tape, her eyes staring straight ahead. In the back, Grant was holding Jane French tightly against his chest with one hand and holding a pistol to the side of her head with the other. He was wearing the Kevlar vest and helmet he had demanded in negotiations. The pistol was a SIG Sauer P226, a gun Nicky recognized from her training with the Armed Response Unit. It looked small in his big hand but she'd seen how much damage the nine-millimeter bullet could do when fired at close range.

Nicky, standing by the ramp, had met her mother's eyes for a split second as she had turned into the street, just long enough to feel her determination and courage and to garner some reassurance. Dave, standing beside her, had nodded when Grant acknowledged him. The rest of the police, stationed behind cars and barriers, weapons raised, watched, faces unmoved as the man holding three women and a city hostage drove past. In the sky, a helicopter, flying high above the car, had been instructed to keep pace with it as it moved through the empty streets.

The negotiations had been short and to the point. Dave had balked at first. Then Grant mentioned two unsolved murders from eight and ten years ago respectively. He provided exact locations as to where, in one of the cases, another body might be found. In the second case he named the location of the murder weapon. Dave realized the man he'd always considered to be a dupe, a low-level criminal hired to do the bidding of others for little gain, was nothing of the sort.

Two victims in the first case had been killed efficiently and professionally and now there was a third. Grant confirmed with Dave the exact locations where the body parts of the first victims had been discovered, information known only to the police and the killer. Dave remembered the pathologist informing him both men had been killed with a nine-millimeter bullet between the eyes, after some fairly routine torture lasting a couple of hours at most.

They'd been targeted because they were about to grass up a local businessman who was planning to expand his operations into the recreational drug market with the assistance of a Chinese consortium. When their bodies were reassembled in the morgue, they were complete except for their tongues. Rumor had it these had been thrown over the fence into the tigers' enclosure at the zoo.

It took Dave five more years to expose the Chinese connection to the influx of meth onto the local market, but until now there'd been no hard evidence linking the businessman to the crimes and he'd escaped scot-free. Grant had just provided the information needed to tie that man to the murders as well as the meth operation. He'd taken a big risk revealing his involvement in these horrific crimes just to prove how serious he was. Dave had no choice but to take his threats to the hostages seriously and listened carefully to his list of demands and the detailed consequences if these weren't met.

Grant had demanded a ten-minute head start and clear passage to the Frenches' house in Thorndon. Once there he would tell Dave what he wanted next but told him to have two helicopters at the ready.

Dave had then radioed for unmarked cars to be stationed along the route, not only to hold back gawking bystanders but also to manage any hold-ups. The last thing they needed at this stage in the operation was for a member of the public to become unwittingly involved in what was a very dangerous situation. Grant had been very clear about his intentions should this happen.

In the next twenty-five minutes the route between Sage Consulting and the Frenches' home in Thorndon had been closed off. At five o'clock on a Monday afternoon when normally the streets were clogged with rush-hour traffic and pedestrians traipsing to buses and trains, they were now empty. People and cars were held one block back from the quay skirting the harbor by lines of police. Exits and entrances to this narrow city built between the hills and the sea were already limited and now they were choked at either end. Vehicle traffic was locked up for miles in all directions. Only the wily cyclists who whizzed past everyone on the side streets, fists raised in triumph, were getting to their destinations. Wellington was officially in gridlock. Blocked ambulances howled their protest and flashed lights to no avail. No one was driving anywhere, except Grant and his hostages.

Dave had contacted Traffic and the ARU while Nicky had contacted Parliament Security. The route to the Frenches' Thorndon home took the car up the hill past the Beehive and Parliament, and two more of New Zealand's most important institutions, the Reserve Bank and Treasury. Because it was Monday, only the Prime Minister and his cabinet were in the capital, but they needed protection, as did the country's senior financial civil servants and the buildings they occupied.

It had to be more than a coincidence that Grant had chosen the one route most likely to create maximum congestion and at the same time require Dave to deploy police and security service staff at multiple sites. The one positive aspect was that Police Headquarters was in one of the streets blocked by traffic. Dave might have to take calls from the Commissioner but he would not have to deal with him face to face for the time being. Unless the Commissioner was prepared to walk, which based on past experience was most unlikely.

Nicky tapped him on the shoulder and Dave ended his call and looked up. She indicated the waiting car. "It's been five minutes — time to go."

"Your mother was driving the car for Grant."

"I know," said Nicky.

"It didn't and it doesn't look good. She doesn't make it easy to find an innocent explanation for her involvement, does she?"

"She's as much a victim as the others."

"To be honest, Nicky, it doesn't look that way. I've been able to pull in more people, so I'm going to ask you to stand down."

Nicky opened her mouth to protest but realized it was useless. She would have thought and done exactly the same if she'd been in Dave's shoes. He regarded her sadly before snapping shut his laptop then getting into the car he nodded to his driver to leave.

Nicky was left standing alone on the street. Everyone had gone in the other cars behind Dave. She turned and looked up at the windows on the tenth floor. She could just make out Kezia looking down from the boardroom, shoulders raised, hands upturned, just as uncertain as she was. Ben, ordered by Dave to stay at Sage Consulting, was standing behind her, with his hands on her shoulders. Nicky saw Kezia lean back into him. It was as if he was comforting her, reassuring her, and a surge of jealousy welled up in her chest. Ben is supposed to be my friend, she thought.

Nicky heard whimpering and turned to see Petal limping up the ramp with her back foot dragging behind her, leaving a smear of blood on the concrete. She picked up the shivering pug and looked at her back leg.

"We need to take you to the vet, you poor wee thing," Nicky said, cuddling her close. "It'll be all right, Petal, I know it will," she said, trying to feel more confident than she sounded.

Chapter Forty-five

Euphemia pulled to a stop beside the Frenches' front door. It was open, as were the long windows in the living room, the heavy curtains now moving softly in the early-evening breeze. The lights were on in the house even though it wouldn't be dark for another hour. The police who had been guarding Justin had left as per Grant's instructions. If there hadn't been a helicopter hovering noisily overhead, and they hadn't just driven through a cordon of police cars stationed behind the high fence around the perimeter, then the dilapidated house would have looked gracious, even inviting.

As soon as Euphemia turned off the engine, Alison unclipped her seatbelt, opened the door and almost fell into the driveway, she was so eager to escape. Tearing at the tape around her mouth, she ran across the gravel and disappeared inside.

Euphemia checked the rear-vision mirror to see Grant's reaction but he just shrugged. His gray eyes held her gaze while he leaned across Jane and opened the back door, the pistol not moving from her head. Euphemia broke his stare and looked at Jane. She saw the hope fade in her eyes as she hunted her home for some relief and found none.

The thump of the helicopter above was an unrelenting reminder that they were being monitored, recorded, and analyzed, for the slightest weakness, for the smallest opportunity to intervene. Grant had to know that. Euphemia had listened as he negotiated with Detective Inspector Richards. He knew the score, so how did he think he could ever get away with this? How he could think the police would ever let him go? He'd only negotiated getting as far as the Frenches' house. What was to happen after that? It was as if, for him, it all ended here. She didn't want to think what that could mean.

Pulling Jane against him, he got out of the car and motioned with his gun for Euphemia to do the same. With his arm hooked around Jane's throat, the gun to her temple, he backed slowly towards the front door, expecting Euphemia to follow. Overhead the thump of the helicopter reverberated against the house, as it dropped down. She looked up into the noise, but the swirling downdraft brought up a cloud of dust whipping her face and body, forcing her to bend over and cover her eyes and ears with her arms. The glimpse she did manage was long enough for her to see the marksman leaning out to one side, a rifle raised and aimed at Grant. Take him, take him, she prayed. End this for all of us. But she knew the shot was impossible, the risk of hitting Jane too high.

Behind her, the gate at the end of the driveway beckoned. If she ran as fast as she knew she could, she would be free and safe in less than a second. The marksman above would surely cover her as she ran, but it would mean leaving Jane to God knows what. She couldn't do it. She had to see this through. She squinted against the dust and turned her head up to the helicopter again, knowing there would be cameras relaying everything back to a command center somewhere. Cupping her hands around her lips, she mouthed the words 'I love you', hoping this would not be the last time she said this to her family. She then turned and followed Grant into the hall, grateful to get out of the wind and dust and away from the deafening thumps resonating through her chest.

Grant was standing in the hall, waiting for her with legs apart, his pistol raised to shoulder height steadied with both hands, and aimed at her chest. He'd had her in his sights all along, a target he expected to hit should that be necessary. Jane was already in the living room by the sounds of the raised voices inside.

"I'm glad you didn't make a run for it," said Grant, taking off his helmet but not dropping the pistol. "It would have been a tricky shot but I could have had you before you got to the gate, no matter how fast you think you can run."

Euphemia didn't doubt for a moment he was telling the truth and this wasn't the time to find out if she could outrun a bullet, particularly one aimed directly at her. So far none of her so-called superpowers had been much use. It was incredibly frustrating to have to do as she was told when she had so much pent-up energy aching to be released. Later, she thought, I have to go back, replay everything, and see what I could have done differently. There must have been ways I could have used myself better and not let it get this far.

Then she remembered. Two nights before, without meaning to, she'd somehow made Grant and his brother leave her home just when they were about to muscle her aside and grab Jane. She had no idea what or how she'd done it but by making them focusing on her voice, they'd done as she asked. She had to try.

"You must be a good shot, Grant," she said, softly enough that he had to step closer and lean in to hear what she was saying.

"I've had my moments," he replied.

"I underestimated you. I'm sorry."

"It happens."

Euphemia focused on sidling into his expectations, and turning them into her own. She needed to lull him into thinking everything she said was a request he would automatically obey.

She eased her breathing and let tension fall from her neck and shoulders. She felt her vocal cords loosen, felt them relax, so her tone dropped to a lower and softer pitch.

"But it shouldn't. You deserve more respect," she said, watching his body start to respond. She saw his tautness leave him and his center of gravity change as his weight shifted and he softened.

"You must be pleased this is all over."

"Nearly over. Only a couple of things left and I'm gone," he said.

"Leave now. You've done enough." Euphemia watched as stillness enveloped him.

"Can't. No one else knows what to do."

"Alison?"

His tension increased and his breathing quickened as his finger tightened again on the trigger. His head lifted, and she felt their connection weaken.

"Me?" she asked. "Can I help?"

"No, you're the one." He shifted again, as if remembering.

"It's done, Grant. This is over. You can sleep. Remember sleep? You've earned a break. You've done such a good job. You're exhausted, Grant. So tired. You need sleep."

His head sank lower and his eyelids drooped. His finger on the trigger slackened so that the gun started slipping gently out of his grasp.

"Let the gun drop, Grant. It's over..."

"It's not bloody over!" screeched Alison from the living room door.

Grant, instantly alert, squeezed the gun back into his palm.

"I have to do everything myself, don't I?" said Alison. "Always have. You may think you're a super-thug, Grant, but you're only the hired help. She nearly had you. All this would have been for nothing."

"Shut the fuck up, Alison," warned Grant.

"Or what, Grant? You'll duct-tape my mouth again? I'd like to see you try. Justin will have your guts."

"I said shut up."

Euphemia heard the anger in Grant's voice. She could feel his break-point being breached. Alison's harpy words tipping him backwards to a place he loathed and where all restraint was gone.

"Alison, please," cautioned Euphemia. "Leave it, it was my fault. Yell at me."

But it was too little too late. With a roar, Grant pivoted, raised the gun and leveled it at Alison's eyes.

"When I tell you to shut up, shut up! Get inside."

Alison tried to hold her nerve but only managed a few seconds before disappearing backwards into the living room, calling to Justin with a whimpering whine.

"Now, you," said Grant spinning back to face Euphemia. "Don't utter another word. It would be better if you stopped breathing, but I haven't been asked to kill you. I've just been asked to do this."

He grabbed her by her arm and yanked her through the open door and out into the evening dark, out into full view of the helicopter overhead and the police manning the cordon outside the fence. He waited long enough for them to register who was standing there in the glare of the spotlights. Long enough for the police to establish their identities, but not long enough for them to get a clear shot. He pinioned Euphemia back against him with one arm and shot her in the upper thigh.

Grant made sure the police would see the arterial blood spurting from her leg, that they would register the shock on her face as the pain hit her brain, then see her collapse against him, unable to stand or defend herself, unable to function. Then Grant dragged her back inside and slammed the door shut.

Chapter Forty-six

Nicky heard about the shooting over the police-radio just as she left the vet. She heard the words but they weren't real because suddenly nothing around her was real. Cars drove past and disappeared. Pedestrians with places to go vanished into the evening gloom. Overhead the distant thud of a helicopter far away stopped. Below her, in the city, the sounds of angry car horns faded to nothing. The news echoed in her head as she sat alone unable to move, her mouth dry, her gut churning as she tried to process the information.

This victim was someone she knew. Her own mother, no less. Euphemia Sage, a happily married woman who ran long distances and had a dog called Petal. Her mother — the business consultant and her father's wife, a woman who never intentionally offended anyone, an upright law-abiding citizen, the epitome of boring, the first to step back from an argument, the last person to ever make a fuss — had been shot. Killed.

Nicky had joined the police force in part as a reaction against her mother's habit of retreating from conflict. Desperate as a teenager to stand apart from her and show her that withdrawal was not the only way, Nicky had joined the force straight from school, eschewing the university degree her parents had hoped she would do.

Nicky was the one who held the line and who stood up to bullies. Nicky was the last one to back to down, to run away. She was the danger junkie, not her mother.

Her phone rang. It was Dave.

"She was alive when we last saw her. He shot her in the leg. Made sure we would see. The worry is, Nicky, the doc says he got the femoral artery."

Nicky didn't need to be told what that meant. The femoral artery was huge and hard to control once opened. Unless her mother had help within two to three minutes, maybe four, she would have bled out and would already be dead.

"Anything else?" she asked quietly.

"Nothing. He dragged her back inside and after that someone shut all the windows and turned off most of the lights. We have no idea what's happened or is happening. We didn't get the house miked-up in time, Nick, and the long-range ones are too far away to be much use. But we're working on it."

Pictures of her mother flashed through her mind: her mother alive and laughing, hugging her daughters, kissing Kenneth when she thought no one was looking, eating ice creams at the beach, dragging Petal off for a walk when the little dog only wanted to lie on the sofa. She won't be dead. She can't be. It wasn't possible because her mother wasn't that sort of person. She might be quiet but she wasn't a victim. This wasn't part of her world and it didn't make sense. Nicky refused to entertain the idea any further. She needed to take back control and get everyone organized. There had to be something they could do once they were together.

"I'm calling Kezia and Dad. We'll meet you at the house. We'll help. We need to be there when she gets out. She'll be expecting us."

"Nicky, stop. Don't."

Nicky had already ended the call.

Chapter Forty-seven

"What have you done?" cried Jane, when she saw Grant half dragging, half carrying Euphemia into the living room, a veritable river of blood following in their wake.

Grant didn't have time to answer. He knew what he'd done. He knew what it meant to blow a hole in a major artery. He hadn't meant to shoot her that high in her leg. It was Alison's fault. She'd made him so goddamned angry he'd stopped thinking. Anger was a luxury he rarely allowed himself but the combination of Alison yelling at him, demeaning him, and knowing he'd almost been suckered by Euphemia's voice had got to him.

He didn't have time to think about that now. Dropping Euphemia on the floor, he searched for the origin of the artery in her groin and pressed hard. The bleeding slowed but didn't stop so he spread both hands on her groin and prayed. The bleeding stopped but he didn't dare take his hands away.

Jane was the only one of the three who seemed to understand. She ran and grabbed one of the rope tie-backs from the curtains and threw it to him to use as a tourniquet. Grant, desperate for help, looked up for Justin. Unbelievably, the man was occupied closing the windows and pulling the curtains and Alison was no use. She was frittering about beside the piano, pale at the sight of so much blood. It fell to Jane.

"Jane, put your hands here, hard. Don't take them off," he said making sure he was speaking into her good ear. Thankfully she heard and did as she was told while he pulled the tourniquet tight around the top of Euphemia's thigh, as high above the bullet wound as he could get it.

"OK, ease off slowly."

They watched as the tourniquet held. Grant motioned Jane to put pressure back on the groin.

"Just in case."

"She needs to go to hospital, Grant. Please. She'll die otherwise. Look at her," pleaded Jane.

"Not happening," said Alison, brave enough now that the bleeding had stopped to come closer. "Get something to mop up the blood, Jane. It's everywhere."

"You get it. I'm not leaving her. And from what you've been saying you know the house, my home. You know where everything is. Get the first aid kit from the kitchen and towels from the upstairs bathroom. Hurry."

"Those are the good towels, Jane," said Justin. "Alison, get the ones from the kitchen. There are old towels in the tradesmen's bathroom by the back door."

Jane looked at her husband with total disbelief.

"Fuck the good towels!" she yelled. "Do as I say, Alison. Not him. Now. Or else she's going to die and I'll make sure you go down for accessory to murder." Alison gulped and ran out of the room.

Jane took a good look at Euphemia. Her eyes were shut and she wasn't responding to anything or anyone. She was deathly pale with a blue tinge to her lips and she was cold, very cold. Jane bent down to listen for breathing and was rewarded with a faint puff of air against her cheek. Reassured she was alive, she ordered Justin to bring blankets.

"No need to be so bossy, Jane," he said sulkily. "Just because you've done a first aid course, no need to get on your high horse." But he did as he was told and brought back two blankets, putting them down on the only part of the floor not covered in blood. Jane pulled them over Euphemia's body, making sure she left the shot leg free.

"Get that foot stool and put it under her other leg. We've got to get as much blood as possible back to her heart."

"Please. Say please," said Justin. "Manners go a long way, Jane, even in an emergency."

Grant, still kneeling beside Euphemia, adjusted the tourniquet again and looked up at Justin.

"Get it."

Justin was about to reply but was stopped by the sound of Dave Richards on a bullhorn.

"Mrs. Sage needs to go to hospital, Grant. Now, or we both know she'll die. There's a helicopter standing by. Bring her out and it will be better for you later. Better for all of you."

"What does he mean, better for all of us? We didn't shoot her. You did. You're the one who is going to get done for murder, not me. Not Alison. This is your fault," said Justin.

"Bring her out, Grant," called Dave again. "Please. She has two daughters and a husband who love her. Do the right thing."

Alison came back into the room and threw the first aid kit at Jane and dropped the towels beside Grant before taking up her previous position near the piano, as far away from the blood and Euphemia as she could manage. "What are you going to do?" she asked.

"He doesn't have a choice, Alison," said Justin. "He has to take her out. I didn't sign up for murder. All I want is the jewelry, the real stuff, Jane. Make him take her out. She looks terrible, like she's going to die any minute."

"I'm going to do what I came here to do, Alison. I have to," said Grant quietly, ignoring Justin. "You'll be fine. It's me they saw shoot her. But afterwards, I'm going to need you to distract them while I finish up."

"What do you mean finish up? What's he talking about? This doesn't have anything to do with the jewelry, does it?" said Justin. "This never had anything to do with the jewelry."

"One more word, Justin, and I'm going to shoot you in the exact same part of the leg I shot her. Only I doubt that your wife would be as keen to stop the bleeding. Am I right, Jane?"

Jane smiled and shook her head without looking up. Now that the tourniquet was holding, she was too busy tying a thick bandage around Euphemia's leg over the site of the wound to pay much attention. "It'll stop blood going into the muscle, Effie," she explained quietly, as if reading to her from the first aid manual.

Outside, the bullhorn fell silent. It was clear Euphemia Sage wasn't coming out.

Chapter Forty-eight

Kezia and Ben were the first to arrive at the Police Command Center in the large truck parked behind the Frenches' house. Ben had commandeered a motorcycle when he got Nicky's call and it took another fifteen minutes weaving in and out of the stuck cars to arrive at the house. Traffic on the major routes in and out of the central city was starting to move but the roads to Thorndon remained blocked off and there was a one mile cordon around the house itself. Ben flashed his badge at every checkpoint and to those who queried the beautiful blonde woman riding behind him, he just said Kezia Sage and they were let through immediately.

"Have you noticed that as soon as anyone hears my name, they can't look me in the eye?" she asked.

Ben had picked that up but not wanting to alarm her, just grunted. Kezia had never been on a motorbike before and with the stop-start nature of their journey, she had had to put her arms right round him and hold tight. The feel of her body pressed into his back, her breath on the back of his neck, made him want to ride in a completely different direction, far away from the terrible news he was sure would be waiting for them at the house. He didn't want to have to face being there when she was told that her mother had died.

Ben had always avoided 'the knock' if he could. It was that depressingly awful part of a policeman's work when you were the bearer of bad news to unsuspecting relatives. Selfishly, today he didn't want this woman, of all the women in the world, to be told the news when he was there and forever after automatically associate him with her mother's murder.

Ben had never met anyone like Kezia before. She was completely innocent of her effect on men. She was the most intelligent woman he had ever met but, as with her looks, she was oblivious to her talent and assumed everyone was as smart as she was. This afternoon he realized that she thought it was normal to be able to run calculus in your head, and understand the most cryptic of computer codes immediately. And her eyes. Her eyes were pools of blue set into a flawless pale complexion, blushed with the softest pink. He prayed Euphemia was still alive.

Dave Richards was sitting in front of a bank of monitors when the two of them climbed up the steps into the Command Center. It was the size of an average shipping container and draped with wires and satellite dishes on the outside, with a bank of monitors taking up one wall on the inside. Two technicians were seated at the console, talking quietly into their headsets. Neither looked up as they concentrated on the multiple screens showing different views of the house now lit up by spots stationed on the walls around the perimeter. If anything moved, if anyone emerged, they would be seen.

Dave swiveled round in his chair and stood up. He was a tall man but Kezia was taller. In the close confines of the truck he had to tilt his head back to look at her. He wasn't comfortable.

"I'll say more when your father and Nicky get here but in the meantime, I can let you know your mother was shot in the leg and the docs have told us the bullet went through a major artery. We haven't seen or heard anything since she was taken back into the house."

Kezia nodded. That much she knew and was prepared for. She moved on immediately to examine the setup in the truck.

Ben could see her mind computing camera angles and the amount of light on each window, the positions of the spots and where the armed personnel were stationed on the wall. He listened as she asked first about the helicopter, then the range of the rifles and the number of marksmen. Her last question was where in the house they assumed the hostages were being kept and what the thermal imaging had told them.

Dave Richards barely kept up with her questions, they came so fast. When she stopped, he suggested they wait until the others arrived because he didn't want to have to go through everything again. Kezia agreed but reluctantly. Then to fill the silence she asked about Grant, requesting to see any information about him the police had. She scrolled through everything they had, shaking her head here and there, then asked to see the plans of the house and garden, including the fly-through video taken by the real estate agent prior to the house being listed.

Dave hesitated but nothing was happening and he recognized both her need for distraction and the technical expertise she could offer. While Kezia might not be police, she was asking all the right questions and any ideas were welcome. They were at an impasse and his options were limited.

Every possibility he considered risked the loss of more lives as he had to assume Grant wouldn't give up now without a fight. He was up for murder so he had nothing to lose. Dave had seen the amount of blood Euphemia had lost in the seconds before Grant had taken her inside. No one survived a bleed like that without specialist medical help delivered immediately. The silence that had greeted his offer of help more or less confirmed his assumption that Euphemia Sage was already dead. It was the lives of the remaining three hostages that concerned him now.

He stood back and let Kezia take his chair at the console and watched as she quickly brought up and absorbed more information. Both men were bent over on either side of her, looking closely at a screen displaying the downstairs floor plan, when the door opened and Nicky and Kenneth stepped into the truck.

Nicky could see at once what was happening. She'd been usurped and it was Kezia saving her mother now, not her.

"So I'm on the force and taken off the investigation. I'm not allowed to help and my sister, the civilian, is. Thanks a lot, Dave, and you too, Ben. You're both rocks. Both there for me when I need you."

Kezia swiveled round to see her father looking very scared and her sister livid with anger and she promptly burst into tears, then leapt up and hugged them to her.

Chapter Forty-nine

The truck wasn't the place to hold a family conference. Emotions were running high and the news Dave had to give them wasn't good. He suggested they adjourn to a nearby home that had been vacated by the owners at the request of the police. A place where the family would have privacy to come to terms with what he was about to tell them.

Dave had dispatched Ben to get coffee for everyone and the young detective was taking forever. While they waited, he paced the room unable to make eye contact, now and then checking his phone for a message that would give him an excuse to leave but which didn't arrive. He was old school. He figured women were better than men at dealing with tears and grief. Unfortunately, the woman he usually delegated to do the job was sitting looking at him, her face full of hope. He wanted to hug her to him and comfort her but he couldn't. His job was to tell her and her family the facts, answer their questions, and leave them to come to the only conclusion that could be made in this situation. He looked at his watch. The other three hostages, those who were still alive and had a chance — they needed him.

Dave looked at Kenneth sitting on the sofa, a daughter on each side, his broad shoulders dominating the space, his arms holding them close. He saw the man's exhaustion and contrasted this with the memory of his drunken happy voice on the phone the night before. If only a hangover was all he had to cope with. Dave admired his struggle to be brave for the sake of his daughters when deep down the man must know it didn't look good.

If only Ben would hurry up with the coffee. Giving people something to hold, preferably hot, something they had to pick up and put down, helped when there was bad news. It delayed people's reactions and made them pause before they said or did anything rash. Just when he was about to carry on without his favorite prop, Ben returned.

"Right," said Dave, while Ben was handing out the cups, "I know you all want to know if Euphemia is still alive. And the answer is we don't know."

Kenneth slumped back against the sofa with relief. The girls and he looked at each other and smiled hesitantly, hopefully.

Dave continued, "We know she was shot in the leg and we know the bullet pierced an artery and we know she was alive when she was taken back into the house. The man who shot her is still there, as are three other hostages. Jane French and her husband, Justin, and your receptionist, Alison Sinclair. We're doing our best to negotiate a safe exit but at this point in time, the shooter, Grant, is not responding to any of our attempts at communication."

Kezia opened for the family, "Thermal imaging? That would tell us for sure if Mum was alive. You haven't told us what that's showing."

"It's because we haven't got a camera."

Kenneth looked up from his coffee. "What do you mean you haven't got one? Surely a camera like this is standard equipment when there are hostages?"

"Yes, Mr. Sage, it is, but ours is being serviced and we've been told the only other available unit is in use already. In another operation."

Kenneth spluttered, "You've only got two cameras? We need to know if she's alive now, not next week. We need to get her to the hospital while there's still time."

"It's not great, I agree. But we are doing our best. The latest funding cuts haven't helped."

"I don't give a damn about funding cuts. I'll pay anything. Get one now, and God help you and the other people in there if you don't."

Nicky tried to calm her father. "He's trying, Dad, it's not his fault. Support him, don't yell at him."

After this is over, Dave thought, I won't be such a coward. I will ask her out. As to her father, he could understand his reaction.

Kezia was the only one who wasn't upset. Instead, she was busy on her phone, texting furiously.

"I've got one," she said, looking up. "One of the interns at work is a Physics major. You need an uncooled infra-red detector, don't you? He's got one he set up on his drone. Borrowed it from the lab, not legally, so you'll have to turn a blind eye or he won't cooperate."

Dave could have kissed her. A drone already loaded with a camera was just what he needed. It might help let him see inside or it might not, but it was better than anything else he had.

"Don't want to know. Just get him here. He can operate it. As long as he follows orders, we have a deal."

Chapter Fifty

Grant looked down at the unconscious Euphemia. The towels had sopped up most of the blood on the floor and now lay in a congealed heap to one side. Jane's first aid seemed to be helping. The patient was pale but she was still breathing.

Damn it, he hadn't meant to kill her. A flesh wound was all he needed, but she'd got inside his head. For a few seconds her words had soothed him and he'd let his guard down and he was a man again, not a killer. How sweet it would have been to walk away. No more orders from people like the Sinclairs. To be jerked back to reality by Alison had reminded him of his mother and he'd lashed out, nearly ruining everything in the process.

Grant prided himself on his ability to do the work without letting it get to him. He'd mastered the art of compartmentalization, something he'd read about in a psychologist's waiting room when he was twelve. No order was too brutal, no direction too strange. He did as he was told and as long as the money went into his account, he justified everything he did in the name of business.

In the beginning, there had been times when he'd been shocked at some of things he was asked to do, but that changed when he got to know what his victims had done. He realized no matter how much they protested their innocence, they were seeing him because they had offended someone, committed a crime against a crime boss or big businessman, or worse, hurt or abused someone else. True, sometimes an innocent bystander had got mixed up by mistake and Grant would pause for a moment and wonder what he was doing, but this never lasted long.

As the years passed, he was able to ask top price for his services and with that, he ended up working for the worst of the worst. He could use whatever means necessary as long as he was discreet. In the circles he operated in, his reputation was often sufficient on its own to achieve the desired outcome. If that didn't work then a preliminary chat would usually make any problem go away. But if the civilized approach didn't work, he had a system. The bodies were rarely found.

Grant already had a sizeable nest-egg locked away in several overseas bank accounts when he was approached to do what he hoped would be his last job. It wasn't the sort of work he normally considered. He was a professional and took pride in his work. The only reason he agreed to be the enforcer for a couple of amateurs like the Sinclairs was the amount of money promised in return. Half up front was one sweetener, and being able to put Mark, his brother, on the payroll was another, and that clinched the deal.

Mark was a pussycat and people took advantage of him in ways they wouldn't have dared to if it was known they were brothers. Grant also knew at least three people by name who would be delighted to have Mark killed slowly and thoughtfully if the connection to him was made, so he'd put a rumor out that Mark had moved to Auckland as a teenager and then disappeared.

Mark had never understood the principle of compartmentalization no matter how often Grant had tried to explain it. He lacked the ability to separate himself from his victims as Grant did and this had resulted in limited opportunities and increased vulnerability. He was useful in a fight so Grant had got him a job as a low-paid bouncer in one of the small strip clubs on Courtenay Place.

Grant had always protected Mark when they were growing up. He'd distracted their mother when she was in one of her drunken rages when they were little. He was the one who stood in the way and took the beatings from her boyfriends. This seemed to happen a lot, as the men their mother chose were universally quick to use their fists first and talk later, if at all. The boys would be beaten for the smallest of transgressions, such as eating too much food, or watching the wrong program on TV. One of them seemed to object to them breathing too loudly.

Grant also made sure he was the one who went to the woodshed with Uncle Jake, that is until he was old enough to defend himself, and Uncle Jake never came back.

Grant only ever allowed himself to love one person in his life, and that person was Mark. The months they'd spent working together for the Sinclairs had been happy months. The work consisted of looking tough, taking ridiculous orders from Malcolm and Alison, and trying not to laugh when they said stupid things. Sure they'd had to rough up some slow payers but the people they were roughing up weren't criminals and rolled over pretty quickly. Ordinary citizens and business people, it didn't take much for them to see reason and find a mutually agreeable solution, so this was like a holiday job. To be with Mark twenty-four/seven and be paid an enormous amount of money were added bonuses.

But it had to end. Grant knew life wasn't this good and there would be a reckoning.

He hadn't anticipated the reckoning would come from Alison. Over the previous year, he'd watched her go off to work in her cardigans and leggings, moaning as she left about having to run errands all day for the 'high and mighty boss, Mrs. Euphemia Sage'. He had watched her change as the loan-sharking business generated more and more money — money she wasn't used to having. She became the embodiment of a female Jekyll and Hyde — nice receptionist during the day and stiletto-wearing greed freak the rest of the time. Grant had even felt sorry for Malcolm, who resembled a possum caught in his wife's headlights, as she grew more ruthless and demanding.

One afternoon when Malcolm was at golf and Alison had just returned from shopping, Grant was still carrying the bags in from the car when she received a phone call. Suddenly, the woman who had just terrorized the retail staff at the Designer Clothing Gallery on Lambton Quay was no more. He watched as she shrank before his eyes.

"He wants to meet us," she said. "Now."

"Who does, Mrs. Sinclair?"

"My father — the person who pays your wages. The person who made sure Malcolm hired you and your brother. He's on his way. Don't leave me alone with him, Grant, please," she said, then added, "That's an order."

In that moment, Grant had almost pitied Alison. Almost.

Alison's father was a dapper little man, English with a posh accent and very well dressed. He had a very simple request — simple, but weird. He wanted fresh samples of blood taken from Euphemia Sage, arterial preferably, and he wanted them delivered in the containers he handed to Grant at that meeting. He would leave the details to Grant. And she was to be left alive because he didn't discount the possibility he might need more samples in the future. And he stressed *No fuss!* He wanted the samples taken as unobtrusively as possible so as not to alert anyone or draw the attention of the authorities.

It was only after he left that Grant realized the dapper little man hadn't acknowledged his daughter. He hadn't said one word to her. He didn't need to.

Chapter Fifty-one

"Known Simon long?" asked Ben, making sure the others weren't listening.

"About six years. We did Physics together. Total geek. I've offered him a proper job but he prefers independence."

"Very good looking."

"Is he?" replied Kezia, keying information into her laptop. "If you say so. Come and look at this, Dad, Nicky. We're linked into Simon's camera so we see everything the police see. Better than the police actually because I've also downloaded an image enhancement tool."

Nicky made a face and tried to look disapproving but what was the point. The dark screen sprang into color — greens and reds, orange and yellows, in shapes they recognized even though they were fuzzily psychedelic. Against the black background green cars and orange police officers came into view in their positions around the wall of the house. The image changed again as the drone flew in a wide arc towards and above the house, dropping down in front of it rather than taking the direct route. Kezia tapped some keys and the focus changed. The green-yellow of the car their mother had driven from the office took up a lot of room, its heat slowly dissipating in the cool evening. The drone flew over it and three bright red long oblongs dominated the screen.

"The windows at the front of the house," explained Kezia automatically. "Go higher, Simon, get above the roof and see if we can see more that way."

"Won't the roof be too thick?" asked Nicky. "To see people two floors down, I mean."

"Have to try, and then if you're right, Simon can try again through the windows, but there's light coming from inside, which runs interference with what we want to see. That's the problem."

They watched as the screen darkened again. The roof was slate and still warm from the day's sunshine, which meant the camera couldn't get a good image of anything on the ground floor. Kezia tapped some keys and brought up the resolution, then took it down again. She could tell Simon was doing his best to penetrate down to the living room where it was assumed the hostages were being kept, but it wasn't working. They could be pretty sure, at least, there was no one in the attic or on the second floor. They waited as the drone took a dive to the ground again and Simon lined it up in front of the window where the curtains hadn't been drawn as tightly as the others.

"There," said Kezia triumphantly. "There, and there. Do you see them? The pulsing yellow — that's a person, and they're walking." She tapped some more instructions into the laptop and the outlines of two others further back in the room at one end became more obvious. It was easy to see them now. Kenneth leaned over Kezia and pointed at the screen, counting off. Away from the two at the end of the room, there was a third person kneeling beside a weak outline of someone lying on the floor. Kenneth squeezed Nicky's hand so hard she yelped. He thumped Kezia on the back and turned to Ben, his eyes blazing with relief.

"Thank God. Thank God. She's alive. I knew she would be. She's a toughy, your mum. She'll survive anything." His voice cracked as he fumbled in his pockets for something to wipe away tears. Out came a paper serviette from the bar he'd been at the night before, smelling of pizza and whisky.

Nicky's phone rang.

"Your mother's alive," said Dave. "Weak signal, but she's OK.

Absolute bloody miracle. We'll do everything we can to get her out as soon as possible."

Nicky nodded, gulping back tears of relief and happiness.

"Nicky?"

"I'm here. I heard. I'll tell them. Gotta go." She clicked off.

"Look," said Kezia, "where did that one come from?"

Another yellow person, a much larger image, had appeared and was kneeling beside Euphemia and seemed to be doing something over her body or was it to her body? They couldn't be sure. Kezia tried to increase the image quality, but the colors blurred together. The person kneeling beside her had leaned over and blurred with the first person. They were struggling and the first person was thrown off, landing across the room. From the back of the room, one of the standing yellows came and stood over the sprawled figure.

A sudden gush of color pulsed from the prone figure. Nicky gasped and buried her face against her father's chest unable to watch. Kezia took her eyes off the screen and looked up at Ben, her blue eyes beseeching him to do something.

Kenneth watched as the pulsing color grew fainter as the signal from the figure on the floor weakened. He watched the yellow image stand up and walk across the room to a person standing away from the chaos. The two stood unmoving and there was something passed between them or maybe Kenneth was imagining it. The yellow image turned and raised his arm as if saluting. In the other hand he was carrying something, something square shaped with no signal, a black nothing on the screen. Then he left the room.

Immediately, the yellow who had been sent sprawling across the floor scrambled back towards Euphemia. The other two hung off to the side.

The screen pulled back showing more of the house. The large yellow man was moving fast now, negotiating the corridors to the back area where there were no other heat sources, the signal highlighted on the dark screen. He paused only to open doors and was moving purposefully.

"Look, he's trying to escape out the back. At least that's what it looks like. He's nuts."

The drone shot lifted higher to reveal a line of yellow outlines, the police stationed around the perimeter, starting to move, ready to capture the person leaving the house as soon as he in turn moved towards them.

"Got you," said Nicky.

The yellow man vanished. The line of police outside the house ran forwards, yellow images going in all directions as they searched the back of the house, but their quarry was gone. Disappeared.

Chapter Fifty-two

It was the pressure on her leg that brought Euphemia back from the darkness. She felt Jane above her struggling, and heard her protests and then the thump of her landing a few feet away. Someone pushed down hard and she could feel the clot plugging the hole in her artery slipping free as her blood pulsed freely again. It felt so good when the tourniquet loosened but only for a second or two. She felt glass tubes pressed against her bare skin one after the other until she counted three in total. The warm blood cooled quickly in the fresh air as it ran out of clot. Her body was being plundered and Euphemia was powerless to stop it. Cold seeped into her bones as she lay on the hard floor. She wanted to shiver but was too exhausted to summon the strength. All she could do was lie still and trust her body.

It takes three to four days to make and deliver new red blood cells and platelets into the circulation after a big bleed but Euphemia didn't have the luxury of days, or even hours. She needed those new cells in her bloodstream doing their job now. She felt like an observer in her own body taking a tour of the production control centers where she identified the processes that needed activation.

Within seconds of Jane retightening the tourniquet and the bleeding stopping, Euphema was aware which cells needed to go into overdrive to produce the appropriate hormones that would stimulate her bone marrow. Rachel's Switch found the code and in no time protein production had been ramped up in the stem cells in the fatty marrow. The two-day turnaround time zoomed down to two minutes and new cells poured into her arteries carrying oxygen to vital organs that had been shut down for the duration. She felt the repair going on in the muscle in her thigh and then blood vessels opening up again in her feet and hands. Her core temperature returned to normal and with the warmth her senses moved from sleep mode to active, heightened and empowered, better than before. She lay there, concentrating on her body making it work for her.

"It's like this, Jane, tell me where the jewelry is. I get out of here, and you three get to live. The police aren't going to wait. They'll be ready to storm in and take the place by force any minute."

"What do you mean 'I' get out of here? What about me?" asked Alison.

"Really, Alison," said Jane. "You can't still believe he ever intended to include you? Justin's a one-man band, always has been. Didn't you pick that up when you were in my bed with him? Didn't raise alarm bells that the sex was so selfish? You were never anything more than a way to get to me."

Alison turned to Justin, who refused to meet her eye. She pulled at his arm and tried to turn him round, but he shrugged her off.

"Jane's right. Not about the sex, of course," smirked Justin. "You told me I was the best you ever had. Much better than Malcolm. But I can't take you with me. There's not enough money for both of us."

Alison, her head sunk into her chest, wrapped her cardigan tightly around her and walked over to the curtains.

"Don't touch the curtains, Alison."

She ignored him.

"Stop it. Grant gave me his gun. Don't make me use it," said Justin, leveling the pistol at her. "Now why don't you go and sit by Jane, there's a good girl."

"You wouldn't shoot me, you don't have the balls," said Alison.

"Try me."

Alison studied him for a moment and stepped back from the window.

"Go over there and sit, both of you."

Jane checked Euphemia and got up to sit with Alison on the nearest sofa.

"He hasn't got the guts, Jane," said Alison.

"So that's why you're doing what he tells you to do, is it?" yelled Jane. Alison made her get up and they swapped places on the sofa.

"I'm humoring him, that's all. He's such a dickhead."

Justin raised the gun and fired. Plaster from the ceiling billowed down in a cloud of white dust coating his hair, face, and shoulders. When the last of the dust finally settled, Justin stood looking at them, his eyes peering out from a mask of white like two lumps of coal in the face of a snowman.

"That went well, didn't it?" said Alison.

Jane was about to add her bit but couldn't, she was laughing so hard. The two women collapsed in a heap on the sofa, laughing till tears rolled down their faces, the tension of the last few hours relieved by Justin's stupidity. They only stopped laughing when they smelled gasoline and heard dollops of liquid splashing around them, then over them, soaking through their clothes, cooling them before drying their skin and stinging their nostrils and eyes with the fumes.

Chapter Fifty-three

Gasoline. It hit Euphemia's brain like a bullet, triggering memories of teenage driving lessons and school. Maree had made her stop and fill the tank as part of her very first lesson. She remembered the heaviness of the hose and how she'd struggled with the pump handle. Gasoline had gone everywhere, ruining her tracksuit and shoes. The following day at school, the girls had refused to sit next to her as the smell clung to her hair. They'd made jokes about her being a human Molotov cocktail ready to explode into flames if someone lit a match. She was still anxious when she heard the sound of matches rattling in a box.

Now the smell was so strong she could taste it. It tugged at her senses, speeding her back to full consciousness and into the room with the others. The memory of rattling matches receded, replaced by the sounds of Jane and Alison huddled together, weeping.

On the other side of the room there was loud banging and crashing as someone pulled up floorboards. Nails creaked against wood, and she heard a man swearing. She lay still and waited.

"Your mother might as well have sealed the safe in concrete, Jane. How the hell were you ever supposed to get the stuff out when you needed it?" she heard Justin say.

"Skil-saw," said Jane.

"Ahhh, that's right," he paused, out of breath. "You did a carpentry course, didn't you, after she died, and before the upholstery course, then the furniture painting course and then the patchwork class. They went on and on, those bloody courses. And you accuse me of not paying attention. Hah!"

Euphemia opened the eye closest to the voices. The room was almost dark except for a lamp on the floor beside Justin. Old rugs had been thrown aside and he was on his knees with a crowbar, a pile of floorboards beside him and a dark hole in front of him. He staggered to his feet, panting, and leaned on the crowbar. He looked mad, his eyes blazing through dust and sweat as he turned to confront Jane.

"The combination, Jane," he puffed. "Tell me."

"I don't know it," cried Jane. "Truly, I don't."

Justin tried to hurl the crowbar at his wife but it was heavy and fell short, landing with a metallic clang on the floor then skidded in a pool of gas to rest beside the sofa. Alison and Jane clutched at each other whimpering.

"For fuck's sake," he yelled. "Stop it, or I promise you're both gonna burn." He leapt out of the hole in one bound, picked up a Zippo lighter from the top of the piano and flicked back the cover.

Alison screamed, disentangled herself from Jane, leapt up from the sofa, hurdled Euphemia, and had almost reached the door when Justin yelled at her, "I will shoot!"

Alison stopped. "At least I'd die quickly."

"If Jane tells me the combination, you won't have to die at all, any of you. It's up to Jane what happens — not me."

"Jane?"

"I don't know it. Do you think I'd sit here covered in gas with an idiot with a lighter in one hand and a gun in the other, and not tell? I. Don't. Know. It."

"I believe her," pleaded Alison. "And if she doesn't know, then let me go. It's over."

"I'll say when it's over," said Justin flipping the top on and off the lighter, "not you. Where did the old biddy put it, Jane? It'll be somewhere in this house. It has to be."

Jane hesitated. "I might know. I was going to tell you but you started with this lighter thing. Put it down and I'll take you."

"Tell me."

"I'm not certain and if it isn't there, then it might be in another place. I can't tell you each and every place she may have hidden it, can I?"

Jane's logic was indisputable. The question of what would happen to Alison if she and Justin went off to find the combination hung between them.

Justin was the first to move. He grabbed two curtain tie-backs.

"Come here and lie down." He indicated the floor beside Euphemia. Alison reluctantly did as she was told and he tied the cords tightly around her arm and leg and then repeated the knots around Euphemia's arm and good leg. One could not move without the other.

"OK, Jane, show me and hurry bloody up."

Chapter Fifty-four

"Hear that?" whispered Euphemia.

Alison startled, jumped, and the knots binding them together tightened.

"Christ, you're alive," she said turning her head. "I thought you were dead. Or soon would be. It was getting creepy being tied to you."

"I'm not at peak fitness, but I'm alive."

"Father said you'd be amazing when your powers started but I bet he had no idea just how amazing. Hear what, by the way?"

"Outside," whispered Euphemia. "Police."

Alison stifled a sob. "Thank God. If we yell they'll know we're here. Quick before he gets back." As she took a deep breath, Euphemia yanked her arm.

"Stop! Jane! We can't leave her."

"You're such a goody-good. She can look after herself."

"Then consider this. The last thing we need is the police coming into a room soaked in gas with guns blazing. One spark and we all go up."

Alison shuddered. "Well, what do you suggest?"

"We need to get closer to the windows where we can talk without Justin hearing. Do you think you can get some traction and pull us both? My leg is better but it's not back to normal yet."

Alison dug her free heel into the floor and pulled. They moved a few inches. She did it again, her face red with effort, and this time she tried to add traction with an elbow. They moved another few inches.

"Oh for goodness' sake, I didn't realize you were so unfit," said Euphemia. "Bend your other knee, the one tied to mine. Plant it on the floor."

Alison did as she was told and found herself whizzed around so they faced away from the windows. Euphemia kicked off with her good leg and the two of them slid so fast across the floor they would have hit the wall and gone through it if she hadn't pulled their hands up to stop them at the last minute.

"I'm going to be sick," said Alison.

"Shush," said Euphemia, listening for footsteps on the gravel outside. When she heard them directly through the wall she called out softly, "Officer. It's Euphemia Sage. You can't storm this room. There's gas everywhere. We're soaked in it. Any explosions, any sparks, and we'll be incinerated. Got that?"

"Acknowledged. Can you get out?"

"No, we can't leave Jane. She's upstairs with Justin. He has a gun. I think the house is booby-trapped. Tell Dave Richards."

The officer spoke softly into his mike and there was a moment of quiet then she heard him give the order to pull back.

She counted ten people crunching softly on the gravel as they moved back out of position, away from the house. The soft buzzing of what she assumed was a drone still hovering beside the windows remained. Euphemia heard drawers opening and contents being tipped out directly above her, then cupboard doors opening and slamming shut. She wished the police would hurry up and come back and tell her what they were going to so. They didn't have much time.

"Why did Grant take my blood, Alison?"

Alison took a deep breath. "Father needs it. He's been waiting for years."

"I don't understand."

"Father is behind all this. He made me get close to you. I had to watch and as soon as I saw any changes then I was to let him know.

Typically you took forever. He assured me I would only have to stay until you were fifty-two, the average age of menopause in case you didn't know. But you... had to take an extra year- fifty-three. You really piss me off."

"You've gotta be kidding."

"Father's a geneticist specializing in mitochondrial DNA, the type you can only get from your mother."

"Not totally correct but go on."

"Well, smarty-pants, as usual you don't need me to tell you anything, do you? I'll shut up."

"I'm sorry, Alison. Tell me. I don't know much, just what I learned from Wikipedia. You've been brought up with it. Please?"

Alison couldn't resist showing off. "I do know a bit more than Wikipedia. When I was growing up and after Mother died, it was the only thing he cared about. He worked as a research scientist for his company during the day and then he'd come home and spend all night working in the lab. I had a nanny. Sometimes I didn't see him for weeks. I'd hear his car drive up and him walking past my bedroom, then the door to the lab shutting."

"Sad, Alison, it really is, but there's no time for the movie-length version."

"I thought you might be the one person who would understand but you had your aunt, didn't you. I had no one," said Alison bitterly. "Until one day, he brought your mother home and everything changed. He spent less time in the lab and suddenly we were a family. I had to be nice to your mother, make her want to stay. It was all down to me, he said, to keep her happy. He'd found out your mother had some sort of magical DNA. She'd been drinking and started talking about her family — Rachel and a switch — you know the rest. He thought he'd lucked onto something huge. For a time, we were happy. Father didn't spend all his time in the lab. We even ate meals together. She told me about you and how she couldn't wait for us to meet. She said you were more special than she would ever be. Something to do with your father."

"My father? She told you about my father?"

"That was it. But according to my father, it didn't make sense."

"What was she like? Did she really say she was coming to get me?"

"She'd even booked the tickets. She was great, but only when she was sober. You've seen the photos of her partying... she used to get totally smashed. She was scary. Father would get angry, there'd be a scene and then deadly quiet the next day. She couldn't stop herself, she said. We'd have a few weeks of calm and she'd be nice again."

Alison paused and smiled remembering. Euphemia nudged her sharply. "Hurry up, finish. They'll be back soon and I need to know."

"They were the happiest months of my life. Then she caught him drugging her and taking her blood when she was out to it and it all went pear-shaped. There was a huge fight and she stormed out threatening to go to the police. Father grabbed his bag and went after her. I saw him come back later that night. He thought I was asleep and didn't see but he was soaked to the skin and the next thing the police were there telling us your mother ran the car into the duck pond and drowned. They said she was drunk but I know she was totally sober when she left. Father wouldn't let the police talk to me. Told them I was too fragile."

Euphemia could feel the sadness in Alison's body.

"He told me over and over again it was my fault, and that if I'd been nicer to Fredericka, she wouldn't have run off. He said I had to make it up to him. Said I had to come here, to New Zealand, to the ends of the earth and find you. And I did, but even that wasn't enough. He made me marry Malcolm because Malcolm had been to school with Kenneth. He thought that would make us closer, you and me. He didn't know what Malcolm was like. Thank God I didn't have kids. That would have been the end, having lots of little Malcolms running around."

"You did all that because your father told you to? I don't believe it, Alison."

Alison wriggled to get comfortable but only succeeded in tightening the cords. "Surely with your superpowers, Euphemia, you could bust us out of these?"

"I wish. I'm still recovering. But we can sit up." She planted their joined legs on the floor and pushed them both back, sliding up so they could lean against the wall.

"Tell me when you're back to normal. I don't like being this close. You're the reason I've had to stay here, miles from home, and why I had to put up with Malcolm Sinclair. I don't especially like you."

"Mutual," said Euphemia, "but as long as we're tied together and waiting for Justin or the police, whoever comes first, tell me exactly why your father wants my blood. Surely he got enough from Fredericka?"

"That's the problem. She died too soon. She hadn't started menopause and so the switch hadn't been activated. Whereas you..." she left the sentence hanging.

"Whereas I have. You spied on me and told your father that it had happened."

"Grant has taken enough blood to make my father very happy. At least I hope to God it's enough. I want a life."

Euphemia shuddered. She felt violated. How dare he? Later, she told herself, later when you're out of this, when you can think properly, his time will come.

"So what are you planning now you've fulfilled your part of the deal, Alison?"

"I'm free. Father has what he wants and he doesn't need me or want me, I guess. Justin and the jewelry were supposed to be my ticket to a new life. You can see how that's turned out."

Euphemia tried to muster some sympathy but couldn't. Sure, Alison had been manipulated by her father. But she had to have understood what he was doing and that helping him was wrong. No one has to marry anyone. She could have left or got help. But then, thought Euphemia, who would have believed her? Lying in wait for a woman to go through menopause so her blood could be stolen to find the secret of eternal youth, oh and the switch to turn on superpowers? She realized if it hadn't been Alison, her father would have found someone else. He would have stopped at nothing to get what he wanted. He was the real villain.

"What's his name? Your father's?"

"Varies," said Alison. "I think he's using Paul Spooner at the moment, but he changes it all the time. Other people know he's onto something and are after him, he says."

Euphemia touched Alison's hand, curling her fingers around Alison's, but got no response. Turning her head, she saw the muscle at the side of Alison's mouth flicker leaving behind the remnant of a smirk.

Chapter Fifty-five

"So what are you going to do?" interrupted Kenneth.

Dave Richards was briefing the family. Telling them about the gas-soaked living room hadn't been easy. They'd been happy when he arrived, knowing that Euphemia was alive and, by the strength of her thermal image, getting stronger every second. It was remarkable. Amazing. A miracle even. And very hard to explain. How could a middle-aged woman survive a normally fatal gunshot without medical help?

"Everything has changed," he said. "I can't risk sending in the assault team. One spark and that old house will go up like a Guy Fawkes bonfire. You've been watching so you know two of them are upstairs. Euphemia told us it was Justin and Jane. We heard a gunshot so we think Grant gave Justin his gun. No, we haven't found Grant yet, but we will."

Silence greeted his summing up of the situation.

"So what else did Mum tell you?" asked Nicky.

"She said she wasn't leaving Jane."

Kenneth groaned. "Bloody woman. Stubborn as all hell."

Together Nicky and Kezia turned to their father, hoping he would have the solution. He'd had the answers to their problems when they were growing up, after all. But for the first time either of them could remember, he shook his head.

Ben broke the silence and pointed to the screen. "Focus in on the two upstairs," he said. "Watch. They're searching for something by the looks of it. I reckon when they find it they'll go back to the living room. That's our chance. But we'll need to be ready and we'll need to be fast. Do we have any stun grenades?"

"Yes but we can't use them because of the fire risk."

"Maybe not in the room," said Ben. "But we could set them off outside, on the driveway. The windows are huge and would easily transmit the blast but any spark would stay outside."

"We need the curtains out of the way, but I get what you're driving at."

"We set them off as close as possible to where Justin is standing. And a team goes in and extracts the hostages, hopefully before he can light the match."

"It could work," said Dave. "Ben, come back to control with me. The rest of you stay here."

"But..." said Nicky.

"Nicky, you need to stay out of it and be here with your family."

"But..."

"Drop it. We don't have time," said Kenneth. "Get on with it, Dave. Nicky, I need you here with me."

Ben and Dave had already left.

Chapter Fifty-six

"Remember," said Euphemia. "Lie still. When Justin gets back, it's really important he thinks we're still tied up and even more important that he thinks I'm still unconscious."

"You don't need to go on and on about it. I'm not stupid."

Euphemia bit her tongue. She had no choice but to trust Alison not to give them away. She was gambling that Alison had weighed up the risks and that for the time being Team Euphemia gave her better odds of survival than Team Justin.

Upstairs she heard a muffled but triumphant yell. Justin must have found the combination.

"Hear that? They're coming back. Now lie still and look convincing."

"Didn't hear a thing, but no doubt you have super-hearing powers along with everything else. You make me sick."

"Just stay quiet and remember what I said."

"You think you're just amazing, don't you? You and your super-hearing, your super-strength, your super-healing. Wait till my father cracks the code... there'll be so many people with superpowers, you'll just be one of many."

Euphemia put her free hand over Alison's nose and mouth and squeezed tightly. "I said shut up and I meant it." Alison tried to wriggle free. Euphemia had had enough and, raising herself on her elbow, leaned over and lightly head-butted her. Dazed and limp, Alison was finally quiet. Pity it's only temporary, thought Euphemia.

The door opened and Justin pushed Jane ahead of him towards the hole where the safe had been concealed. In his haste, he made only a cursory check of Euphemia and Alison. He pushed Jane into the hole with his pistol.

"Open it. Hurry."

Euphemia peered over Alison's chest and watched as Jane did as she was told. Poor Jane. Silent tears were streaming down her cheeks as she turned the dial and the tumblers clicked into place one after the other. She pulled up the heavy door and handed Justin a box, identical to the one that had contained the fake jewelry. Justin grabbed it from her and tried to open it but it was locked. There was no key. He howled in frustration and slammed the box down on the piano, setting off a sour bass chord that reverberated around the room.

He grabbed Jane by the collar and lifting her off her feet and out of the hole, pulled her face into his. "Where is the fucking key, Jane?" he yelled, sending spittle over her face.

Jane looked straight back at him, unblinking. "I swallowed it. Upstairs when you weren't looking."

Justin opened his hands as if an electric shock had gone through them and Jane dropped to the floor. For a moment he was puzzled. How could this woman, his wife, do this to him? She wasn't anything like the woman he'd married. She was staunch and willing to thwart his every move even when he had a gun, even as she shivered in her gasoline-soaked clothes. He shook his head and looked at her, not knowing her after all, and turned and picked up the box.

Step away, Jane, thought Euphemia, willing her to move. Jane did exactly that, inching backwards to the windows, closer and closer to the heavy curtains. Justin, absorbed with opening the box, didn't notice until he glanced up. Furious, he took his lighter out of his pocket.

"You deserve this. Beg, Jane, beg for your miserable life." And clicking the lighter, a flame shot up.

Euphemia rolled away from Alison and stood up. She tested her weight on her leg. It was strong — stronger in fact, as was her whole body. There was someone outside the window Jane was standing next to. She heard the word stun grenade whispered once, but once was enough.

"Go, Jane, now!" yelled Euphemia, then she ducked down behind the sofa putting both arms over her face and ears. Jane, wresting her gaze from the flame, pulled back the curtain at the exact same time as a hand punched through the glass and pulled her backwards through the window and out into the night. Justin looked in shock at the dark hole where only a millisecond before Jane had been standing. Hearing the breaking glass, Alison sat up to see what was happening, just as the first grenade exploded outside.

Not as effective as if it had been detonated in an enclosed space, the intense flash of light was still enough to blast the backs of Justin's eyes setting every nerve ending alive simultaneously, completely blinding him. One hundred and seventy decibels of sound, partially neutralized by the night air and largely rebounded off the walls of the house, still managed to penetrate the living room and stretch his eardrums to breaking point, the pain searing into his brain, incapacitating him, dropping him to the floor. As if it were a candle on a child's birthday cake, the lighter was extinguished by the wave of sound and clattered harmlessly to the floor beside him.

Chapter Fifty-seven

Two officers dressed head to toe in black stepped through the broken window, weapons raised, torches on full beam, and scanned the room. Glass crunched beneath their feet as they slowly moved forward. Euphemia had weathered the blast reasonably well but her ears were still ringing when she stood up behind the sofa, arms raised, eyes blinking in the bright light of their torches. She could feel the nerves in her ears repairing themselves but she wasn't yet able to hear clearly what they were saying. She watched as they mouthed the words 'Get out, get out now' to her.

Behind her, Alison was writhing on the floor, screaming that she was blind and was dying. Sitting up when she did, she like Justin had taken the full brunt of the explosion. One of the officers went to her and tried to reassure her, but Alison, unable to hear or see anything, recoiled in fear when she was touched and curling into a ball, promptly wet her pants. It took three officers to get her to sit up and then they had to pick her up and carry her out to safety, her wailing and screams echoing around them.

Distracted by Alison and delayed somewhat by her relief that it was finally over, Euphemia stayed where she was. She wanted to see the officers arrest Justin and get him out of the house before she really could believe it was actually over.

One of the two officers who had come through the window was standing over him, nudging Justin with the barrel of his rifle, while the other picked up the pistol and removed the cartridge chamber.

Justin hadn't moved. He lay face down on the floor just beside the hole in the floorboards, arms tucked underneath him. The officer nudged him again with the end of his rifle and waited but there was no response. He knelt down, gripped Justin's shoulder and rolled him onto his back.

From across the room, Euphemia saw Justin smile just before he clicked the lighter and his body erupted in flames. The officer hadn't noticed the pool of gasoline he was kneeling in when he'd turned Justin. His trousers caught and he too was engulfed. His partner, about to come to his aid, was beaten back by flames which snaked across the floor barring his way and setting the furniture alight around him. Justin screamed as his body crackled and spat in the heat, blackening lips peeling back against his white teeth in a horrible grimace.

Euphemia leapt the sofa, picked up the burning officer and carried him out the window into the cold night air, dropping him onto the gravel, spinning him over and over to put out the flames. Others arrived as if by magic from the darkness and took over, rolling him on the ground, then covering him in foam. She ran back into the room, which was now well ablaze, smoke billowing above the flames, choking the oxygen from the atmosphere, burning her eyes so she could barely see. She couldn't drop low because the tinder-dry floorboards were now well alight. She had to rely on feel, the feel of the movements of air, indicating an obstruction that something solid was in front of her or to the side. Every sensory organ was on full alert, feeding information to her brain as she searched for the second officer. She found him where he had collapsed, having got as far as the door into the hall. Slinging him over her shoulder, she ran out through the hall into the night air, happy to feel him coughing and spluttering against her as he gulped oxygen.

Sirens and flashing lights pierced the night. One side of her body was cooking in the heat from the fire and the other was freezing in the cold. She shivered and turned back to look at the house licked by streaks of orange and red against the black. The sound of the fire as it roared through the old wood was deafening. Beams cracked, then crashed, sending showers of sparks pluming into the darkness. Windows in the living room popped and shattered glass rained onto the gravel.

She turned at the sound of someone calling her name. Through the smoke, Euphemia saw Kenneth and the girls running towards her, laughing and crying, relieved to see her alive. She opened her arms and they fell together, hugging and weeping with joy.

Kenneth felt Euphemia tense in his arms. Over Nicky's questions and Kezia's assurances of love, Euphemia heard a cry for help, away off inside the burning house. A chill went through her as she recognized Ben's voice. He must have been searching upstairs when Justin had lit the fire, and was now trapped. She could hear his cries for help, soft, his voice hoarse with smoke. There was nothing she could say. She kissed Kenneth and extracting herself from the arms of her family before they could hold her back, she ran around the side of the house. Her silhouette briefly lit against the flames and disappeared into the darkness.

Chapter Fifty-eight

The noise of the fire and the firefighters made it difficult, even for her, to identify exactly which part of the house Ben was trapped in. She called out to him to tell him she was coming for him and to stay where he was, even though she knew he wouldn't be able to hear her. She had to trust he would keep yelling, keep trying to survive.

Luckily the fire had started in the front of the house and had not yet reached the back, although it wouldn't be long. Smoke was pouring out of the gaps around the upstairs windows, which thankfully were smaller on this side of the house.

Two firemen had just been detailed to this area and were training a single hose on the back wall, soaking the roof from behind to contain the blaze at the front. They were concentrating so hard on what they were doing, they didn't see Euphemia until she was halfway up a drainpipe next to a small window, which she assumed would be a bathroom which was directly above the back door.

One of them yelled at her, ordering her to get down, as the other radioed command. Then they did exactly what she'd hoped they would do. They tried to hose her off the wall, soaking her clothes and every part of her with freezing water. Hand over hand she easily pulled herself up the pipe, grateful for her wet clothes, and then swinging herself up, she kicked her legs through the window. Her body followed and she was inside. The men gaped in astonishment, unsure what they'd seen, each checking with the other. As one they moved the hose again, this time training the water on the smashed window and into the house behind. Neither said anything. They were too experienced to think this would end well.

Smoke was curling up under the door into the bathroom. Euphemia stopped and listened. She heard Ben. He wasn't far away. She tried to recall the layout of the house but, never having been upstairs, all she could remember was the second floor balcony leading off the staircase under the stained-glass window. She assumed it must lead to bedrooms, and Ben must have been searching these rooms.

Euphemia looked around and found a pile of what Justin had called the 'good towels' on a stool beside the basin. Snowy white and thick, they'll do, she thought, and she threw some on the floor where the hose was sending in gallons of water. Others she dropped in the basin, then turned on the tap. The water spilled out onto the floor and soaked the towels in no time. She wrapped one around her head and over her mouth leaving a gap for her eyes and ears. Peeling off her top she draped wet towels front and back and pulled her top back on to hold the wetness against her skin.

As she opened the door cautiously, the heat hit her like a tidal wave, melting the mascara on her eyelashes. Searching out a path to her lungs, the dried air instantly stripped whatever moisture she had in her throat and lungs. She dropped to her belly and started crawling towards where she guessed Ben had to be. Below her, the floorboards were getting hotter. Nails popped out of their holes and bounced against the underside of rugs. She pulled one rug along with her as protection, grateful again for the thickness of Justin's good towels.

Ben's voice was non-existent by the time she finally found him. She pushed open the door to the last bedroom and there he was, lying semi-conscious trapped under the collapsed corner of a four-poster bed. He jumped, banging his head on a railing, when her hand touched his leg through the smoke. She pulled out the wettest towel and started draping it around his head. He caught on quickly and took over, struggling, his eyes widening with the relief of the moisture.

Euphemia felt the building shudder. She heaved the bed off Ben and pulled him towards her but she saw his eyes roll back in his head. Lapsing in and out of consciousness, he wasn't in good shape and would need her to get him back to the bathroom. How she was going to keep a hold of him was the problem. He was too weak to hold on to her and she needed both arms to elbow her way across the floor. His weapon was so hot it almost burnt her hands when she yanked it free and unclipped the strap. Lengthening it she looped the belly of the strap under his arms and clipped the ends together around her neck. It would work but it wouldn't be comfortable.

Ben did what he could when he came to but the smoke soon overcame him and again he lost consciousness, his dead weight pulling hard and painfully against her throat every time she moved. She lifted the strap up against her chin and then against her forehead where it seemed to work, although rather frustratingly it slipped off again and again and she would have to slide it back before pulling Ben forward, inch by painful inch, to the sanctuary of the little bathroom. The roaring noise above told her the fire had reached the ceiling space. Roof tiles dropped randomly, burning hot into the ceiling plaster, but luckily, it held.

On one side Euphemia heard the lead in the stained-glass window melting, the glass buckling and bowing as it too melted or cracked and slid to the floor, the night air sucking the flames from above, out through the holes. The noise was overwhelming.

Euphemia looked down at the floorboards turning black under her body. The smoke was curling even more thickly up through the gaps by the time Euphemia had pulled Ben into the sanctuary of the bathroom. She slammed the door shut behind them just as there was an almighty crash. She felt the house waver, and figured the staircase and the balcony, the internal support, had finally given way and crashed onto the floor below. It wouldn't be long before the outside walls followed, taking the bathroom with them down into the fiery pit that had once been Jane's home.

The air was slightly clearer near the window, but only just. She ripped the towel from Ben's head, grabbed him under his arms, lifted him up and draped him face first across the sill, unconscious but alive. It was in this moment that she realized the little room wasn't full of smoke. It was full of steam. Every surface was soaking wet. The men outside must have sent a tankerful of water into the window after she disappeared. She would have cried with relief, but there was no time. She could hear the fire behind her, tugging at the door, banging it against the frame. Pulling herself up beside Ben, who was straddled on the windowsill, she was immediately drenched. Below her, the firemen — astonished but ever professional — kept their hoses trained on the walls and roof above the window, raining water down onto them, steam rising in clouds from their clothes.

Euphemia could have jumped then. She could have leapt to safety first. It would have been easy. She could have waited on the lawn while the firemen brought their ladder into position and rescued Ben. That would have been the sensible thing to do. But of course she didn't, couldn't do it. She had to stay with him until she was certain he would be OK. She had to ignore the sound of the flames battering the other side of the flimsy bathroom door and make sure he got out. Only then could she look after herself.

She watched as a ladder was braced against the wall and a fireman in breathing apparatus ran up it. She helped lift Ben further out over the sill and onto the fireman's shoulder and waited as they descended. Ben being still unconscious made this no easy task, so she stayed and held the ends of the ladder hard against the wall, steadying it so it didn't slide or tip and send Ben and his rescuer hurtling to the ground.

"Euphemia, for God's sake, jump, jump now!" she heard Kenneth calling. There he was standing on the grass, their daughters beside him, waiting there for her, as he'd always been.

She heard the building groan and buckle as she balanced on the sill, and felt a suck of air pulling her back. She launched herself out into the night just as the entire wall tumbled inwards, falling to the ground in sections like so many Lego bricks, taking the ladder with it and sending up showers of sparks and flames around her.

Euphemia Sage soared away from the flames, away from the empty hole where a house had stood only seconds before and landed on the lawn beside her family as if she had just stepped off a train. Momentum sent her straight into Kenneth's arms and he didn't let her go.

Chapter Fifty-nine

Jane was sitting up in her hospital bed wearing every piece of jewelry she owned when Euphemia arrived. The box lay empty beside her.

Diamonds and sapphires glittered around her neck and wrists. She had hooked her earrings one after the other into long lines of golden jewels, which dangled gaily from each ear over her shoulders and down the front of her white hospital gown. The extravagance of the pieces contrasted oddly with the bandages swathing her nose and mouth. Her hair, unwashed and still sprinkled with yesterday's debris, stuck out wildly from under a modest tiara overwhelmed with the pieces that didn't fit anywhere else. She looked like a very expensive Christmas tree and all the lights were flashing.

"Look, Effie," said Jane loudly, "the police found the box in the rubble and brought it over this morning. Aren't they marvelous?" And I produced the key only half an hour ago. Brilliant timing.

Euphemia shut the door and, pulling up a chair, sat down beside the bed and put a finger to her lips.

"Sorry," said Jane, "I keep forgetting. The doctors told me it might take a few weeks for the ringing in my ears to go away and they're not sure the hearing will ever come back in the left ear, but hey, Effie, we're alive."

"Thanks to you," said Euphemia, picking up her hand thick with rings. "I wouldn't be alive if you hadn't looked after me."

"Forget it," said Jane, her attention on her other hand, which she was holding out admiringly in front of her turning it this way and that. She was staring lovingly at the diamond engagement ring the police had removed with considerable difficulty from Alison the night before. "Look, I got my watch back too."

"I'm pleased for you."

"What did you say? I didn't hear you?" yelled Jane, tearing her eyes away from her booty.

"I said I'm pleased you got it all back. You fought mighty hard to keep it."

"I did, didn't I? I'm quite proud of myself. For once I didn't roll over and give in to him," she said quietly. "I spent my whole life doing that. You'll think I'm awful, Effie, and don't tell anyone, but a part of me is glad he's dead."

Euphemia got up and walked over to the window. The morning breeze was tossing cherry blossom petals in drifts of pink across the lawn below. The sun was shining and across the street past the cars, she saw Kenneth waiting for her, his hands laden with bags of fresh vegetables he had bought at the Tuesday farmer's market on the reserve. He was so handsome, better looking now than when they first met. She raised a hand and waved but he didn't see her.

"Part of me isn't though," said Jane. "Pleased, I mean. Justine is going to pop in later on the way to the airport. She was always a daddy's girl and I have no idea what I'm going to say to her."

Euphemia turned back to the glittering Jane. "Don't you think she deserves to hear the truth?"

Jane looked shocked. "I don't think so. The less she knows what really happened, the better."

"Won't she find out from the papers or the net?"

"She won't get a chance. She's brought her trip to New York forward. When I rang and told her that Justin had been killed in the fire and that the house was gone, she was upset, naturally. She hung up but then ten minutes later she called back and told me she'd changed her ticket to tonight. The young are so resilient, aren't they?"

"Justine is remarkable, Jane. She isn't worried about you?"

"I told her there was nothing she could do now and it's best for everyone if she gets on with her life. She's going to do so well in New York, Effie. I know she will and I don't want to hold her back. She said I could come and visit when she's organized."

"I hope you do. It would be good for you to get away. You've been a great friend, Jane. Thank you."

"Don't be silly, you don't need to thank me. It was me who got you into this mess. Though, I hate to think what would have happened if I hadn't done that first aid course."

They sat together in silence looking at each other.

"Look at my jewels, well, Mummy's jewels.

Aren't they gorgeous?"

"They're magnificent. I'm just not sure if they're worth everything we went through."

"I'm not either."

Jane glanced at Euphemia. "I didn't know Justin hated me so much."

"I don't think he hated you. I think he hated himself and couldn't see any way out of the mess he'd got you both into."

"That's it. Probably. One day I'll think about it but not now. It's too much. I can't wait to see my girl. She's going to do so well in the Big Apple. They'll snap her up. At least we did one thing right, Effie."

There was a knock at the door and the dinner lady barged in holding an iPad officiously in one hand. "Pumpkin frittata or the fish?" she demanded.

"What sort of fish is it?" asked Jane.

The lady looked up, annoyed that someone was asking the same question she had answered twenty times already this morning. The sight of the grandly bejeweled and bandaged Jane sitting up in bed made her pause but only for a moment.

"Cod."

"I'll have the frittata."

"Right. Twenty minutes." The door closed behind her.

"Alison is locked up pending charges. And Malcolm, they arrested him at the airport," said Euphemia.

"Good. That's where they both belong, and I hope they put them in the same cell. Just what they deserve — each other. And Grant?"

"They found a tunnel in the old coal shed behind your house. Did you know about it?"

Jane thought for a moment. "News to me. Hold on. I remember, about three months ago, Justin said there were problems with the drains and we had workmen there for weeks. Do you think they dug it out then?"

"Must have. It led out under the wall and then down under the street for about half a mile. Came out in the blind garden just near the tennis club and the American Embassy. They're getting the CCTV tapes later today. Dave says he'll be long gone."

"I don't understand why he wanted your blood, Effie. In fact, there are a few things I don't understand."

Euphemia stood up and looked at her watch. "The nurse said I wasn't to stay long, so I'll let you rest. We can talk later," she said walking backwards to the door.

"But Effie."

"Jane, it's a small point, I know, after everything we've been through, but please, could you please stop calling me Effie. My name is Euphemia."

Chapter Sixty

"Are you going to tell me?" asked Kenneth, from behind the paper.

They were sitting in the garden in the sunshine, the morning's breeze having died away. They'd had lunch and Petal was lying on a red cushion at their feet, looking adoringly at them over the round plastic collar that stopped her from tearing at the bandage on her back foot.

"Tell you?"

"Tell me. Everything."

"Jane is coming to stay with us until she finds somewhere to live. She had nowhere else to go and I felt sorry for her."

"I understand, and that's fine. She can stay as long as she likes. No, I meant, everything else. You need to talk to me, Euphemia."

"Did I tell you how much she snores? We'll need earplugs, industrial strength."

Kenneth folded the paper up and, taking off his glasses, put them both on the table and stared at her.

Euphemia sighed. "I don't know it all yet so I can't tell you absolutely everything. And you're not allowed to tell anyone else. I don't want Nicky and Kezia to find out until I have the facts. This affects them too, especially Kezia, maybe Ben. Have you seen the way he looks at her and more importantly how she looks back at him?"

"Euphemia."

"In the beginning, I thought he was keen on Nicky but they must only be friends."

He folded his arms across his chest and glowered at her. Years of marriage told her this was not a good sign.

"OK, this is it and don't laugh because I know it how it sounds. I have superpowers. They started a few months ago when I had my first hot flush. I can see better, hear better, and smell better than any human — better than any dog, which is saying something, isn't it, Petal? Not always a blessing — the smelling part in particular. So I try to ignore that. I am now stronger than most people, yes, you included. I can run as fast as I want to and don't think I've reached a PB yet. I can sometimes control people with my voice. Oh yes, and I'm a fast healer. That's it for the time being. I'm still working it out. There may be other things I'm good at but I don't know them yet."

Kenneth waited.

"It was all in Maree's letters, just not in any detail, and it wasn't until I started menopause that I could trust she was telling the truth. She didn't know this but there is a type of DNA passed down from mother to daughter, which is triggered by menopause. The family calls it 'Rachel's Switch'. She was one of my grandmothers, way back when they used to dunk witches. Well, the women they thought were witches. But this isn't magic, it's genetics."

Only then did she look up at him and saw that he was laughing. His shoulders were going up and down and tears were rolling down his face. He had stuffed the sleeve of the jumper draped over his shoulders into his mouth to muffle the sound.

"Oh, and I have a ring which I'm not completely sure about but I can't get it off." She held up her hand and showed him the dark sapphire.

"It's not funny, Kenneth. I told you in good faith and look at you. This affects all of us."

"I know, I know, but who would believe it?"

He stopped smiling, took her hand and pulled her onto his lap, putting his arms around her waist.

"I'm sorry, but I really didn't think life could send us any more surprises. Anything else I should know?" he asked, nuzzling her neck.

"Yes, there is a mad scientist, geneticist actually. He's Alison Sinclair's father and when I was unconscious he got Grant to steal my blood because he wants to find the secret of eternal youth in my DNA. He could be a problem. So could Grant."

"That's it?"

"I think so, don't you?"

"Yes, that's enough. So let me understand the important bits first. Jane is coming to stay with us for an unspecified time and she snores like a back-row prop. We aren't going to get a good night's sleep until she finds her own place. And my wife is a superhero."

"I've thought about it and I prefer to be called a 'super woman'. Two words, lower case, no capitals, maybe 'superwoman', haven't thought the name through yet."

"Two questions. One: Does this mean we should make love now before Jane arrives? And two: Will super woman — two words, lower case — use her powers to overwhelm her husband in bed and make him her sex slave? I only ask the second question because I don't fancy super-sex. Well, not today. I prefer the old-fashioned kind, slow and magnificent. The way we've always done it."

"Two answers," said Euphemia, feeling heat rising in her belly as his lips moved across her neck to her throat.

"One: Definitely yes, definitely now." She breathed. "Right now. And two: No, I won't use my superpowers in bed. We've been through enough this weekend. Today, magnificent, slow sex sounds perfect."

Kenneth stood up, still with Euphemia in his arms, and carried her into the house.

Petal watched them leave. For a dog with a sore foot wearing a large plastic cone around her neck, she had surprisingly little difficulty leaping up and onto Euphemia's empty chair. It was so easy then to reach over and lick the last of the food from the plates.

About the Author

Rosy Fenwicke is a doctor, writer and mother of three adult children. She has worked in women's health, occupational medicine and general practice for most of her career, and edited *In Practice: The Lives of New Zealand Women Doctors in the 21st Century* (Random House, 2004).

Rosy lives in Martinborough, New Zealand where she enjoys reading, gardening, running and writing.

For more about Rosy and her writing, visit rosyfenwickeauthor.com.

Acknowledgements

As with any work, there is never just one person who sees it through to the end. I would like to thank the very patient readers of the first drafts, Josie and Georgie Fenwicke, Charlotte Calder, Felicity Cuzens and my sister, Janet Dysart. You all made suggestions but most importantly to a new author, you were always encouraging and resolutely enthusiastic. Janet also did the final read and corrected many errors. I thank you all for your support.

I would also like to thank Jeroen Ten Berge for his cover design, Emma Chan for proofreading and Martin Taylor of Digital Strategies for helping me through to final publication.

Made in the USA
Monee, IL
15 August 2021